Osric's Wand:

The Wand-Maker's Debate

Jack D. Albrecht Jr.

&

Ashley Delay

ISBN-13: 978-1466269477
ISBN-10: 1466269472

<u>DEDICATIONS</u>

My daughter Molly is, without a doubt, the greatest blessing in my life. I hope that she can be as proud of me as I am of her. I love you, Jelly Bean!

~ Jack

Family is thy beginning, thy middle, and thy end; such a story shall be blessed. I cannot even begin to put words to my gratitude, but each of you have had a hand in my tale.

~ Ashley

ACKNOWLEDGMENTS

Edited by Kris Kendall of www.final-edits.com

and by

Scott Alexander Jones at www.scottalexanderjones.com

Cover designed by Rodrigo Adolfo at www.roadioarts.deviantart.com

Many thanks to the family, friends, and strangers who contributed their time and talents to help us along the way. We want to extend a special thank-you to all of our beta readers. Samantha Pugsley, your expert eye and meticulous grammar were a lifeline in a sea of inexperience. We wish you luck with your own novel and with all of your future endeavors.

Preface

There is a time when history begins. A time when those who live feel the need to write their story for those who come after them to read. When recollection of events of importance cannot be left to one's offspring alone but must be shared with all.

Then there is a time when history transcends into legend. When strongly held beliefs are tried by fire and traditions are questioned. There are beginnings that truly are beginnings and those that were only thought to be.

This is that world. This is truly their beginning. What they thought was knowledge was only a foundation. They will delve into a depth they have never known, discover things they never thought imaginable, and struggle to uphold the truth rather than be consumed by it. With magic in its infancy and a world in turmoil, an endless chain of possibilities lies dormant. Rousing them has the potential for paragon or chaos, and only time will tell.

Just as Leonardo da Vinci mapped out the human body, and the world began to discover the mysteries within, so it is on Archana. With the rudimentary structure of magic in place, they now have what it takes to discover what it can do, both with the mundane and with the divine. Lore begins in these days, and mythology will forever echo their names.

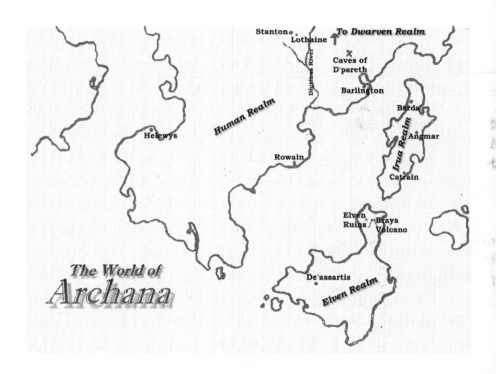

Stanton

Lothaine

To Dwarven Realm

Djanus River

Caves of
D'pareth

Barlington

Human Realm

Helewys

Barda

Irua Realm

Angmar

Rowain

Catrain

Elven
Ruins

Braya
Volcano

De'assartis

Elven Realm

The World of
Archana

Chapter 1
At Round's End

A large explosion ignited the sky in a vibrant display of color. Osric looked up and smiled as he walked into the market district. A crowd of upturned faces surrounded him, all with expressions of awe and excitement. Three giants were hurling boulders a hundred strides into the air, while an enchantress waved her wand to trigger the eruption of the rock into light and ash. Osric took a few more steps toward the square and felt a tug from under his boot, accompanied by a loud squeal.

"Hey, watch where you are stepping! Damn humans!"

Osric looked down in embarrassment and lifted his foot off of the tail of an angry squirrel. It took a swig from a thimble of mead and staggered away, obviously intoxicated.

"My apologies. With all that is going on, I allowed myself to be distracted for a moment." He would have to pay more attention to where he was walking.

The morning parade had left remnants of jubilation on the ground. Food vendors wheeled their carts wherever a crowd could still be found. The entertainment and creativity displayed at this unprecedented occasion were spectacular. The duels and displays of unique magical gifts were awe-inspiring. The noise could be heard for miles, and crowds here and there were amused by the activities still taking place.

Wizards and witches were trying to make names for themselves with their most impressive feats of magic. Giants were arm-wrestling, and kids were playing carnival games. A crowd of children surrounded the most popular game, which involved levitating a shaking bucket full of water and trying to fill up a moving bottle.

Near the end of the market district on the way to the palace, Osric slowed to watch as a lion demonstrated his ability of fire-telling. His deep voice rumbled as it captured the imagination of the children watching his story come alive in the flames of the nearby fire. He was walking around the firepit near the middle of the square, placing his massive paws carefully to avoid the toes of the children eagerly awaiting his words. The inflections of his voice guided the figures and images created by the flames, and shadows played on the buildings and shops surrounding the show. The lion was telling a traditional story of how men and lions learned to respect each other after witnessing the hunt that each performed.

Osric had been captivated by fire-tellings since he was a child, and this was one of his favorite stories. He had loved watching it each year at the start of hunting season. As young boys, he and Kenneth had been taught by the traditional fire-tellings to always behave honorably in a hunt and to respect the last wishes of their prey. They had loved to sit for hours watching the figures of flame act out the narration in the fire. Then they would sneak away with their fathers' spare bows and practice until their mothers called them in to bed. His childhood had been fun and carefree, although brief.

The scene in the fire brought back memories of his parents, who had both been killed when he was fifteen by a lion hunting to feed his family. They had been traveling to Lothaine, a small town just a day's walk from Stanton, where Osric's parents were raised. Once a year, they would travel back to the Lothaine Temple to give thanks to Archana for their blessings and to confer an offering of gold to the Temple Attendants.

That year, they had left Osric behind in Stanton, and prey had been scarce on the grasslands. Osric had been in the training arena, sparring with Kenneth. They were practicing DuJok, a form of unarmed combat that all Vigiles had to be proficient in, when the lion had come to thank him for the sacrifice that fed his hungry family. He had brought Osric his father's short sword and returned the gold that they had planned to leave in tribute at the temple. It had been a considerate gesture, maybe, but a devastating moment for a young Vigile recruit. Osric acknowledged the lion's gratitude stoically, while inside he wailed with agony at being left alone to face the world. His parents would never see him achieve his goal of becoming a Vigile, or be there to guide him when he had children of his own. Osric was glad he had been training in DuJok, for if he had been armed he might have given in to the temptation to avenge his parents, rather than afford the lion the respect of a grateful hunter.

After mourning his parents in private, Osric had poured his grief and frustration into his training. He had quickly become the best swordsman in his class of recruits, and with his best friend Kenneth training with him, he soon had his sense of humor back, along with a sense of purpose. Kenneth's skills with a bow and arrow always surpassed Osric's, and they made a formidable pair. Later that year, they both joined the force of Stanton's Vigiles.

In the absence of his parents, Osric had matured under the guidance of his Vigile superiors. Midway through his twenties and half a head taller than most people in his town, Osric was now the Contege, the leader of the Vigiles. He swept his sandy hair back from his jade-green eyes and paused to watch his favorite part of the tale dance through the flames. Resuming his patrol through the square, he stretched his arms behind his back. His lean, muscular build from years of DuJok and swordsmanship, paired with his personable smile, made him stand out in the crowd. The eyes of every available young woman followed him as he crossed the square to the outpost, and he nodded to the lion as he walked by.

His promotion to Contege had come abruptly. Contege Thamas had gone missing just after Stanton's Ryhain, Domnall, announced that the ratification ceremony would be held in their palace. The Hain of Domnall's staff contacted Osric to inform him that he was being promoted to Contege for his outstanding performance and loyalty to the Vigiles. As Ryhain, Domnall was the highest authority; it was an honor to be called into his company and accept the position directly from him.

Osric did, at times, feel as though the position was a bit much for a young man to handle, but his superiors quickly dismissed his concern. They assured him that he would grow into the job. Still, he sometimes wondered why they had chosen him to lead an elite team of security officers.

Osric had been serving with the Vigiles, in one form or another, for ten years. Although he felt confident in his job performance, the leadership was not something he was accustomed to. The Vigiles were professionals, and they carried out their duties relentlessly. Commanding men more than ten years his senior was not an agreeable feeling, and Osric would rather be taking the orders than giving them. His skills in swordplay and hunting had contributed, yet if promotions depended on skill alone, they would have chosen his friend Kenneth. There was, of course, his innate magical ability to consider. It had certainly served him well as a Vigile.

As a security officer, his magical gift was of great use, and he was superb in its execution. Osric was a Portentist. He had the ability to know when something was about to happen—something momentous or dangerous. He could even feel the threatening intentions of others. A Portentist was a rarity and most often worked in some sort of security position.

Several murderers had been caught due to his diligence. In fact, an attempted assassination of the Chancellor of the Wizardly Union had been foiled by him, just months before. That, more than anything else, had led to his new position. He was proud of his advancement, even if he couldn't quite shake the suspicion that his superiors weren't telling him everything.

The night was cold, but that was to be expected in early fall. He wondered if he would wake up to snow the next morning. After his rounds, Osric was looking forward to warming up with a hot mug of rulha. His broad shoulders fit well in his new, dark-brown tunic. With his standard-issue tan breeches and the ornate V stitched on the upper right breast indicating his rank, he cut an impressive figure. His heavy, leather boots crunched on the gravel as he skirted the crowd, preferring to scan the shadows both with his gift and with his highly trained eyes. Most criminals could easily blend into a crowd, but they tended to slink along the perimeter, where there were multiple escape routes and fewer people to bring attention to them. That kept them isolated and made it easier to pinpoint them as the source of a potential threat.

Passing by the cart of a young Wand-Maker, Osric ran his finger along the hilt of his short sword. He had gotten into the habit of making sure his wand was still securely bound to the hilt. It was an Eni wand, a gift from the Chancellor for saving his life. He had been meaning to buy a leather pouch to carry it in, but since his promotion, he had been tied up with all of the preparations and had neglected to buy one. So, he bound it to the hilt of his short sword by winding a leather cord around them both. Unfortunately, it had a habit of coming unbound. He made a mental note to seek out a leather vendor after the signing; the new wand was too expensive to risk losing. With his wand securely in place, Osric felt the pride of the day coursing through him. He walked into the last security outpost on his way to the palace and warmed his hands at the fire by the door.

"Report!" he demanded with a stern look. Osric watched as the two Vigiles, each dressed in a light-tan tunic with a small brown V on the breast, jerked around with wide eyes. They had been watching the lion's fire-telling out a back window, across the small room from the door.

"Archana's bones!" Gordyn's voice rumbled from his barrel chest as he swore at Osric. He had been standing guard since before his new Contege could draw a bowstring, but Osric knew he meant no disrespect. Gordyn had never been one to hold Osric's age or inexperience against him. "You shouldn't sneak up on new recruits, sir. They may wet themselves."

4

By the nervous look on the other Vigile's face, Osric was afraid that this might have been more truth than jest. He allowed a smile to return to his face and let out a warm laugh. Slapping the young man on the back, Osric felt a pang of pity for the harassment the recruit likely suffered from Gordyn.

"Relax, gentlemen. It's been a long day. It won't hurt to enjoy the last few hours." He kept his hand on the young man's shoulder. "What is your name?"

"Dru, sir, from Dangsten."

Osric hadn't heard of the town, but he imagined it must be small. He got the impression that Dru wasn't used to the city yet.

"Well, Dru from Dangsten, if Gordyn gives you too hard of a time, you just let me know, and I will deal with him. It wouldn't be the first time. He may have helped train me in DuJok, but it's been years since he could beat me."

Gordyn's only retort was a loud grunt and an exaggerated roll of his eyes.

"Yes, sir," Dru replied, grinning shyly.

As Osric crossed the room to warm his hands near the hearth, he heard Gordyn grumbling under his breath to Dru.

"Don't believe that dribble. I let 'im win to build his confidence. I could pin 'im with one hand behind me back. Taught 'im everything he knows, and look where it got 'im. He should be thanking me for that pretty new tunic." Dru laughed, and they went back to watching the celebrations out the window, both with one eye on the door. They wouldn't be caught off guard again.

Running the security for the peace ratification was a great endeavor. Osric was proud of his men; they had done a superb job. Thankfully, there had been only minor issues. One irate woman had caused a scene when she caught her large, hairy husband looking at another witch. It took five Vigiles to get her off of him. The witch's wand was confiscated until the next morning, when she could pick it up after paying her fine.

There was a theft of herbs at one of the shops, as well as a stolen wand at another, but both crimes had been resolved quickly. The culprit had been discovered when an observant Vigile witnessed an odd limp. It turned out to be a man with an umbrella wand stuffed down his pants. In a strange turn, he had stolen the herbs as well. Massive puss-filled boils covered half of his body as the result of an anti-theft charm at the herb shop. He had then stolen the wand from the esteemed Wand-Maker Eni, because his own wand would not channel magic well enough to heal himself. Yet, why had he chosen an umbrella wand? Osric thought he would have been better suited stealing a quill, spatula, or knife wand; he might have gotten away with the theft if he had. Osric could understand the man's desire to have an Eni wand. The man had owned a wand from an unknown maker; no wonder he could not heal himself. It looked as if it were a child's attempt at a wand—just a stick, by any true way of measurement. No finish, no style, and no autograph.

The best Wand-Makers liked to leave their autographs or initials on their product so people knew who made them—all except for Gus, of course. Gus didn't need to sign his wands; one could tell a true Gus by the bolt symbol. A few peddlers here and there claimed to sell them, but the bolt never looked quite right. Everyone knew that a true Gus wand could only be purchased from Gus himself. He could afford to be that picky, as he was the world's best Wand-Maker, and his wands were quite valuable.

Osric had spent enough time by the fire. His hands were warm, and he needed to be in the throne room before the signing took place. All was well at the outpost, so he would leave the men to enjoy the story.

Gasps of excitement and awe came from the crowd, which Osric guessed was due to a display in the fire. He pulled his leather gloves on tighter, hoping to keep the warmth in longer on the last stretch up to the palace.

He approached the cart of a portly man he knew well. James had red cheeks and big brown eyes with more eyebrow than mustache. He waved and smiled at Osric, drawing attention to a disproportionately small chin for such a large man. He had an odd-looking cart that he had made himself years before. It didn't look terribly sturdy, but James liked to brag about how he had reinforced the corners and walls with metal bars. That had allowed him to make a larger cart that was much lighter than that of his competitors. The sign, however, simply said, "MEAT." When Osric asked about the sign several years back, James had told him he had made it as a child with the help of his father. It was out of sentiment that he had never replaced it.

Frequenters of James's cart knew that he sold a whole lot more than meat. His four-course meals were known to be the best in the region. James was, in fact, also a trustworthy source of intelligence for Osric. He had provided him with a great deal of information on the assassination attempt that had led to his promotion to Vigile Contege. Nobody was afraid to talk to a man behind a cart.

"I'm not used to seeing you so far from the dragon platform, James, but a scent that enticing can only come from one cart. How are you, my friend?"

"Thriving, sir! I haven't seen a crowd this merry, or this hungry, in years. It was well worth rolling this beauty to the market. Have you time for a meal?" James motioned to a large slab of meat and a pot of vegetables. Osric's stomach grumbled at the scent of succulent tubers, sweet young corn, and earthy green beans mingling together in the pot, with the subtle aroma of thyme and rosemary and just a hint of lemon.

"To my despair, not now. It's about time for the signing, so I must head up to the palace." Osric smiled back and leaned in to examine the food, and he whispered, "Have you heard anything of note?" In a city the size of Stanton, there was always a criminal population. Most of them were rather boastful of their intentions, unless a Vigile was nearby.

"Not a peep, good sir. Are you sure you are not hungry?" James was a great salesman, and he had worn down many customers with tenacity alone, as if the food was not good enough already. "As you can see, I have one of the best cuts of meat I have had in some time, as well as greens. I'll even throw in a honey cake. For you, free of charge—for the cake, that is."

"I never said I wasn't hungry," Osric said, shaking his head. "To be truthful, I am famished. However, I don't have time; that is the issue. Would you mind coming up by the palace in a bit? I am sure there are more than enough customers up there for you, and when I am done with my rounds, I will be one as well."

"Thank you, Osric. You are a good man. I will be there. You can count on me." James put a thick hand over his heart in a dramatic display and smiled his most thankful smile. After all, no carts had been allowed up by the palace all day—just another layer of security added for the occasion.

Osric said his farewell and began to walk to the palace, his stomach objecting to leaving behind such impressive fare.

"Good sir!" James shouted after Osric. When he turned around, James tossed him a piece of dried meat—a thank-you for the business he knew awaited him at the top of the hill. None of the food would go to waste that night.

"Thank Archana, and thank you," Osric said as he walked away and took a bite.

"And thank you, my friend!" James said from behind the meat cart.

Osric was starting to feel as though he should be at the palace. Something was not quite right, but the feeling was not urgent, so he thought it must be nerves. It was, after all, a very important day. Ambassadors from every tribe, tongue, and species in the world were attending. The ratification ceremony had been almost a thousand years in the making, and he was in charge of the safety for everyone in attendance. Osric was taking the responsibility seriously.

He had personally met with each of the representatives gathering for the signing and had sensed no danger. If any of the ambassadors had any desire to bring an end to the treaty-signing, he would have known.

Osric took a bite of the meat James had thrown him, savoring the texture and taste as he walked. It had a rich, smoky flavor, and he looked forward to seeing the man again later for a real meal. The rough gravel path would soon turn to grey stone and be easier on his tired feet. Right then, he would welcome any comfort.

The night was not yet over, and Osric still had a nagging feeling that something wasn't right. His pupils contracted, and his muscles tensed as he slowed down and looked around. He tried to focus with his gift to locate the source of the feeling, but it was vague and he saw nothing out of the ordinary. The feeling passed and he felt his muscles relax and his heart rate slow. Maybe it had just been his nerves, as the time for the signing was fast approaching. He would stay alert for anything unusual, but he hoped nothing would go wrong this close to the conclusion of the day.

He passed an old witch and overheard her teaching a group of children: "We are all granted the same measure of magic. It is how well you use it, and your *wand*, that makes you a better witch or wizard! The gift is what differentiates everyone. You are born with your ability, and you must learn to master it. For example, a Wand-Maker is the only one who can make wands." She went on describing different gifts as Osric walked out of earshot.

He had to dodge a woman who was chasing her children and shouting, "If you don't get back here right now, I'm going to sick a paun on you!" Osric laughed. The boys must have really been misbehaving for her to say that. To imply the threat of a supernatural beast was the way of most mothers, and even Osric's mother had attempted to scare him into good behavior on occasion.

The paun were something of a myth. They killed quickly, regardless of the size of the group, and never left survivors—or so the story went. The trouble was, nobody had ever actually seen one, so their existence was questionable. Still, anytime someone came across a gruesome scene of unexplained death, they blamed the paun.

The truth of the matter was that not every creature lived by the Hunter's code. It was popular, and most societies upheld the practice, but occasional offshoots killed more than they needed and left the remains to rot in the sun. They killed without honor and refused to thank families for their sacrifices. It seemed unnatural, but it happened.

Shortly afterward, he passed by a heated scholarly debate on why unicorns could not—or would not—speak. Two elderly gentlemen had strong feelings on the subject; it was a common topic at any celebration. Only one fact was known and agreed upon by all: unicorns could not be killed.

He took a short detour around a scuffle over a game of lucky dice. One man felt that the other had used his wand to influence the roll. His Vigiles quickly confiscated the wand, however, impressing Osric with their prompt response.

At last, he could see the door to the palace. Osric's best friend Kenneth stood to the left side of the entrance. His Profice, Toby, second in command to the Contege, stood on the right. They saw him approaching and quickly ended their conversation, squaring their shoulders and gazing straight ahead. Osric was looking forward to the warmth of the palace. He had to school his expression to hide his eagerness as he walked the last few yards on gray stone worn smooth over the years by the passage of many feet.

"Toby, Kenneth, is it safe to assume that you haven't had any trouble up here?"

Kenneth casually waved his hand in the air and leaned back against the cool stone of the palace wall. "A couple deliveries are all we have seen in the last three hours, Os—not even a dancing lady or a fire-teller. Could you move a meat cart up here at least? We're withering away to nothing while you enjoy the festivities." He indicated the meat in Osric's hand with a nod of his head, wiping imaginary drool from his chin.

Kenneth was lean with dark features and brown eyes, and his corded muscles were a little too close to the surface of his skin. He kept his long black hair tied back, and he usually had enough weapons on him to arm a small army. Between the sharp blades and his thickly veined, broad neck he could appear dangerous when he chose to. His fellow Vigiles would have feared him were it not for his disarming smile and quick sense of humor.

Whoops and gasps could be heard in the distance where the crowds were gathered. Osric looked at Kenneth with feigned sympathy and took a big bite out of the meat.

"It's true. It's been all dancing girls and feasting for me today. I'm sorry you missed it." Then with a wink he said, "Toby, how do you put up with this guy?"

Toby was several inches shorter than the other two men, but his intimidating presence made up for what he lacked in stature. His smooth, shaved head was oiled to a high sheen, in stark contrast to the thick mustache and beard that shadowed his jaw. A thin scar crossed his cheekbone just below his right eye, and two-thirds of his first finger was missing from his left hand. He liked to tell new recruits the elaborate tale of how he had lost his finger, and nearly his eye, hunting drogmas in the swamps east of Catrain. However, an Empath friend of Osric's had discovered it had really been a drunken brawl with an angry dwarf. An empty bottle of spirits was no defense against a sharp axe. Around his neck was a twist of colored thread his son had made for him, and a gold unity chain adorned his left wrist. Toby's skin might have been hard as nails, but he had a soft spot for his family.

Toby shot Kenneth a sarcastic grin. "After years of listening to Old Thamas grumble about his aching bones and tired feet, Kenneth's immaturity is a refreshing reminder of his youth, sir." Toby had been Contege Thamas's Profice for seven years prior to the Contege's disappearance. After his promotion, Osric was afraid that Toby would resent him for passing him in the chain of command. Toby was more than qualified for the position, and he was the obvious choice for Contege. On Osric's first day in his new post, Toby stood across from him, placed his palms flat on the surface of the desk, and looked intently at his new Contege. Osric had tried to appear less nervous than he felt, but after a few moments Toby smiled and said, "I am sure you are wondering why I am not sitting in that chair. They offered me the position, and I declined. I would much rather leave the joy of dealing with our superiors, and the responsibility for any failure, on your young and capable shoulders. I would be happy to advise you, but let there be no doubt, I do not envy you this promotion." At first, Osric wasn't sure if he had meant it, but Toby had been an able and willing source of advice on everything from new-recruit training to social etiquette.

"Well, gentlemen, it won't be much longer until you are able to go chase off the last of the fire-tellers and head home for the night," Osric said, slapping Toby's shoulder. He couldn't help adding, "This is the end of my rounds, and my feet are killing me!" Then he walked through the large oak doors that were standing open to let the crisp evening air inside. "Hey, Kenneth." He turned back and motioned up the path. "James will be here soon. I made arrangements for a meal after the signing."

"I knew I could count on you, sir." Kenneth laughed.

"How many times do I have to tell you?" said Osric. "Don't call me sir."

"Sorry, sir!" Kenneth said with feigned fear in his voice. The men laughed as Osric walked into the entrance hall, shaking his head.

The sound of Osric's footsteps echoed back to him from the arched ceiling high overhead. In the short time it took to cross the room, he absorbed each detail around him. Smooth, white granite walls climbed thirty paces into the air to meet the unique stone ceiling. Pale-colored stone was intricately layered to create an elaborate scene of wooded hills, yet the stone was so delicate that the sun illumined the scene, adding depth and shadows to the detailed carvings, and its path could be traced across the ceiling to mark the time of day. At mid'day, sunlight streamed in through a great domed skylight, casting a halo of golden light upon the throne on the raised dais in the next room.

Behind him, to either side of the wide oak doors, hung elaborate tapestries. Each told its own story with richly dyed threads. The women of Stanton had woven one to depict the First Hunt: Braya with his head bowed and a drogma at his feet, offering its heart to his blade. The other was woven by elven hands and had the haunting illusion of movement in its pastel depiction of Er'amar entering the Grove of Unicorns.

Directly in front of him, a wide staircase led up to a balcony that spanned the width of the room and overlooked the adjacent throne room. The brown marble stairs were wide enough at the top that four men could walk abreast, and they widened gracefully to three times that at their base. Oak handrails curved majestically alongside the steps, anchored by twisted columns of white marble. Four arching doorways, two on the wall on either side of the staircase, separated the entrance from the throne room. A

11

massive crystal chandelier was suspended in midair above the stairs, holding hundreds of lit candles, and torches lined the walls, casting a golden hue to the air itself. Servants went about their business, whisking platters full of food between the throne room and the kitchens.

He ascended the steps to get a good look at the throne room and to oversee the Vigiles from the balcony. He noticed a discreet couple standing in the shadows on the far side of the balcony, exchanging whispered endearments over goblets of mulled wine. A young boy sat on the bench before an elegant grand piano. It took a second glance for Osric to realize that the boy was not playing the piano but rather watching entranced as the keys danced before his eyes of their own accord.

As Osric approached the railing to view the proceedings, he again felt an alarm within him. His muscles tensed, his eyes focused, his hearing sharpened, and it was as though his skin was on fire. Something was not right, and the Portentist gift ignited within him. All the joy of the few moments with friends at the door disappeared. As the banquet went on, preceding the greatest peace treaty signing the world had ever seen, Osric gave hand signals to the Vigiles to begin subtly searching the room. He would not be a good custodian of this new post if he did not act when he felt his gift surge within. The high-society guests would hardly notice them searching the room noninvasively.

He watched the ambassadors' tables as they went about eating and drinking. The magical harp in the corner behind the head table was producing a soft, soothing tune that grated on Osric's nerves. He needed all of his senses focused on finding the source of the warning that kept building within him. His men were busy searching, and he could not get their attention. There was a threat and he had to stop it. Something dangerous would happen at any moment.

Time seemed to stop in the moment as he took in the scene. The faces of every ambassador showed joy. He saw representatives of the irua and weasels, who always seemed to side with each other; the councilors for the elves, lions, dwarves, and the groundhogs, who had stayed united as long as stories had been told; and the Wizardly Union all gathered together in comraderie. Down the line—every face, every voice filtered through his gift—no danger was present. He needed to get down into the room and search for himself. His Vigiles did not have his gift. They could look right past something, especially if it was small and well hidden. He made the choice, but there seemed so little time.

His Portentist gift prodded him, along with an urgency he had never experienced. His heart raced as he approached the stairs at a run and jumped. His legs slid over the highly polished oak railing. Lightning-fast, his body propelled down the length of the railing as he tore off his right glove. He slid along on his right hip until he was near enough to the ground for his legs to have a chance to carry him on after the drop. He gripped the railing hard with his right hand, his momentum swinging his body around to face the doors to the throne room. His feet hit the ground smoothly, quickly propelling him through the opening. He could hear a gasp from Kenneth back at the entrance, and his gift enticed him in that direction, as well. *Two pulls? That's a first.* Osric never hesitated; he knew he needed to continue toward the threat. The pull from behind him was peaceful, but the draw from the throne room was danger, and it was his job to deal with it. The strength of his gift was just as great in either direction, and his head felt like it was splitting in two.

The crowd was loud as he entered the room, and many people looked up in response to the way he ran in. He allowed his gift to guide him toward the danger, and it led him straight toward the head table. The pull from behind him was getting closer, and he thought he heard hoof beats coming up the path. Panic rose up inside of him as he rushed deeper into the room. There were so many people there, all joyously awaiting the signing of the treaty. He felt the danger rising, but he could not locate the source. The faces of the seated crowd to each side of him lit up with amusement, and they began to gasp and point. It all seemed to move so slowly, as he finally spotted the danger. A soft glow was coming from a goblet full of pearls on the head table. The crowd erupted in applause.

"The pearls!" Osric yelled as he slid to a stop and reached for his wand. The exclamations of awe continued from the crowd. He had no time to see what they were reacting to. His Portentist gift told him it was important, yet non-threatening; that would have to wait until he had dealt with the threat. He planned to cast the pearls out of the windowed dome, high above their heads. As his hand felt for his wand, despair filled his heart. His wand was gone! He looked down at his side to see if it had fallen. He heard the sound of hoofs seeking purchase on the slick marble, and the tip of a ringed horn just miss his shoulder. He was propelled forward a few feet as something collided with his right hip. Light filled the room from the direction of the pearls, and a concussion wave ripped through the palace. Osric felt the cold marble floor, smooth against his cheek, as the blast forced him down. *This can't be the end,* Osric thought, as he felt his consciousness fading. Panic, frustration, pain, and fear overwhelmed him as everything went black.

Chapter 2
The Meadow

In his old age, Gus was not much for celebrating. There was no need for him to go to the ratification ceremony, so he would leave it to the young to socialize and celebrate. He felt that his day would be better used searching for wand materials.

He preferred to spend his time pondering wand theory as he walked in the meadow, his favorite wand at his left side in a leather pouch that Lady Carrion had made for him. He wasn't carrying anything but a sack for the sticks he collected. Gus was serious about his work. Best to carry light and lengthen the time of productivity.

He had a large family to provide for, after all. His species was known for having many offspring, and he was no exception. Gus had lived a very long life, especially for a prairie dog. He had survived three wives, the succession of two Turgents, and a brief yet terrifying excursion in an elven prison cell. Years of gathering raw wand materials had left him slightly kyphotic, and he moved a little slower than he used to, but even hunchbacked he stood taller than any other prairie dog in his colony. His coat had lightened over the years and was mostly grey, except for a few dark patches on his shoulders and legs. He stretched his aching back as he placed a perfect stick in the satchel at his side.

It was getting late and his bag was full. The meadow was not far from his colony, but there was one more stop to make before he went home. It was only a short detour, and his empty stomach would thank him for it. He hoped that he could catch Lady Carrion at her evening meal. He did love her food, so much that he made it a regular habit to arrive around mealtimes. Like all prairie dogs, his typical menu consisted of a variety of plants and insects. However, over time he had developed a taste for other foods. He was frequently invited to dine with his customers, but he had yet to find a chef who could top Lady Carrion's chicken stew. His youngest son, Pebble, shared his love for a variety of fares, and he often brought him home remnants of his dinner.

He had grown quite fond of Lady Carrion since she had arrived in the meadow, and for her he had made an exception to one of his foremost rules. For the first time in his life, he had made a wand out of a spatula. She had wanted one so badly, and he had taken advantage of her generosity many times. She could not afford an Eni spatula wand, so he had fashioned one for her. It was a fine wand, but it drove him to fits to see her carrying it in her belt for all to see, with his bolt on the handle. There was no end to the amount of pestering he had to endure because of that one moment of benevolence. "No, no, no!" he thought out loud. That was the one and only spatula wand he would ever make.

Sticks were the only material to use to create a proper wand. All that other fancy stuff seemed pointless to him. Why you would want to make a wand out of something that already had a purpose was beyond him. Sure, he made exceptions on special occasions—a high-paying request, a ceremonial sword, or things of that nature—but those were really just novelties. Sticks, however, had no purpose, and he thrived on giving them new life. The throngs of admirers who begged him to make a wand out of a hammer or a quill were merely looking for something to show off. They could patronize his competitor, Eni, for all he cared.

Creating a wand from a stick was easy. Interlacing the magical strands to make the constricted shaft for the power to be propelled through was the difficult part. Of course, you had to use sticks that were sturdy and had an appealing shape, then clean and polish them before creating the magical structure within, but that was all just pointless aesthetics to please the buyer. The raw structure of a stick could easily contain the magical strands that those gifted with the ability of wand-making manipulated. Only Wand-Makers were able to see the magical strands, and they could draw them from Archana, mold them, and bind them to create a wand.

Gus and Pebble were the only ones in his colony who could see into that realm. He had devised a game to train his son in the art of wand-making. He would locate an item or a creature with a specific pattern of magical strands, and Pebble would have to guess what it was he had chosen based on clues. Pebble was young, however, and he often tried to play the game with his siblings, who could not see what he saw. Gus had to remind him often that it wasn't fair to make them guess something they couldn't see.

He was heading south, parallel to the tree line, in the direction of Lady Carrion's cottage. He thought perhaps she would be preparing a potato soup, as the young tubers were most succulent that time of year. Suddenly, a noise from the woods caught his attention, and he looked left and stood upright in fear; just in time to see an arrow released from a bow. Gripped with terror, he was rooted in place. This is going to hurt, he thought. The arrow struck his leg on the back side of his thigh, nearly severing the muscle. He screamed out in pain and fell to the ground, swearing at the hunter.

"You imbecile. Have you ever shot a bow before today?" he shouted, as he reached for his wand and began to heal his wound.

"I am sorry, sir!" he yelled, as he ran up to Gus. "I beg your forgiveness. I am so hungry that my arms are shaking at the tension of the bow."

"Well, that will happen if you are stupid enough to hunt this meadow!" He frowned up at a very apologetic man. "May Archana place many obstacles in your path as you hunt." He continued to work on his wounded leg. "How long have you been hunting this meadow anyway?"

"'Bout three days now, sir. I fell asleep, and I awoke just moments ago and saw you—"

"And you had to bloody miss, didn't you?!" Gus interrupted.

"Well, sir, you don't present a very large target."

"I am a full eighteen inches, as you can easily see. I didn't even move!"

"Yes, sir, but you only weigh about three pounds."

"I was eighteen inches!" Gus interrupted again. "Now I'll be seventeen and three quarters and lean to the left, thanks to you!" He had stopped the bleeding and was working with his wand to end the pain. He mumbled under his breath as he worked, "They will have to change my name to Eileen. I've never seen a worse hunter in my life. I could have fed a starving man. My pups would have been proud. But no, this idiot had to miss a perfectly easy shot."

He did fear dying, as anyone in the sights of a hunter would, though he feared aging to decrepitude more. In all of the stories told, very few people, prairie dog or otherwise, had made it to that sort of an end. The tales of those who had lived to old age all spoke of the pain they experienced. Some of them lost their mental capacity or control of bodily functions. There were terrible tales of disease, of the sadness of seeing all of their children die before them, of loss of eye sight, and of being dependent on their family and friends to survive. Gus wanted to die nobly, to nourish an honorable hunter, but he feared it would not happen.

Gus was aware, due to an encounter with a See-er in his younger years, that he was destined never to be hunted. He was determined not to die a sad, lonely death of old age and incapacity, and although it was an

17

honorable goal, when a See-er showed a person their death, they rarely escaped it.

When a hunt had been botched, there was nothing left for the hunter. Honor would not allow him another shot—at least not at the same target. So, all that one could do was hope that his attempted prey would point him in the direction of a food source.

"My apologies, sir," the hunter said, trying to appease Gus. "I assure you I would have honored you if I had bested you in the hunt. If you were incapacitated, I would have."

"Yes, you proved that by not killing me after your display of incompetence!" Gus yelled back.

"Once again, I beg your forgiveness, sir. I will leave you to heal and be on my way." He roused himself to leave.

Still healing his leg with his wand, Gus watched as the hunter gathered his belongings. Healing a severed muscle took time, even with a great wand like his. His anger had finally begun to subside as the man headed back into the trees. Honor got the best of him, and he hated himself for giving in to it.

"Wait, hunter!" He watched as the man came striding back.

"Sir?" He halted about halfway back, afraid he would be verbally assaulted again.

"You are the world's worst hunter!" Gus barked at him. The man looked thoroughly annoyed, and Gus knew he should feel happy to have survived their encounter. For a long moment, each stared hatefully at the other. "But you showed honor in your hunt," Gus said with less anger, pausing again. "If you travel in that direction, you will go another three days without food."

"I will be in your debt, indeed, if you tell me which direction to travel." The hunter approached, and knelt in front of Gus.

Gus took a deep breath, angry with himself for giving up the information. The hunter did not deserve it, after the terrible way he had performed with his bow, yet Gus felt pity for the young lad.

"A short walk to the northeast." He shook his head, not believing he was helping the fool who had put him in such a foul mood. "There is a meadow, slightly larger than this one." He got up, testing his weight on his leg and wincing. "There are about four hundred prairie dogs living there."

The man stood, looking in the direction he had indicated, eager to leave yet aware that Gus had not finished.

"Listen up, boy!" Gus was angered by his inattention.

"But the light is almost gone!"

"Yes, and sight is only one of your issues. That lousy aim of yours is another. So listen to me!" Gus paused and pointed at the ground for him to kneel again. The hunter shot him an irritated look, but he did as he was told. "Twenty minutes in that same direction, you will find a raspberry bush. Stop. There. And. Eat!" he said, gritting his teeth. Then Gus walked close to the man and kicked him in the knee with his newly healed leg. "Then rest! You will hunt much better if you can handle the tension of the bow, you fool!"

"Yes, you are right. Thank you, sir. You honor me." He bowed to show respect. "May I have your name?"

Gus looked at the man, weighing whether he should tell him. Deciding it would be more torturous if he did, he quickly replied, "Gus."

The man's face went white, and he said, "The—"

"Yes, that is me," Gus interrupted, shaking his head. "And no, I'm not going to be making you a wand today! You have gotten quite enough out of me already, haven't you?"

The man backed up, nodding in agreement. "Yes, sir!"

"Now, be off with you." The man began to walk northeast. "You might be able to curry some favor by ridding me of another mouth to feed, mighty hunter!" he called with a snort of bitterness as he resumed his walk south toward Lady Carrion.

He hoped that he would catch her making dinner for herself. Although she would gladly make him dinner if he asked, it did not feel the same as showing up just as she pulled a minced meat pie out of the oven. She was a talented cook, and he knew she loved to be appreciated for it, so they both benefited from the arrangement. Besides, the minced meat pie was well worth the gas it gave him. After the incident with the pathetic hunter, Gus figured he could use a warm, home-cooked meal. It was shortly after eight, by his reckoning, and that was about the right time. His evening might still have a high point left.

Time passed quickly as he complained to himself while walking toward her home. As he approached, he could smell freshly baked bread and beef stew, and he could see the smoke coming from the brick chimney as he made his way to the cobblestone path that led to her door. His mouth watered in anticipation of the meal.

A bright flash in the western sky, in the direction of Stanton, stopped his progress. *That's odd,* he thought. He did not see any clouds. *Perhaps they are setting off some more fireworks.* As he approached the steps, a strong gust of wind punctuated the chill from an already cold day. He could not wait to step inside, feel the warmth of the fire, and eat some of the delicious food he could smell. At last, he came to the door and pulled on the rope she had dropped down for when he visited, and a bell chimed within the house.

"Come in, Gus," announced a delighted voice from inside. Gus walked in through the small door she had hinged especially for him. "You are just in time. I was pouring a bowl of stew. Would you like some?" she asked knowingly, as she ladled soup into a second bowl. Her light-blue dress and white apron swirled around her ankles as she gathered dishes and bread to accompany the stew. Her long brown hair was tied back in a tail to keep it out of her way while cooking.

Not wanting to give his intentions away, and acting his role in their mutual arrangement, Gus spoke with an affectionate flare, saying, "Why, Miss Carrion, I was just in this area and wanted to see if I might borrow your sink to wash my sticks before I brought them home." He swept one paw out before him and bent his small body in an exaggerated bow as she turned toward him. "However, I would be a fool to turn down such a delightful-smelling meal from a beautiful lady such as yourself!"

"Oh, Gus, you are such a flatterer," she said with a genuine smile, as she moved to make sure her spatula wand could be seen in her belt. "My days of being a *miss* are long since over, as you well know," she said, shaking her finger playfully at him. "But I am delighted to have your company, as always." She turned back to cut bread for them both. Gus set his satchel of sticks on the ground in front of her sink and climbed up to the table while she finished preparing their meal.

Hearing a commotion outside, he stood erect on his hind legs to allow him to see past Lady Carrion out the window. Several men were running through the meadow. One man stopped, catching his breath, and spoke to her nearest neighbor. His arms waving wildly and pointing in the direction of Stanton, he appeared to be in a panic. Lady Carrion cast a confused look at Gus as they watched a second man run up to her house and knock frantically at the door.

"Come in," she said timidly, not knowing what to expect. To better see the man as he entered, Gus remained standing.

The man opened the door only enough to stick his head in, and reported, "Something occurred at the palace during the ratification ceremony. The palace collapsed in on itself. We are asking all who are able to lend aid to report immediately. The situation is dire." Then, just as quickly as he had arrived, he fled, running toward the tree line to continue spreading the news. Lady Carrion looked baffled, but Gus patted her hand and then jumped down to the floor.

"Do you still have the wands I left here for safekeeping?" Gus asked, thinking quickly.

"Yes, of course."

"Give me a lift to the sink. I'll rinse these sticks while you grab the wands and your bag." She lifted him gently and went to find the wands. When she returned, he had a pile of clean sticks sitting on the edge of the counter. "Put the wands in at the bottom, and make sure they are covered; I don't want to mix these up." She did as he said and held her bag at the edge of the counter so he could push in the sticks and jump in himself. "You will pardon me for hitching a ride? My left leg isn't what it used to be, and I would just slow you down." She grabbed her cloak and the bag and headed out the door. "I'll have these made into wands by the time we arrive in Stanton."

"Why so many?"

"Because today, I am giving them away."

Chapter 3
Rude Awakening

This is not what I expected, Osric thought as he lay motionless, his head pounding in rhythm with his heartbeat. He could hear voices, but they sounded muffled and far away. *This feels more like waking up than dying.* He was certainly in enough pain to be dying. He had always imagined that death was a release from pain and suffering, but every muscle in his body ached as he strained to breathe. *Breathe? Do the dead breathe?* Reaching up to rub his temples in an attempt to ease his headache, Osric grazed his knuckles on stone. His eyes jerked open, but in the dark he could not perceive anything to determine his surroundings. *Dust. I smell dust,* he tried to call out, but his throat was dry from the cloying dust, and he managed very little sound. *I survived? I can't believe I survived!*

What could have happened? Osric was mystified. As he moved his hands along the ground beside him, he felt debris scattered on the smooth marble floor he lay upon. How could he have lived through the explosion? He had no wand. He was so close to the source, there was no way he could have survived such a blast. Yet there he was, still on Archana—or at least he thought he was.

He thought through the events leading up to the explosion, and the two pulls of his gift had him baffled. He had never experienced two simultaneous events triggering his Portentist gift. Thoughts continued to cycle through his head as he tried to unravel what had caused it, but he had no information except for the crowd looking behind him with excitement. Whatever they had seen, they did not seem to fear it. He had felt, with his gift, that what was happening behind him was momentous, but it had not felt threatening. Perhaps later he could learn more; right then, he needed to focus on where he was and how to get out.

He seemed to have a fair bit of room on each side of him. Above was another story. When he tried to reach up, his hands encountered stone within a hand's length above his waist. He pressed against it with as much strength as he could at the awkward angle, but it did not budge. His sword was still at his side, secured in its scabbard. He could hear movement near his feet, but he couldn't see anything. Without his wand, he could not move the stone that trapped him. Hopefully, what he was hearing was an attempt to find survivors, and hopefully they would be able to free him. If not, it could be days before he died of dehydration. As the worst parts of that death started to cycle through his mind, he felt a sharp pinch at his calf.

"Ow!" Osric yelled, instinctively kicking his leg. He felt his leg connect with something just below his knee and assumed it was the creature that had bitten him. Getting eaten alive by rats had not even crossed his mind; he was sure that would be worse than dehydration. He tried to pull out his short sword, but the hem of his tunic got caught on the guard, and he tugged it halfway up his chest trying to get the blade free. However, there was no room to swing it, so it was useless.

"Thats was rude!" a young voice cried out, "I am's just checkin' for survivors. What'd you's kick me for's?"

"Well, you could have asked if I was alive. You did not have to bite me!" Osric was not in the mood to apologize to his assailant.

"Well, you's did not move when I came's in here, so's I thought you's were dead." Osric did feel a little bad for kicking a child; the voice could not belong to anyone over the age of six. "Was bitin' you's so's I could wake you's if you's was just sleepin'."

"I can't see in here. I thought you were a rat!" Osric slid his half-drawn sword back into his scabbard. The guard was cold on his skin, but there was not enough room to pull his tunic down.

"You's shoulda lit your wand."

"I lost my wand before the explosion." Osric was growing tired of explaining himself. "Look, are you going to help me or question me all night?"

"Night?" He giggled. "It's is mid'day already. This is my second time through's the bottoms of the piles."

"And am I going to be rescued or what?!" Osric was tired of the word play. He needed to get out and start an investigation into who had caused the explosion, but to do that he needed a wand.

"Oh, yes, I hope's so. I gotsta wait for the go-go so's I know nobody will be smooshed when I lifts this wall off of you's. It could makes another guy go smoosh if I do's it now," he said, lighting the tip of his very short wand.

Finally, seeing he was talking to a prairie dog pup, Osric stopped thinking about being eaten alive. Osric guessed him to be about seven inches tall, and very plump. His fur was mostly dark brown, but it lightened to tan on his belly and paws.

"How many survived?" Osric asked, looking around in the poor light. He could barely make out a pair of legs to his right; the rest of the man was doubtless pinned beneath tons of stone wall and ceiling. Osric looked away, not wanting to see what could have been his fate. It was a gruesome sight. He tried to focus on the conversation instead.

"So's far, just you's."

"How old are you?" Osric asked, letting the annoyed tone in his voice die. After all, if he had to wait until help actually came, he could at least be polite company. The young prairie dog jumped down to flat ground behind Osric's head and linked wands to communicate with someone outside the palace. Light emanated from the diaphanous image hovering over his small wand, but Osric could not see from his pinned position on the floor who he was conversing with.

"I found a live one, Pa. I'll wait for you's to tell me it's a'right, I'm's puttin' up a marker so's you know where I am." Then he sent a bright blue light with his wand through the stone above them after the image had disappeared. As he turned back to face Osric, he said, "I's four, but my Pa says if I keeps practicin', I can be makin' wands better'n Eni in a couple years!"

Osric held in his laugh. He had owned an Eni wand. Very few Wand-Makers could boast of being able to make one better.

"And what's your name?" Osric asked, to keep the conversation going.

"Pebble," he said, slightly ashamed. "But when you's have two hundred pups, you's run out of names to think up!"

"Well, I guess you would." Osric thought it strange that a prairie dog could live long enough to have that many children. He had hunted prairie dogs, and they were not difficult prey. "Who is your Pa?"

"You's don't knows my Pa?" Pebble spoke in astonishment, his small mouth dropping open and eyes going wide.

"Well, I only just met you, so I am not sure how I would." Osric thought it was cute that the pup thought the whole world would know his father. He hoped one day to have a child that thought that much of him.

"Yeah, but… but everyone knows my Pa." Pebble sounded a bit more serious.

Osric could only think of one famous prairie dog in Stanton. "Is your father"—he was doubtful, but he asked anyway—"Gus?"

"So you's do know's him!" Pebble jumped up and down, thrilled to have his faith in his father restored. "I knew you's did. You's a silly fooler!" Pebble laughed, and the lit tip of his wand flickered with the sound of his giggle.

"Well, I have never actually met him," Osric stated with a smile. He could not help thinking that if he could meet Gus, perhaps he could replace his missing wand. Here he was, sharing a confined space with the son of the world's greatest Wand-Maker. He wished for just a moment that the rescue scenario was the other way around. "But I do know of him, that's for sure."

"Well, duh!" Pebble giggled again. Osric laughed with him.

"Yes, I know, and I would love to be able to buy one of his wands someday, just like everyone else." Pebble gasped and scampered back into the rubble near Osric's feet.

"I's sorry." He was making his way back, dragging something behind him over the broken pieces of stone. "Pa said if someone's can't find their's wand, I's supposed to give's 'em one." He pulled a wand, longer than himself, over the debris to reach Osric's hand.

"Really?" Osric could not believe his luck as he tried to get his arm in a position to take the wand. He wanted to jump for joy, but there was no room. Everyone wanted a Gus wand, and anybody who had one had paid dearly for it. They were the finest wands ever made. An inexpensive Gus wand would have cost him a year of his pay, and it was just being handed to him.

"I's supposed to say that they's is not pretty yet 'cause Pa made 'em on his way here." Osric ran his fingers over the length of his new wand. "But it works really good! Pa had me checks 'em first!" he said with pride, puffing his chest out.

"Thank you." Osric was genuinely grateful, and his excitement was clear in his voice. He was still caressing the wand, though it was nothing special to look at—just a stick the length of his forearm, probably broken from a tree in a recent storm. The bark was rough under his fingers, and he was afraid the wood would splinter where a knot ran through it if he wasn't careful. He would have to seal it when he got out of there, or maybe Gus would finish it for him if he got the chance to thank him. It didn't even have Gus's lightning bolt signature carved in it, but if Gus had made it then it was surely a great wand.

The first spell with a new wand was a learning experience. It needed to be something simple, as you and the wand had to be introduced. It had to feel your power, and you feel its resistance. It was called a power lock, because you could not disengage yourself from it. It was usually brief, but the more powerful the wand, the longer it lasted. It had taken almost ten breaths to light the tip of his Eni wand, compared to the two breaths or so it had taken with his first wand. It was pleasurable if done correctly, but it could be painful if done wrong. Focus wasn't possible during a power lock, and Osric was hesitant to engage with the wand for the first time in this restricted space.

"Well?" Pebble said impatiently, rolling his eyes playfully at Osric. "If you's gonna help me wit' the wall, you's gotsta lit the tip now." His childish sarcasm made Osric grin.

I'm going to like this pup, he thought. He had spent a little too much time admiring the amazing gift. Most would have initiated the power lock immediately.

"Thanks, Pebble. It has been a rough day so far." Osric's Portentist gift ignited with a singular intensity, peaceful but nonetheless important. He drew a breath, closed his eyes, and attempted to relax. Holding the wand in both hands on his chest, he lit the tip.

The pleasure he felt was intense. It was above and beyond anything he had ever experienced before. Pebble's giggling seemed to transcend into the sound of water trickling along the smooth stones of a brook. The cold floor against his skin was like the caress of water after diving into a mountain lake. The smell of the dust in the air intensified and became the sweet cloying scent of lilacs in full bloom. The feel of his tongue in his mouth, his teeth, his hands on his chest, the way that the guard of his short sword felt against his side—every single part of his body was in ecstasy. He shook with the power of it. The wand had so much more resistance than it should have had, and it was taking a lot longer than normal for his power to sync with it.

Reds, blues, and greens intertwined with each other, flashing before his eyes in a spectacular display. Breathing became difficult as the feeling built. He could not hear, see, or feel anymore, and he lost sensation in his entire body. As time went on, his head jerked back and forth. Sweat rolled off of his body, and every nerve suddenly came alive, making him want to cry out with rapture. He could not take a breath or withdraw his power. He was certain that the strength of the power lock would kill him if his own power did not conquer the wand soon, but he felt no fear.

Just when he thought his heart would beat out of his chest, the power lock stopped, and Osric lay panting on the cold marble floor.

26

"Wow!" Pebble shouted, amazed, as Osric focused on breathing. "That's was *awesome!*" He was dancing around in circles with excitement. "It didn't do's that for me. Try this one! Do's it again," Pebble said, offering him a second wand.

"No," Osric wheezed, struggling to catch his breath. "As much as I would love to experience that again someday, now is not the time." His whole body throbbed. Muscles that only moments before had reveled in pleasure were screaming in objection to the tiniest movement. His head ached worse than ever—from his gift or from the power lock, he did not know. The frequency with which his Portentist gift was activating troubled him. He could not recall ever feeling it trigger twice in a week, and now he was losing track of the number of events that had set it off over the course of two days.

He wondered if that intense of a power lock was what everyone experienced with a Gus wand. Remnants of colored light were still dancing before his closed eyes.

"Are you all right, sir?"

The voice came from above him. His ears were still ringing, but it seemed the stone that had trapped him was speaking. Too tired to focus, he cracked one eye open to reassure himself that someone had indeed called out to him. Sunlight greeted him as he looked up, glaringly bright after the darkness of his entombment. He saw the silhouettes of several men standing at the top of the slanted slab of stone that was once the ceiling of the throne room. Finally! Someone had come to get him out of there.

"Thank Archana!" he exclaimed.

Pebble bounded over to his side and looked up.

"He's a'right. I told him to's lit the tip, not burn's a hole in the roofs. It's not my fault!" Then he looked at Osric. "Got so's bright in here you's sword look'd bright too!"

This makes no sense. I burned this hole? Osric's thoughts raced as the bright light made his head pound even harder.

"You did this, didn't you?" Osric asked the men standing above him.

"No, sir." Osric recognized the voice of the recruit, Dru. "We came rushing as fast as we could when we saw the bright light shoot into the sky. The section of stone that is gone from here is just dust, scattered all over out there now," he said, motioning behind his head. "We thought you must be dying, and so you did this to get help in a panic."

Osric's mind reeled as he tried to process all that had happened. Too many unexplained magical events had taken place lately. He sat up slowly, feeling each muscle protest in agony.

"Did Kenneth survive?" Osric suddenly had a terrifying vision of his best friend being crushed by the walls of the palace. "Was he thrown far enough away to avoid falling debris?"

"Thrown free, sir?" Dru sounded as confused as Osric felt.

"Of the explosion!" he shouted. "What do you think caused this?" He indicated the rubble surrounding himself and Pebble.

"We don't know, sir," he stated, apologetic yet defensive. "Kenneth said nothing about an explosion, sir. Neither did James. They said they were just standing there"—he parted his hands in explanation—"when four unicorns came running up. Three stopped at the door and the other one ran inside." He hesitated before continuing. "Then, moments later, the entire palace just collapsed in on itself."

Chapter 4
Questions

It was a unicorn? That would explain the horn I saw. What were they doing here? Osric recalled being pushed forward as the unicorn collided with him. If not for that, he would have been crushed, along with that unfortunate gentleman next to him. He could not begin to make sense of the questions circling in his head. He pulled his tunic down between his skin and the cold hilt of his sword as he stood stiffly, examining the hole in the stone. He still couldn't believe that his simple spell had caused it.

After Pebble helped Osric out of the rubble, the prairie dog pup left to continue looking for survivors. Osric surveyed the devastation before him. Once he got his bearings, he realized it was as if every wall in the palace had fallen in the direction of the goblet of pearls, starting with the throne room, then the entry walls, the kitchen, the servant quarters, the library, and out to the guest quarters and wash facilities. They would have been digging for days to get to that spot. If it were not for the hole in the roof, they would have had to uncover everything else before they got to him. The more he took in, the more questions he had, but he thought he knew of a good place to start.

"Somebody take me to Kenneth."

"Yes, sir!" Dru jumped forward eagerly.

He led the group carefully across the top of the rubble, sliding down a slanted wall to the path Osric had traversed the night before. Osric saw three unicorns lying gracefully on the grass alongside the path. They seemed to be waiting for something. Unicorns did not typically stay in one area for long, and they were gazing patiently in the direction of the palace. What they were waiting for, he did not know.

There was no disturbance to any of the surroundings or foliage. As Osric was led to the last outpost, he surveyed the lack of devastation along the way and realized that only the palace had been touched. *What could have destroyed the palace but not touched any of the surroundings?* Upon opening the door, he saw Kenneth, asleep and looking very disheveled but in one piece.

At seeing his oldest friend safe, Osric said in a coarse whisper, "Kenneth?"

Kenneth's eyes popped open and he sat bolt upright.

"Os!" Amazement and relief filled Kenneth's face as he made his way to his feet. "I thought you were dead!"

"I thought so too." Osric was combing his hands through his hair, dislodging dust and stone.

"Who else made it?" Kenneth asked with a hint of hope.

"So far, just me. All of the town's council, Ryhain Domnall, and nearly a hundred representatives from other lands are still unaccounted for in the palace's rubble." Osric knew he needed to get some answers, so he pressed on. "I am sorry to have to do this now, but I need to ask you a few questions, my friend."

"Yes, sir," said Kenneth. The sooner Osric was caught up on the investigation, the better.

"I was told you did not hear the explosion. Is that correct?" Osric was aware that he had to ask the right questions, otherwise he would end up getting useless information that would bring about more unanswered questions. As soon as he asked this question, he knew it was the wrong one.

"Explosion?! What?!" Seeing the look on Osric's face, Kenneth changed his answer. "I mean, no, sir. I heard no explosion."

Osric was relieved to be questioning his friend. Nobody else would have recognized Osric's distress and reined in their curiosity like that.

"Did you feel anything outside the palace?" Osric probed again, trying to focus on the interview rather than his sore body and pounding head.

"No, sir." Kenneth could tell that Osric was in pain, and he wanted to make their conversation as brief as possible.

"What did you see?" This was the only question he knew for sure would yield results. He needed to hear it directly from Kenneth, and in his own words. Even the smallest detail could make a huge difference.

"Nothing inside the palace, sir." Osric had suspected that, but Kenneth continued. "But outside, I was standing at my post talking to James, and we saw four unicorns come strolling up the way." Osric was careful to note that he said *strolling*, not *running*. Kenneth pointed toward the market district as he described the scene. "And, I'm not sure why, but they were still a fair distance off and they started running, and I mean a *dead run*! The three on the right stopped at the door, and the one on the left just kept running, straight into the palace. We didn't know what to make of it." He paused, replaying the moment in his head. "I heard the walls crashing

30

down. I tried to come in to help, but the unicorns had blocked the door. No matter what I did, they wouldn't let me through, until all the walls had fallen." It was apparent that he was upset at not having been able to save anyone. "Then they went over there and lay down in the grass." He indicated the three creatures they had passed.

"Thank you, Kenneth. You did everything you could, my friend. I need to find James and ask him if he remembers anything else." He hoped that he could learn more by comparing their stories, but he doubted it.

"No, good sir." Osric hadn't even noticed James enter behind him. "Sorry if I startled you, but I saw you walk in here from just over there"— he motioned to a tent set up near his cart—"and I got here just in time to hear the story. Every word is exactly as I would put it—every word, good sir. I mean, they just showed up and everything went crazy. You do not see unicorns that often, and when you do, you don't see that many of them. It was like something out of the fire-tellings." James set a plate of warm food down in front of Osric as he finished speaking. "You must be famished after your nap in the rubble."

"Thank you, James." Osric suddenly realized how hungry he was. Dru sprang forth, drawing his coin purse from a pocket to pay for the Contege's meal.

"No need for that, son. I will donate the food to any man who will aid Osric today. I hear rumors of war," James said in hushed tones.

"War?!" Osric gasped.

"Yes, good sir. I took my cart back to the Dragon Deck to sell for the day, as the messengers for the peace envoys were boarding to leave. Each accused the other factions of causing the walls to fall." James pointed his fingers at each man in the room, reenacting the scene he had witnessed. "Each one swore retaliation from their people. Only the messengers were left, you see; everyone else was in the palace when it fell. They were nursing their heads from their own celebrations in the square, and tempers were flaring. The weasel and irua messengers were shouting at those of the elves and humans, and I nearly had my head taken off by an angry lion. It was a good thing the dwarves allowed the humans to represent them for this. If a dwarf were here, there would have been trouble, even if they sent only a messenger. The dragons took off with their passengers before there was bloodshed!" he exclaimed, hammering his fist into his open palm.

The silence that filled the room was palpable, as the enormity of what had been spoken set in. Osric eyed each man in the room, seeing his own

31

thoughts reflected in their expressions. There had never been a war on the scale of this one, were it to happen. Most of the wars of the past had occurred before the advent of wands. The death toll of those wars was notable, yet relatively small, considering magic could not be used effectively. It came down to who had the largest force. The wars that had taken place since the creation of wands were over quickly. The death toll was minimal, as wand wars were usually ended by a quick strike to the opposing leadership. One side, with clever tactics, could overwhelm the opposition quickly, with very few losses.

A world war would be different; billions might die. Wands had made magic readily available for the first time in history. Not that Archana's inhabitants did not have magic already within them, all species did, but the creation of the wand made it possible to use magic effectively as a weapon. Since their creation, magic had grown at an exponential rate. With that growth, all sorts of applications had been devised, from the helpful to the unthinkable. The introduction of this kind of force on a worldwide arena would lead to death on a scope never before imagined. Osric knew he could not dwell on his fears. He hoped there was still time to discover what had happened.

"Thank you, James. If you hear anything else, you will be sure to tell me?" Osric asked briskly. He still had to focus. If the culprit was located then the whole disaster could be averted.

Osric consumed the meal James had provided, quickly yet savoring the man's culinary skill. There was herb-crusted fish, roasted potatoes, corn, and honey cakes. He didn't know how James prepared such delicious fare on a rickety cart, but Osric was thankful for it. While he ate, they talked about what must be done. He explained what had happened in the throne room, when the unicorn had collided with him and the pearls had started glowing. He sent Dru back to assist with rescuing the survivors, and he asked Kenneth to find out who had brought in the goblet of pearls. That would free him up to figure out what had happened to him, why he had survived, and what had caused the strange event with the wand he was given. He figured he should start with Gus, since the unicorns did not speak. After making the plans, he again thanked James for the meal and the information. James promised to keep his ears open and to hound all incoming messengers for as much information as he could pry from them, and they all set out on their respective assignments.

Osric followed the path toward the edge of the forest along the east side of the palace grounds. Kenneth had seen Gus casting stabilizing spells along the weakest points of the collapsed palace earlier that day. As he passed by the group of unicorns in the grass, he paused to watch them for a moment. Their white hides glistened in the sunlight, muscles rippling with each graceful movement. They alternated between grazing on the wild berries growing near the path and gazing longingly at the toppled palace walls. As one of the magnificent creatures crossed the expanse of grass to another berry bush, it seemed as though rather than walking on the ground, the unicorn willed it to move underneath him. The fourth unicorn had saved his life, he was sure of it, but he didn't know why, or how, or what had happened to it afterward.

Osric continued along the path, and the sound of someone shouting caught his attention. He veered off into the trees to investigate.

"You're an idiot! You cannot have me arrested for giving away free wands!" Osric recognized Eni, the Wand-Maker, and he assumed the gruff-looking prairie dog yelling at him must be Gus. At least he would not have to waste more time finding the maker of his problematic wand.

"Yes, I know, but I can have you arrested for breaking the Eni wands they owned before giving them yours!" Eni stood with his hands on his hips, staring down at Gus with an angry snarl. His barrel chest was straining his tunic as he bent over to poke Gus in the belly, nearly toppling forward from the effort. Gus responded by biting the man's finger.

"Those wands did not belong to you, so you cannot raise the accusation, and I do not hear any of them complaining about a broken piece of refuse." Before the scene could escalate any further, Osric stepped up and cleared his throat to get their attention.

"Ah, Contege Osric, thank Archana you are here!" Eni exclaimed. "You must do something about this rodent. He is breaking my customer's wands again!" His whining tone reminded Osric of a defiant child. "I made several complaints to the former Vigile Contege before he went missing. I demand action, now!"

The last thing Osric needed right then was Eni pestering him for justice. He put his hand on the man's shoulder and spoke to him reassuringly. "Eni, I am so sorry you have suffered for his actions. You can be sure that I will handle the situation. The rescue efforts could greatly benefit from your expertise. Why don't you go assist them at the palace?" Gus paced back and forth angrily, screaming obscenities at Osric for believing Eni. Osric went to reach for his wand to immobilize and silence the offensive prairie dog, but thought better of it, as he had no idea what would happen if he tried to cast another spell with his new wand. Instead, he reached down and picked Gus up by the scruff of his neck and held him out at arm's length, as he watched Eni depart for the palace with a wide grin. "Wand-Maker Gus, I am taking you into Vigile custody for questioning in the investigation of recent events at the palace. Stop struggling or I will drop you."

"How dare you! You know very well I had nothing to do with that. Put me down!" Gus yelled.

Osric set him briskly back on the ground.

"I am sorry that I had to restrain you, but I needed to get rid of Eni." Osric looked at him scoldingly. "I do not have time for his complaints. Why were you breaking his wands?"

"Wands?! You call those things wands?" Gus protested with passion and disbelief. "Those were trinkets! Garbage! Half of them were no better than paun droppings!"

"Fine, but why did you have to break them?" Osric was beginning to sense that a reasonable conversation with Gus was unlikely. "Couldn't you have just given them new wands without angering Eni?" Eni was indeed a handful, but hopefully he had prevented him from causing another outburst about Gus at the next council meeting, if there were any council survivors.

"He is a pompous idiot and deserved every bit of what I did!" Gus did not want to give an inch.

"Lucky for you, not one of them complained. I have something more important to discuss with you." Osric looked down at him, hoping that the authority associated with his uniform would encourage Gus to cooperate.

Gus stuck out his small chin in defiance. "Go ahead and arrest me then. Your superiors in the palace will let me out the second we free them. You see, I am somewhat popular among those with authority. Being a world-renowned Wand-Maker has something to do with that, I am sure!"

"I would rather question you here than in the dungeon, Gus, and I do not have time for this banter. Let's dispense with the sarcasm. Did Pebble tell you what happened to me in there today?" he asked, pointing at the pile of stone that was once Stanton Palace. He did not want to get into a test of wills. He needed to get some answers from him, and after all, Gus was probably correct about his superiors.

"Well, aren't we grumpy today."

"I am sorry if I sound rude. I am dealing with much more than a defective wand, and I have only moments to discuss this before I have to resume my investigation into the sabotage of the palace. My time is short, so if you could please cooperate."

Gus eyed Osric carefully, and in a short span decided that he had done him a favor when he made Eni stop pestering him, so he would comply with Osric's inquiries. He was tired of arguing anyway.

"Yes, Pebble told me everything. That wand is not defective. You should have known better than to use such a powerful spell. Vaporizing stone, indeed!" Gus looked him right in the eye and said, "Very impressive, though. Don't think that one has been done 'til now, so you can name it." He took a short pause then started again. "Trouble is, you did it for your first spell with the wand, and it caused you to go into spasms or something. Pebble thought it was an incredibly long power lock, but I straightened him out on that. I don't know what more I can tell you." Osric had to keep himself from screaming at the ridiculous accusation that he had intentionally used such a spell to initiate his link with a new wand.

"First of all, I did not attempt to vaporize stone. I lit the tip," Osric stated through clenched teeth, and Gus rolled his eyes in annoyance. "Then I was locked in; I don't know for how long. All I know is I didn't want it to stop, ever, and it almost killed me."

"That is absurd. You have no need to feel ashamed, boy. Do you think you're the first to make the mistake of using too strong of a spell as a power lock?" Gus tried to dismiss the claims quickly, but Osric would have none of it.

"I am telling you, I lit the tip. Can you just look at the wand and tell me what is wrong with it?" Osric took his new wand out and handed it to Gus.

"Oh, right, because it makes so much more sense that I, the greatest Wand-Maker on Archana, gave you a bad wand?" Gus examined it with a concentrated gaze. Then he reached behind himself and produced another wand, and held it next to Osric's. "No. They are identical! Well, mine is more attractive and has my bolt and yours doesn't, but the magical structure within is every bit the same. Obviously, you messed up, not me." Gus tossed his wand to Osric.

"What is this for?" Osric looked at it with surprise.

"Well, if this wand gave you an extensive power lock, so will that one. Go ahead; light the tip, if that is really what happened." Gus eyed Osric with displeasure. "Go on, boy; show me how *defective* my wands are."

Osric felt like strangling Gus. How could someone that small look down his nose at any man? There he was, calling Osric a liar and talking to him like a child. Osric did not want to endure another power lock that intense. At least, the rational part of him did not want to. Yet Gus was standing there, daring him to do just that.

"Do you have any idea how draining that experience was?" Osric tried to reason with him.

"Well, I can only guess, having never been foolish enough to try a spell such as that, when I knew a power lock was inevitable," Gus taunted.

"You have no idea what you are asking me to do!"

"Oh, I disagree. The question is whether or not you are willing to repeat your incompetence to prove yourself right." Gus gave Osric a smirk that dared him to do it.

"If this kills me, I will haunt you for eternity!" Osric knew the only way to end the debate was to endure another power lock. Then hopefully he could find some answers.

Osric lay on the ground, expecting the same physical assault he had experienced before. If Gus was right, and the wands were identical, he knew what would happen when he lit the tip. Once he was relatively comfortable, he gave Gus a disdainful look and lit the tip.

Power coursed through him and began to build. Osric felt his skin tingle as the flow of magic met the resistance of the wand. The sensation intensified, every nerve coming alive, and the tip of his wand began to glow. Osric smelled the sweet musk of the pine trees, and the muted greens and browns of the forest sharpened. The tingling grew stronger, and he knew any moment the intensity would become overwhelming. Osric took a deep breath to prepare for the coming strength of it, and the power lock stopped.

"Twelve breaths. Now that is a great wand!" Gus said pridefully as he reached down and exchanged the two wands.

"I... I don't understand." Osric desperately searched his memory for an explanation. "I lit the tip! I know I lit the tip!"

"Well, at least we know you are not a complete dolt. You didn't repeat the same mistake." Gus eyed Osric with condescending amusement.

"There has to be another reason?" *Archana's bones! Did I light the tip?* The thought crossed his mind briefly that he had accidentally cast a different spell. He shook his head as he stood up, brushing debris from the forest floor from his clothing.

36

Gus ignored him, clearly distracted, and Osric followed his gaze through the trees and saw what had caught his attention.

Chapter 5
Interest and Intrigue

The three unicorns were striding purposefully toward the toppled palace, accompanied by a beautiful woman. Her russet hair flowed freely down her back, and her modest gown of variegated earth tones clung gracefully to her figure. Hues of amber and olive, bistre and emerald shifted with each movement as she approached the palace grounds. Osric had the same impression of the ground gliding beneath her as he had while watching the unicorn.

In the distance, Osric saw something jump down from the rubble, right where he had descended that morning, and make its way toward the woman and her unicorn companions. It moved with the same majestic grace as the three unicorns crossing the field. Its white coat gleamed with the same unnatural shine, but its forehead was unadorned by the distinctive spiral horn of a unicorn.

Osric stepped out from the trees and crossed the expanse of manicured grounds; he had an overwhelming urge to be closer to the woman. The closer he got to her, the stronger it was, and he was unsure if it was his Portentist gift pulling him or something else entirely. He was hypnotized by her elegance as he watched her examine the animal. She traced her hand delicately up its muzzle to its forehead, and rested her palm at the point where the horn would be. Osric stood, transfixed, as he reached the strange group, unable to take his eyes from her movements.

Gus had been only a step behind him, and nearly collided with Osric's boot in his eagerness to perform his own examination of the beautiful animal. Gus was a flurry of movement, running around the hoofs of the hornless unicorn, and weaving about the legs of the other three in his excitement.

However, the woman was a vision of calm. Her gentle hands moved purposefully, inspecting the animal without fear. A pleasant, peaceful smile adorned her thin lips, and lit her delicate face. Her bright blue eyes shone with knowledge and confidence that belied her youthful appearance. Her long dress was cinched at her waist by a jeweled belt, securing a silver dagger and several bottles of herbs and tinctures. Standing near her, Osric could see shades of gold and honey in her hair, softening her commanding

38

presence. Osric suspected he knew why she moved with such grace, but he had thought those women only existed in stories.

"Is it a unicorn?" Osric asked, taking a step closer to her.

"Yes." She smiled over at him and his breath caught in his throat. "She will heal."

"So, the horn will grow back?" Osric asked, while Gus finally stopped running around in circles and stood on his hind legs, gazing at each of the four animals.

"Of course it will." She said with a soft laugh. "I am pleased to hear your concern, but these creatures cannot be killed."

"I think this one saved my life." He said.

"Oh?" She turned and looked directly at Osric. "It is possible."

"A lot of strange things have happened lately." Osric was remembering the pearl, the split pull of his gift, surviving the explosion, and the power lock. "Tell me something," He paused, trying to word his question in a way that would get him an answer without having to explain everything that had happened. "What would cause it to lose its horn?" He asked hopefully.

"There are several possibilities." She said, turning her attention back to the unicorn. She untied one of the bottles from her belt and sprinkled something into the palm of her hand. As the unicorn nuzzled at her hand for the substance, she rested her forehead on the place where the horn should be, sighing softly. A red stone amulet slipped from where it had been tucked inside her dress and rested on the muzzle of the unicorn. "They can shed their horns, or lose them in a massive power usage, or a fight over territory." She said as she straightened, tucking her amulet away, and opening her hand to allow the unicorn to lick the herbs from her palm. She stroked the unicorn's muzzle with her other hand, a faraway look in her eyes.

"So, do you think that she could have shielded me from the blast, and that caused her to lose the horn?" She brushed her hands off and looked intently at Osric.

"To be honest, I am not sure," Osric could see silver flecks in the blue of her eyes. "But one thing is certain; they have taken an interest in you. I am Bridgett," she held out her hand, "Maiden of the Unicorn."

So Osric had been right about her. Stories told of the mystical sect of women who lived among the unicorns, but he had never known anyone who had met one. Osric brought her hand to his lips and brushed it with a kiss. She would know more about the unicorns than anyone else on Archana. Perhaps she could help him find out what their involvement was.

"I am Osric, Contege of the Stanton Vigiles, and so far, sole survivor of that pile of rock that used to be Stanton Palace." He blushed when he realized he was still holding her hand in his.

"I think you have an admirer." Gus had ceased his inspection of the unicorn long enough to interrupt their introductions. "That is so cute!"

Osric's cheeks darkened and he took a step toward Gus. He had a hard time believing that such a small creature could be so brazen.

"I'm reconsidering the dungeons, old man." Osric started to reach for him.

"Now, gentlemen." Bridgett stepped between the two of them. "It seems we have more important matters at hand." She said, addressing Osric.

Gus and Osric glared at each other briefly, then Osric looked back at Bridgett and his expression softened. He still felt drawn to her, and he needed to know more about the strange unicorn.

"You're right. I will deal with him later." Osric sent one last threatening look at Gus.

"What took place here last night?" Interjected Bridgett, cutting off Gus' retort.

"Representatives from nearly every race on Archana gathered to sign a peace treaty. Before the signing could take place, the palace was sabotaged. It collapsed with everyone, including myself, still inside."

"Why do you believe you were saved by this unicorn?" Bridgett asked, stroking her silvery mane.

"Just before the implosion, she collided with me, pushing me further into the throne room. Had she not, I would have been crushed where I stood when the ceiling fell down."

"That was all she did? You didn't notice anything else?" Osric thought back to the previous night, but could not recall anything more.

"No, she ran into the palace while the other three remained outside, collided with me in the throne room, and I must have passed out when everything collapsed. I don't remember anything else. All I caught was a glimpse of her horn before the explosion. I did not even know for sure what I had seen until I was informed by the guard that a unicorn had entered the palace."

"What is your magical gift?" Her sudden change of subject caught Osric off guard.

"I am a Portentist."

"A Portentist?" She asked, with a curious, almost disappointed expression on her face.

"Yes, I can sense intent, and as of late my gift has been triggered more frequently than ever before." Osric replied. "Were you with the unicorns last night when they approached the palace? I don't recall my guards mentioning you, and I think that is something they would remember."

"I traveled with the unicorns for the past three days, but as we neared Stanton they became restless and increased their pace. I was unable to keep up and made my way into town on my own. I arrived late last night and found accommodations in an inn near the market."

Osric's face suddenly lit with excitement, and he asked. "You must communicate with them; can you help me speak to them?"

Bridgett shook her head gently. "I cannot question them for you, if that is what you mean. I am an Empath. It is more of an impression of need or intent, rather than a conversation. I know what they need from me, and I can express myself to them to an extent, but it is limited."

"I understand, but if I could speak with them, it may answer many of my questions about their involvement, and why she risked herself to save me. Does it hurt, for her to lose her horn?" Osric asked with genuine concern.

"The herbs I gave her will calm her, but she is not in pain." Bridgett smiled at him. Most men she came across were far more interested in the idea of the mystical creatures, than in their well-being. "I believe that the unicorns did protect you, Osric, and I am sure they have a good reason for doing so. When they are ready for you to know why, they will show you, somehow. That is their way."

Gus walked back and forth studying the unicorn while listening to their conversation. Experience had taught him that most things are simpler than they appear and he was captivated by the creatures. Being able to view the magical strands that made up the world, he knew that the unicorns were special, but he had never been able to discover their secrets. He was sure that they were the key to the wand debate. The answer was there, in the threads that made up their magic. He just couldn't see it. He suspected that the unicorns intentionally hid something from the rest of the world, and he was determined to find out what it was.

The Maiden of the Unicorn had spent her life with the animals. Gus knew of them, and for years he had hoped to meet one. Perhaps she could provide him with an answer that he couldn't see. Osric's wand was something he was curious about as well. Pebble was not usually one to embellish a story, and even he doubted the simple explanation that Osric had chosen an undiscovered spell to bond with a new wand.

"Well," Gus wanted the chance to speak with them both. "As fun as it is to listen to you two, I think we should all move inside and start making dinner plans." Osric looked up and realized the sun was already making its descent toward the horizon.

"We can speak more in the outpost." Osric agreed with Gus. "My Vigiles should be meeting me there soon to make their reports. I need to learn as much as I can to plan a course of action." He led them back to the path and they made their way to the small building.

Gus asked Bridgett about the unicorns as they walked. "Lovely Lady, forgive me for failing to introduce myself in my excitement. I am Gus, a simple Wand-Maker. I have sought to study these magnificent creatures my entire life, and I have lived a very long time. Do you mind if I ask you a question or two?" Osric was surprised to hear Gus speak to her so eloquently, as he had only heard sarcasm and insult from the old Wand-Maker thus far.

"Pleasure to meet you, Gus. I would be happy to answer your questions, if they fall within my realm of knowledge."

"I have heard that unicorns are present when any new magical gift is born into Archana. Is it true?" Gus smiled pleasantly.

"The unicorns frequently carry Archana's blessing to newborns, but who is to say what motivates them to bless one birth and not another."

"Ah, of course, you can't see if they are born with a new gift, how foolish of me to assume. Can you tell me if they truly use magic intentionally, or do they use it only instinctively?"

"I can only tell you that I have seen miraculous things in the Grove of Unicorns, and instinct does not explain them all."

"Really? Do tell!" Gus was excited to hear examples of the magic performed by unicorns.

"All stories for another day, my friend." She said kindly, as they entered the security outpost and Osric busied himself finding chairs for them.

"Yes, I have heard that it is difficult to pry secrets from the Maidens, but I will hold you to the telling of those stories." Gus stated playfully, then he turned to Osric, "So, do you still insist you are perfect, or are you ready to tell the truth now?" His change in tone left no doubt in Osric's mind that he was addressing him.

"I told you what happened. I lit the tip. Why would I ask you about this wand if I had made a mistake?" Osric slammed the wand down on the table in frustration. He unbuckled his sword belt, leaning the scabbard against the wall, and stretched the still aching and tight muscles of his back.

"Only you can answer that, boy. But speaking the truth; that is something you can control." Gus knew something had happened, and he wanted to know what, but he wouldn't admit that to Osric.

Despite all of the day's uncertainty, Osric could be sure of only one thing; he did not like Gus.

Just as Osric had sent one of the recruits to find them something to eat, Kenneth came storming through the door gasping for air.

"Thank Archana I found you." He burst out, leaning on the door post to catch his breath.

"What is it?" Osric asked, rushing to his best friend's side.

"Well, Sir," he addressed Osric, "I have spent the day so far, talking to the volunteers as we worked to uncover the palace. As I struggled beside them, we began to unearth survivors. They had taken to cavities created as the walls fell. Not many, mind you, but there were survivors."

"Survivors!? That's wonderful!" James came rushing in just in time to hear the news firsthand, a stack of wooden plates and utensils in his hands.

"Well, as we uncovered the wash facilities, we discovered a servant woman who saw something suspicious." All eyes in the room and every ear waited in anticipation as Kenneth tried to hurry the story along. "She said that she was in a room changing out the linen when she heard two voices in the hall, whispering about plans to escape. She was afraid they were criminals from the dungeons so she walked to the door to get a closer look." Osric offered him a chair while he continued his story. "She could not see them both, as one of them was on the other side of the wall, but she saw the other. He talked about burrowed tunnels under the throne room. One led directly under the head table."

Osric couldn't believe what he was hearing. He would have sensed it if he was there. Why did he feel the need to make rounds then? Why didn't he stay at the palace the whole day? He tortured himself for that choice.

"He said he would go through, jolt the table and cause the pearls to fall off of the table, and then throw his on the floor to join the others." Kenneth said, looking sad. "She has known for two days now. She thought it was a prank, a noisemaker. She had no idea this would happen, so she said nothing."

Osric stopped berating himself. That could have happened at any time. They could have done it in the night, and a servant would have placed the pearls back on the table, not thinking anything of it. *I wouldn't have sensed danger from a spelled pearl until it was activated. The pearl was not dangerous; the one who triggered the spell was.* It was beginning to make sense to him. He must have sensed them walk past him in the market, which is why he felt danger there.

"Who did she see?" Osric asked. "Who was it?"

"It was a weasel and a female who spoke in an airy rasp." The description indicated an irua, the subterrestrial race that occupied the same region as the weasels, far to the east.

"The irua! I should have known they were involved!" Osric burst out. "Bring the irua and weasels to me, if any are left. I need to question them!"

"That's just it, Sir." Kenneth looked as if he had been asked to do an impossible task. "There are none left. I have spent the day searching. They all fled, speaking of war."

Osric was furious. A hope for resolution was there; it flashed before him, tauntingly, and simply faded away. If war erupted, it would come to Stanton. He walked to the window of the outpost to look out at his city. There were people who had spent all day working on the palace making their way home, and relief help coming to the palace to aid in the search for survivors. The thought of those people he had known his whole life witnessing their loved ones' deaths in the horror of battle was appalling. If they had to face the wrath of an angry world at their doorsteps, they would all be destroyed. They were the people he and his Vigiles were sworn to protect. No, he could not allow that to happen. He would do what was needed. He would end it. He grabbed his wand and summoned his sword belt.

"Then I will go to them in Angmar! James, can you provide me with food for two weeks travel and summon a dragon? Can you see to that?"

He requested, as he fastened the belt around his waist. He could not believe the ease of the wand. That had been his first act with it since the palace, and it was effortless. It was ideal resistance. He could feel the power surge forth from him in perfect control.

"Yes, of course." He said, with only a moment's pause. "I can have it for you in a couple hours."

"Thank you, James. Kenneth, can you go get Toby and meet me at the Dragon Deck? I will need to speak to him before I leave." Kenneth immediately turned and rushed back the way he had come, followed closely by James. "Bridgett, if there is anything more that you can learn from the unicorns about why they are here, and what it has to do with me, I would be eternally grateful for the information."

"I should be getting back to them anyway. I will do my best to learn more about it." She swept gracefully through the door, and Osric was surprised to find the room seemed dull and colorless without her. He shook his head to clear the thought of her from his mind, and mentally prepared a list of what he would need for his journey. Gus started for the door, and Osric stepped in front of him to stop his progress.

"Where do you think you are going?" Osric asked, seeking to put as much authority in his voice as possible, "I suspect you believe me and refuse to admit it, but I need to know that I can depend on this wand. What did you really see when you looked at it?"

"You're worse than a flea I can't shake off. I told you that wand is the same as this one, how many times do you need me to say it, boy?"

"Until you can explain why this wand reacted the way it did to a simple light spell, you will just have to stay with me. You have a short time to figure it out, or you will spend my days away in the dungeon after all."

"Staying with you? I think that may be a worse punishment than the dungeon could possibly be. But if you don't believe me, why don't you ask Pebble? He will tell you the same thing I have, you stubborn fool!" His low, crotchety voice intensified to a growl.

"I have a better idea; we will stop and ask Eni on my way home to pack!" Osric glared at Gus, "If anyone will tell me what you won't, it will be him. Let's go."

Chapter 6
All Aboard

Osric shoved a change of clothes and some hard bread into his pack. He had been sure that Gus was toying with him, but Eni had stated that he saw no difference in the magical makeup of Gus's wand and his. Rather than explain the situation, Osric had thanked him quickly for his assessment and stormed off in frustration. Gus had been surprisingly reserved in his gloating as they had walked to Osric's home, but he had a hard time stifling his laughter at the angry expression on Osric's face.

Osric gathered the last of his things, including a bow and quiver, a few cooking utensils, and silver for supplies, and sat down at his small table. He pulled out a map of Archana and began planning his route to the irua territories. Depending on the dragon, he could make the trip in as little as a month and a half, but he would need to prepare for unforeseen delays. He hated leaving town while so much needed to be done there, but Toby was more than capable of overseeing the Vigiles and the excavation of the palace. He had to find out who was responsible for the attack on the treaty signing before one of the races decided to seek their own revenge.

"Are you going to stare at that map all day, or can we get you to your dragon so I can get back to work?" Gus was annoyed by the length of time spent in preparation, and the sooner Osric left town the sooner he could go back to his life.

"As old as you are, I would think you would have learned patience along the way." Osric stood and folded up the map, tucking it into his pack with the other supplies.

"There is a fine line between being patient and tolerating incompetence, boy."

"You seem to think everyone but yourself is incompetent, Gus. Maybe it is a reaction to the company." Osric took one last look around his modest home and shouldered his pack and his bow. "Let's just get to the Dragon Deck so I can be on my way. Do you think you can stop insulting me until then?"

"If you stop acting like a dolt, then yes." Osric sighed audibly and led the way out the door.

Osric had never left Stanton before—no further than Lothaine, that is. He wasn't sure what to expect, but as the Vigile Contege, it was his duty to investigate. All of Stanton's governing body had been in the palace, so he knew he must carry on without orders.

He stopped at a tanner's shop and purchased a leather pouch for his wand. The last thing he wanted was to lose another one. Things would have happened much differently if he hadn't lost his last wand in the palace. As they passed through the town on their way to the Dragon Deck, Osric's temper cooled and his frustration waned. He had lived in Stanton his whole life, and he knew every building and alleyway. He recognized the smell of the blacksmith's wife's famous corn porridge and the sound of their children's laughter, as he passed their home. He saw the garden where he and Kenneth had picked raspberries every summer in return for a slice of the baker's berry pie. He knew the trip would be dangerous, but he had to believe he would see his home again.

As they approached the Dragon Deck, Osric looked off toward the palace. In the moonlight, he could see people hard at work. Many were casting spells to keep the rubble from collapsing further, while others levitated pieces of the palace walls. Chunks of stone were being lifted away, floating through the air and piled nearby. Osric climbed the steps to the stone platform and found James waiting for him. He could see Kenneth and Toby striding toward them from the palace grounds.

"Osric! Do you have everything you need?" James inquired when he saw they had arrived.

"Yes. Were you able to gather enough food?" Fatigue was apparent in Osric's voice. The day's stress was taking its toll.

"Three weeks of dried meat, hard rolls, and about a week of honey bread," James said with a smile. "All good energy food."

"I only asked for two weeks," Osric protested.

"Yes, but your journey will take nearly two months. Dragons can't fly for days on end. The last thing we want is for you to end up starving to death in the desert of Angmar. You will have to resupply in Barlington, anyways."

"Thank you, James." Osric dug out the silver he had gathered from the house and offered it to James. "This is not enough for all you have done, my friend."

"No need, sir. We all must do our part." James waved away the payment.

"You will need it to resupply your cart. There will be many in need of your services over the next few weeks. Take it. That's an order," Osric said with a grin.

"I wish I could go with you. This should be quite an adventure," James said, reluctantly accepting the payment.

"No, James, I need you here. You have a gift for hearing things of importance, and I need to be kept informed," Osric explained. "Now take out your wand so I can reach you."

James shrugged and took out his wand. He could never leave his cart behind anyway. He held it out and Osric touched the tips of the two wands together and cast a spell of recognition so his wand would link with James's. He would be able to speak with James from anywhere by using a communication spell. As they completed the link and replaced their wands, Kenneth and Toby joined them on the platform.

"Which dragon is ours?" Kenneth inquired.

"The large grey, over there," James said, pointing across the platform at the dragon, which had several deck attendants fastening seats to its back. "Her name is Greyback." Osric raised one eyebrow at Kenneth.

"Ours?"

"Well, yeah. You didn't think I was going to let you run off to Angmar without me, did you?" Kenneth was equipped with what looked like every weapon he owned.

"This is a diplomatic mission, Kenneth, not an invasion. If I bring you and your army of weapons with me, the irua will accuse *me* of starting the war." Osric grinned and slapped his best friend on the shoulder. "I will be happy for the company, though." Kenneth crossed the platform to check on the supplies being loaded onto the dragon, and Osric turned to Toby.

"I am not sure how long I will be gone. Will you keep things in order around here for me?"

"Of course, but hurry back. You know I don't want to do your job any longer than I have to."

"You will need to oversee the cleanup at the palace, and Archana willing, you will find more survivors in the rubble. If you learn anything more about the origin of the blast, or who was responsible, contact me immediately." Osric linked his new wand with Toby's and then crouched down and spread the map out on the stone platform. He was describing his intended course to his Profice when the smell of lavender broke his concentration. He looked up to find Bridgett smiling down at him.

"You have gained the attention of the unicorns, indeed, Contege Osric," she said. He stood quickly and returned her smile. "I was unable to learn much more about their interest in you, but they will not allow me to travel with them."

"Have I angered them in some way?" Osric asked, his smile fading in confusion. "Why would they turn you away?"

"Actually, I believe they want me to travel with you."

"Bridgett, this could be very dangerous. I can't expose you to such risk. We have no way of knowing what we will encounter, and it is not likely that the irua will welcome our visit."

"I understand the risks involved, Osric. I will not be a burden to you, and my abilities as an Empath may be very useful. If you feel that the unicorns' presence here is unimportant, leave me behind. If you believe, as I do, that there is more to it than curiosity, then let us be on our way." Osric ran his hands through his hair in frustration. He knew he needed to know why the unicorn had saved him, but he also wanted to protect her.

"I am sorry, Bridgett. I can't allow you to risk your life by accompanying me. Please, if it is the will of the unicorns to help me, stay here and wait for my return. We will find the answers once I have prevented this war."

"I will try, Osric." She turned and walked across the platform briskly, and Osric was overwhelmed by a sense of doom. His Portentist gift was screaming within him to stop her from departing.

"Bridgett, wait!" Osric ran after her, and she turned back to him. "I do not know what will happen if you come with me, but I know if you stay it will end in disaster. Gather your things. It seems you must travel with us, after all."

Bridgett searched his face for signs of sincerity and then grabbed her pack and approached the dragon.

Osric called out orders to the deck attendants to prepare the dragon for the extra passengers, and he requested that James seek out the extra supplies they would need.

"The large grey" was a very good description. The dragon was massive. She could have curled up in Osric's house, but she would have been unable to spread her wings within his walls. The heather-grey scales were nearly the size of Osric's torso, and they had an opalescent sheen in the moonlight. The dragon's wide, fleshy wings were tinged with green, and heavily veined, showing red where they came close to the surface.

At Osric's command, the attendants had rigged seating for four passengers on her back, rather than two. The double row of spikes that stood on either side of the dragon's spine ran between the two rows of padded, wooden seats. They were secured by soft leather straps that wrapped around her body, aligning them with the wings for stability. To the rear of the wings were two wooden chests for supplies. The dragon folded her wings, resting the tips along the ground. The trisected, bony structure of the wing created a ladder of sorts for reaching the passenger seats.

On long trips, dragons were usually mounted with windscreens for their passengers. Osric asked the deck attendants to remove it in the interest of speed. Everything extra was just more weight and made for longer recovery time for the dragon.

"What a marvelous creature!" Gus exclaimed, as he joined Bridgett by the dragon. "Just look at you! Greyback is your name, is it?"

Glowing, the dragon said in a much softer voice than expected, "Why, thank you, sir. Yes, that is my name, but for someone as kind as you, it is simply Grey." Greyback lowered her head to the ground to be closer to Gus.

"Oh, you do honor me indeed, my beautiful Grey," Gus said, and without fear, he approached the dragon's head and rubbed the end of her snout.

"Will you be one of my passengers today, sir?" Greyback raised her thick eyebrow in a curious expression.

"If only that were possible," Gus spoke with great enthusiasm. "I would not miss a chance to travel on you for the world." Osric thought Gus was being far too congenial to be genuine. Greyback beamed at Gus with a frightening smile.

Kenneth and Bridgett started making their way up the dragon's folded wing to her back. They sat in their seats, after securing their supplies in the chests, and strapped themselves in with leather straps for flight. Gus and Greyback continued with their flattery.

A familiar feeling rose up inside of Osric. His Portentist gift had stirred within him again, but it was not indicating a threat. His eyes focused, and a calm quickly overcame his emotions. His breathing became smoother, and his mind sharpened to allow for greater observation. It was drawing him toward the woods behind the Dragon Deck. Noticing the look in his eyes, Kenneth immediately began to get out of his seat.

"No, Kenneth. There is no danger." All eyes, even Greyback's, watched Osric as he stood at the edge of the platform, a stone's throw from the forest. They stared in confusion as an old witch hobbled out of the woods toward him. Her shuffling gait and sturdy walking stick gave the distinct impression of blindness, yet she moved directly toward Osric. He stood, waiting. Feeling the gravity of the moment, he began to sweat with anticipation.

"Osric, I presume." The old witch spoke with a tired, raspy voice, as she peered at him through closed eyelids. Her long, flowing dress was ragged and dirty, and her white hair was tangled and matted to her skull. The leathery skin of her face was heavily wrinkled, and dark circles rimmed her sunken eyes. Rings pierced her nose and heavily adorned her ears. If it had not been for his gift reassuring him, she would have frightened him.

"Yes," Osric croaked.

"My identity is not important." He felt as though time were slowing around him, and he wasn't sure he could have asked her name if he wanted to. She had to be a See-er. "I have a message for you, my dear." She levitated onto the stone platform and reached toward him, grasping him on either side of his face. She pursed her lips as her eyes opened, and Osric was drawn into her vision…

He saw himself standing next to a fire talking with Gus, watching through another's eyes. He observed the actions of himself and his companions and became increasingly aware of his hunger. He waited for a chance to jump. *I will eat them all before they even know I'm there.* Osric was disoriented by the thoughts in his mind, obviously coming from another. He stood there, crouched in anticipation, eyeing himself as he argued with Gus. *The lady looks tasty too!* Bridgett was sitting on a fallen tree, watching them argue with an endearing smile. After a few moments, Kenneth and Pebble came out of the woods with a rabbit.

As they all looked up at Kenneth, Osric felt himself leap forward in the foreign body. *Now is the time, while they are distracted.* He watched helplessly as he charged, intent on killing, on feeding. *They can't see me, and I will kill them all!* he heard himself think, unable to control his movements or desires.

Osric was filled with horror as he tore his own body to shreds, followed by those of his friends. He saw the blood as it sprayed on the surrounding trees. He experienced the heightened bloodlust as his claws

51

ripped through their flesh. Blood ran down his body, and Osric was disgusted, even as he reveled in its warmth. Chunks of bone and flesh littered the ground in the aftermath. Not even Pebble escaped the massacre. He could taste their blood, feel the texture of raw meat in his mouth as he devoured them. Bone, muscle, sinew, and cartilage mingled vilely on his tongue. He had laid waste to them all. Blackness descended on his vision, and he heard the weary rasp of the old witch in his mind.

Victory cannot be achieved until the wand that is not a wand is known by all on their path. It will be wielded in practice by two, known by one but not known. Triumph will not turn your path from battle, for this is the second making of seven sevens. Only two of which will be wielded by man. For in man rests the hopes for all. Even now, it grows stronger.

Osric was himself again, but he was covered in blood and had to wipe it out of his eyes. He was still standing on the edge of the Dragon Deck, shaking. He felt his gift subside slowly and looked around to see expressions of disgust apparent on everyone's faces. He turned back to where the witch had been standing, and she lay dead in a crumpled heap on the ground. Her remains began to hiss and smoke, and soon all that was left of her was a pile of ash and some dirty rags. He looked down at his own body in revulsion. Blood was spattered over nearly everything he wore: his tunic, breeches, wand, and sword. But his face had taken the brunt of it. He had no wounds as he examined himself, wiping the blood from his hands on his tunic.

"What just happened?" Osric looked around pleadingly. "Did any of you see that?" They all nodded in affirmation.

"Yeah, she spat blood on you and died," Gus yelled out. "I imagine that's how I'll be going out too, if I have my way!"

"She what?"

"She spat on you, and then she died!" Gus repeated.

"You didn't hear her speak?" Osric was in shock and had a hard time moving.

"No, but she was a See-er, you fool! Only you experienced whatever it was she showed you. That's how it works." Gus hoped that this would not delay Osric's departure.

Osric repeated the prophecy but was hesitant to explain how he had been in the attacker's mind when it had killed them all. When he had finished relating the words he had heard her speak, he asked, "What do you think it means?"

"I think it means you should get on that dragon and get far away from here," Gus chimed in.

"You said there was nothing unique about this wand, but what else could she be talking about? You must have missed something, Gus." Osric held the wand out before him.

"Ah, Archana's bones, boy! If anything is off about that wand, it is the man who wields it. Get on the dragon. We should go before it gets any later," Gus shouted. "What do you mean, *we* should go?"

"Well, what do you know about wands, other than how to make one go screwy? A 'wand that is not a wand' sounds like my realm to me. If there is anything to learn about it, I can't very well learn it from here, now can I?"

Osric was terrified that if he allowed them all to accompany him, their journey would end in the bloody scene of his vision, but he was overwhelmed by the idea of trying to solve the riddles by himself. He would just have to find a way to prevent the vision from coming to fruition.

"I am sure Eni will thank me for taking you along, but you better figure this out or the dungeon will be your permanent home when we return." Osric picked Gus up by his scruff and hoisted him up onto the dragon's wing to find a perch on her back, ignoring his expletives of protest. He inspected the gear one last time to be sure everything had been stowed properly, and climbed agilely up the wing.

After the goodbyes had been said and Osric was safely secured in the front row of seats, his short sword strapped tightly between the dragon's spikes, he wiped himself clean as best he could with a cloth James had tossed to him. He took off his boots to make himself comfortable, and tied them to the straps of his seat to keep them in place. Gus took his place in Bridgett's lap, who looked at Osric with sympathetic eyes. There were no more preparations to delay their departure. Osric hoped he would find some answers along the way.

Osric wanted to delve into the mystery of the wand immediately, but Gus insisted that they needed sleep and they would be much better off figuring it out in the light of day. After all, a fatigued mind would often draw the wrong conclusions.

Gus made sure, through incessant flattery, that the dragon would wake them at first light on the flight. Greyback had agreed and assured them that they were safe in her care, and they took to the air.

Osric watched the scenery unfold beneath him as they flew. He could not see much in the moonlight, yet scattered across the landscape were noticeable flickers of light. Torchlight and campfires dotted the darkness below. The steady flapping of the dragon's wings mesmerized him as they flew. His mind wandered back to the vision and the prophecy, as the lights started to waver in his vision. After the stress and strain of the long day, he could no longer hold his eyes open, and sleep took hold of him. His dreams were filled with mysteries and the horror of the witch's vision.

Chapter 7
New Ground

"It was a vision, and a prophecy," Osric said, as they again listened carefully to his explanation of what he had seen. He had to speak loudly, due to the rush of air.

"Indeed, it was," Gus said apologetically. "It does not happen often." He looked at Osric. "But it appears that I was wrong about you. Perhaps there is something unique about that wand of yours." With his apology over, he continued in his typical manner. "Now, let me take another look." For the first time, Osric wished he had not asked for the windscreen to be removed. He handed Gus the wand, fearing the wind would tear it from his fingers, although he needn't have worried, as Gus handled it well. He took it in his paws and activated his gift. A focused glaze came over his eyes as he peered into the very essence of the wand. After a few long moments of inspection, he handed it back carefully.

"Well?" Osric inquired.

Looking almost sad, Gus sorrowfully said, "As much as I would love to have made a wand of the magnitude hinted at in that prophecy"—he exhaled with a sigh—"it is just like every other wand I have ever made." His face took on a confused expression.

Osric was not completely surprised to hear him say this. He kept thinking through the words of the prophecy. *Victory cannot be achieved until the wand that is not a wand is known by all on their path.* Would he have to prove to them in some way that the wand was different? Pebble believed him; he had seen it himself. He almost wished the little guy were there with them. *It will be wielded in practice by two.*

"Both Pebble and I used this wand. 'Two will wield it in practice.' That is what the prophecy said. So, that has to be what it means, right?" he argued, not even convincing himself.

"Yes, but it must also be a wand that is not a wand," Bridgett stated with sympathy. "And that is most certainly a wand. It has to mean something more."

"It is also a stick! Prophecies are always cryptic, are they not? It could be that simple," Osric protested, pleading for someone to agree with him and justify his reasoning.

"Well, there is a chance that it was all just a bunch of paun droppings," Gus considered. "I mean"—he paused briefly—"wasn't Pebble in the vision? Take a look around. My pups didn't even know I was leaving." He shrugged. "There is a high possibility she was just a crazy old blind woman talented in deception."

"I am not a fan of watching my friends get ripped apart right before I die, so I am with him," Kenneth added casually. "Besides, you are a Portentist! How could a beast sneak up on you anyway?" He had hunted with Osric his whole life. Nothing could surprise Osric in that manner.

Osric was shaken by their logic, though he felt certain the vision had not just been a ruse. As he sat there thinking their arguments through, he had to admit that they made sense. Pebble wasn't there. How could a wand not be a wand? How could one know it and not know it? And how could a creature kill him without him sensing it coming?

The fact that so much had happened to him in a few days was a bit overwhelming, and the double pull of his gift still bothered him as well. So, he decided that he would take a different approach. He would figure out how to prove it was the wand by learning what he could about the wand-making process. It just so happened that the world's leading authority on wands sat in the lap of the beautiful woman sitting next to him.

"Gus," Osric said, "I guess the only way to figure out if the prophecy is real would be to figure out if the wand's existence is at all possible, correct?"

"Well, yes, boy. That is what I am trying to tell you," Gus said tolerantly. "It is simply not possible! Wands are just channels through which our power travels." His lecturing tone reminded Osric of the witch in the market district teaching the young children.

"Yes, I understand that." Osric tried the polite path, in spite of his desire to throw Gus from the dragon because of his attitude. "But could you explain the process of wand-making to me?" After all, they had nearly a month of dragon flight ahead of them. Watching the scenery pass by would grow old quickly.

Gus seemed to enjoy the chance to show off his knowledge, as his whole countenance changed.

"So, you wish to be a student?" Gus asked with an arrogant smile.

Osric cringed, but he knew he needed the knowledge, so he went along with it.

"Yes, if you would be so kind." He would have to play the game for a long time, but it was a necessary burden.

"Well, what you need to understand is"—Gus paused, ensuring he had their attention—"these concepts have taken me a lifetime to learn. I will not be able to teach you everything in a month."

Osric nodded in agreement. He was just hoping that Gus sharing his knowledge would make him realize how the wand was different.

"Of course, Gus. We will learn what we can in the time we have."

So Gus set to work describing the process of activating his gift and weaving the strands of magic after drawing them from Archana. He explained how he fashioned the constricted shaft of woven strands that turned an object into a wand, and then attached it to the core of a stick in a way that would reinforce the structure of the wood. The whole process made the wand more difficult to break.

Every ear was glued to the lecture. Though none of them had the gift, it was thrilling to learn how the Wand-Makers' power worked. Most Wand-Makers would highly guard their skills to keep others from besting them. Their livelihood relied on their ability to keep their secrets away from snooping ears. However, on the dragon's back, nobody could hear his secrets, so Gus was more than willing to share why he was superior. The day passed quickly, as he explained every detail of the process, and how doing one step or another incorrectly led to an inferior wand.

"Why does it need to be constricted?" Osric inquired.

Gus looked at Osric in surprise.

"Boy, you are proving yourself brighter than I expected." Osric felt pride swell within him as Gus continued. "That was the perfect question! When you think about *your* magic, you must think of it as a lake." Gus paused for effect. "Your wand acts like the lake's dam, with a hole in it." He smiled, as he jabbed his claw into the air to punctuate his last words.

Every face looked confused by Gus's statement; even Greyback peered back at his odd imagery. Gus continued excitedly, "If the hole is too big, the water falls to the ground immediately under its own weight. If the hole is too small, it sprays out uncontrolled, and you never know where it will land." Their confusion cleared, as one after the other, they began to understand. "However, if the hole is just the right size, the pressure of the weight of the water behind the hole will cast it out in a tightly formed stream."

"Even a tight stream of water will eventually fall to the ground," Bridgett added.

"Bright and beautiful!" Gus quickly pointed out. "You two are a good match, boy." He patted Osric's leg with a mischievous smile. Osric flushed in anger and embarrassment, and Bridgett looked away shyly.

Noticing their reactions, Kenneth interrupted, "But that can't be right. Water could only travel, at best, a few hundred strides. I have cast spells five times that far in the past." He knew Gus would insult him, yet he wanted to take the focus away from the embarrassed passengers in the front seats.

"Osric, you really must look for brighter friends." Gus glared at Kenneth as he explained, "Magic has very little weight, so it can travel great distances. Yet even magic will fall and rejoin Archana after a time," he said in a quick and condescending manner.

Osric nodded in appreciation to Kenneth as he looked up at the sun's position in the sky and realized that it was already mid'evening. He was surprised at the amount of information involved in wand-making, and he thought that they should be landing soon so the dragon could rest.

Truth be told, he would be glad to stand and stretch his muscles after a long day of sitting. He had not had a chance to spar with his short sword for days, due to the preparations for the ratification ceremony. His arms ached to feel the weight of it again, and too much time without practice would rob his muscles of their memories of the movements. Many years of disciplined practice had made him a great swordsman, and it took hard work to maintain his skill.

"Greyback," Osric called out politely.

"Yes?" she attentively replied.

"I am sure you would appreciate a night's rest?"

"Oh yes, sir," she responded gratefully.

Weighing the information that he had gathered, Osric decided that he needed some time to think. So far, he had not heard anything that would explain his wand's reaction to his first spell. A couple of hours of swordplay and a night of rest should give him the time he needed to clear his head.

"Please, find us a good camp site and we can all rest."

"I can see a nice one now, sir. There's a good-sized clearing next to a river, with a blackberry bramble not too far away." Sounding fatigued, Greyback added with relief in her voice, "Only a few minutes away."

"Very good, you beautiful beast," the overly adulatory Gus asserted again.

"That would be wonderful, Greyback." Osric was looking forward to being on solid ground. "We are grateful to you." He had heard that dragons had excellent sight, but he was impressed by Greyback's ability to locate a campsite from the air. From their height, all Osric could see was a solid sea of foliage.

Soon enough, they began to make their way down to the heavily wooded area. Dense trees covered the landscape with an array of bright yellow and orange leaves. The sun sat low in the western sky, producing vivid orange, blue, and purple hues as they descended through the clouds.

They all seemed to relish the thought of feeling the soil beneath their feet, except for Gus, who had fearlessly made his way up the dragon's neck. He scratched the crown of her head, as he insisted repeatedly that he had never had such a pleasurable flight.

They swept in low near the edge of the clearing, and the landing was surprisingly graceful for a beast of that size. They all unfastened their harnesses, eager to disembark. Osric collected his gear and strapped on his sword belt as he stretched his legs and glanced around at their campsite from the height of the dragon's back.

He strung his boots together and slung them over his shoulder, as he ambled his way to the folded wing and made his way down to the ground. He relished the feel of it on his naked feet, letting the soil slip through his toes. The grainy texture of the dirt with the slightly damp leaves and twigs was refreshing. He crossed the small clearing, noticing that all of the aches of the previous day were gone, and his muscles felt fresh and strong. He made his way to the stream, hearing the various calls of the birds in the trees and noticing how the light played off of the leaves. Even the air seemed to empower him as he drew in each breath. It sent chills up his spine as he filled his lungs, heady from the strong smell of loam and pine needles stirred up by his steps.

Upon reaching the stream, he knelt to wash his face, scooping cold water from the edge with cupped hands. The chill of the water on his skin was invigorating, and he had to resist stripping down and diving in. He stood, stretching his back and shoulders, and noticed Kenneth standing nearby.

"I feel different."

"I do too!" Kenneth stated enthusiastically, examining his hands in awe. "And I like it!"

From his perch on Greyback's neck, Gus was watching them flex their muscles. "You're a bunch of..." he started to insult them, and then he examined his own body. "Yes, yes, it appears you are correct again, boy," he said happily. "Now, let me take a look at the two of you." He slid along Greyback's neck and began hopping down the bone ladder of her wing to make his way toward Kenneth and Osric so he could examine them with his gift.

"There is no need for that, Gus," Bridgett stated. "I can explain what you are all feeling," she said, pulling the red amulet out from between her breasts.

"Indeed," Gus said with reverence, approaching her. He examined its fibers as he walked ever closer. There was an obvious structure—not the ruby itself, but inside of it. It was an orb of magical energy that held a charm and made the necklace an amulet. "It is beautiful, Bridgett. What is it?" he asked, intrigued.

"It is the Aduro Amulet—a gift from the unicorns," she revealed as she went on. "It amplifies the magic in its host as well as their companions. I am surprised you have not felt it before now, but I suppose our thoughts have been preoccupied."

"What an amazing trinket!" Gus was still gazing intently at the amulet.

"It amplifies my Empath ability," she said, "allowing me to communicate more effectively with the unicorns." Bridgett looked at Osric attentively. "That was how I knew they were interested in you."

"Enough!" Osric was tired of being the center of attention. He was a decent Vigile and nothing more. There had been so much focus on him these last few days, as though he were someone great, and that frustrated him. He decided to set up camp and let Gus and Bridgett discuss it without him. "I am not special!" The amulet's power seemed to intensify the anger he felt for being put in an awkward position of importance. Realizing how ridiculous he sounded, he took several deep breaths before continuing. "I'm sorry. I just need some time to think. I meant no disrespect." He headed off quickly to avoid making a bigger fool of himself.

Kenneth joined him in setting up the camp. He could sense how his friend needed to work to feel better, and he assisted him in silence. They unloaded the storage crates strapped to Greyback and sent her off to hunt for her meal. Sorting through the supplies allowed Osric some time to work off some steam.

"Tell me, my dear, how long have you been with the unicorns?" Gus asked Bridgett as they gathered wood for the fire.

"I have lived among the Maiden of the Unicorn for fifteen years," Bridgett replied, as they watched Kenneth and Osric setting up camp. "My mother was a Healer, and when we discovered my ability as an Empath, she sent me to study with the Healers of Araseth." She had a faraway look in her eyes as she related the tale of her childhood.

"Remarkable! I have heard of their existence, but I've never met anyone who studied with them." Gus was very interested in hearing more.

"I resided with the Healers for four years. I learned their ways of identifying and harvesting herbs and medicinal plants. They taught me to seek out and rid a body of pain and disease, and they showed me ways to use my Empath abilities to communicate with the world around me, with Archana itself."

"Communicating with Archana? Er'amar's Wand, woman! What does that mean?" Gus stood up rigidly, but his ears twitched with the intensity of his curiosity. He could hardly stand still at the possibility of such a thing.

"Araseth Empaths attune their own magical power to that drawn from Archana for weaving spells. The way you are able to see the strands, I am able to hear them. It is not a conversation like you and I are having, but rather an understanding of the world around me. I can feel the needs of the trees and express myself to the lesser creatures when needed. It is rather empowering, to help a seed to grow because it asks me to."

"Archana's bones, it has been years since I have been this excited about something new. I apologize for my language and for taking this conversation in a new direction, but I will ask you more about that another day." Gus bowed out of respect and lowered himself back to the ground. The effort he put into hiding his interest was apparent, as his right ear quivered when he spoke. "With all of that excitement, what brought you to the Maiden of the Unicorn?"

"The unicorns were frequent visitors to our valley, and as my powers developed, I spent more and more time among them when they came. They took me further outside the Healers' valley over time, showing me where to find rare plants and leading me to sick animals who needed my help. On the four-year anniversary of my arrival in the Araseth Valley, they gifted me the amulet, and we traveled two days to a small mountain lake. Death and decay were spreading from its waters, and many creatures had been sickened by drinking from it. It took everything within me, but I was able to heal the waters. From there, we traveled to the Grove of the Unicorns, and they welcomed me among them." Bridgett smiled at the memory, resting her free hand over the hidden amulet at her chest. "I have always suspected that if I had failed to cleanse the lake of its sickness, they would have returned me to the valley instead." Bridgett piled the wood they had gathered in the clearing and went to the stream to collect water for their meal.

"Marvelous," Gus exclaimed, following her toward the water. "They must have wa—"

"Whoa!" Kenneth shouted, interrupting Gus and Bridgett's conversation as he dropped the lid back onto one of the chests. His face was white as he drew his long sword and spun around. He began to frantically search the perimeter of their camp.

Osric drew his sword and wand and came rushing to his side, along with Gus and Bridgett, each one of them trying to see what had raised the alarm in Kenneth. It was dark and visibility was low.

"What is it?" Osric questioned him quickly as he gazed out into the darkness.

"Look in the chest, all of you!" Kenneth pointed behind him.

The three of them backed slowly toward the chest, keeping an eye toward the dark forest. Osric lifted the lid for Bridgett and Gus to peer in while he kept a lookout. Bridgett gasped and Gus swore as they both stepped back in shock.

Osric watched their faces drain of color, noticeable even in the twilight. He dreaded what he would find as he turned to look. There had been too many mysteries and so few answers. He did not think he could bear another one. As he looked within the chest to see what had sent his friend into a panic, and blanched the faces of his companions, the memory of the vision sent shivers across his skin.

"So much for the elaborate prank," he whispered to himself. Pebble lay asleep in the bottom of the box.

Chapter 8
Fear Filled Flight

"I's was on my's way home," Pebble explained between sobs, hanging his head, "an' I see'd my Pa talkin' to's the big dragon, so's I came to see's it."

"By the strands, son, how did you end up in the box?" Gus shouted, terrified of what Pebble's presence meant for the fate of their party.

"I hided inside when the scary lady showed's up, and the lid's falled down so's I's couldn't get's out." Pebble covered his eyes to avoid the stern looks directed at him. He was unsure what he had done wrong, but he knew from the look on his father's face that he was in trouble. "I's sorry!" Tears flowed freely down his cheeks as he looked around at their surroundings. The trees on the edge of the clearing towered above him, and he trembled slightly in awe. He realized it must have been the dragon's flight that had rocked him to sleep, and he felt small and very scared waking up so far from his home. He wished everyone would stop looking at him so angrily. After all, he had not meant to stow away in the crate.

As the sky deepened to shades of purple and grey and the moon began to rise, they tried to settle into their places to rest. Each of them was keenly aware of how the situation had changed. It would be a restless night, and Gus was taking it harder than the rest.

"Don't try to sleep by me! You are in so much trouble!" Gus shouted at Pebble. "Ask someone else! Be careful or they just might skip you across the water." His face held anger, but fear and love were in his eyes as well. Perhaps a child would miss the underlying emotion, but the rest of them saw through the mask. Gus was terrified that his son would die on their journey.

Pebble looked despondent as he glanced tentatively toward the other members of their group, who had all settled inside their thick woolen sacks. His big watery eyes looked around to see if anyone returned his gaze, to plead without voice for warmth and rest.

"Over here, dear," Bridgett spoke sympathetically. Pebble began to slowly and cautiously make his way to her.

Softly and fearfully, he asked, still just out of her reach, "Is you's gonna"—he breathed in with great effort, choking back his sobs—"toss'ed me crossed da water's?"

"Oh no, dear. We will keep each other warm, all right?" Bridgett spoke softly but cheerfully, encouraging him to trust her. "Now come on. Hop in here. I'm getting cold." She opened the blanket slightly to give Pebble a place inside to sleep.

Pebble ran inside and cuddled up close to her and began to cry. Bridgett ran her fingers down his back to sooth his nerves. She looked up to see Osric watching her, and they exchanged sympathetic smiles. He could not seem to tear his eyes from her kind face. She stared back at him, understanding how he felt, perhaps better than he did. She felt drawn to him as well, and they allowed themselves a moment of shared comfort.

A realization came to Osric as he gazed into her blue eyes. He held up one finger for her to wait. He climbed out of his sack and walked quickly in the cold air to the chest that held the food and supplies. Osric poured a small amount of water into a dish and grabbed a honey cake, then made his way back to Bridgett, who smiled broadly at his consideration. He broke the cake in half as he knelt next to her.

"Pebble," Osric called softly to him. "I have some food and water here for you. You really should eat. Would you like some?" He smiled at Bridgett again and then gave her the biggest half, allowing his fingers to brush the inside of her wrist.

"It's honey cake." Bridgett held the sack open slightly for Pebble and peered in.

"I cannot finish this whole thing by myself, and I would not want it to go to waste. Would you eat with me, please?" She held it so he could see.

Pebble peered out cautiously as he wiped his nose on Bridgett's shoulder. His little brown face wrinkled up as he sniffed back his tears, and alertness returned to his eyes.

"Smells good. S'pose I can eats just a bit," Pebble said with a small amount of eagerness.

Bridgett broke off a little piece and handed it to him, and Osric set the dish of water down in front of them. Pebble's cheeks were soon bulging, and Bridgett giggled as she swept crumbs from the soft wool lining. She felt Pebble snuggle deeper into the sack, until he was curled up against her chest, and soon he was sleeping peacefully.

64

After a moment, Osric stood up and carried the dish back to their baggage. He climbed into his own sack across the fire from hers and noticed a contemplative expression on Gus's face. He turned his back to the old Wand-Maker and fell asleep listening to Bridgett's breathing and Kenneth's rumbling snores. Tomorrow would be another day, and he intended to find some answers.

* * *

Osric woke early, anxious to cleanse the old witch's dried blood from his tunic. After splashing cold water on his face, he stripped the garment off and knelt down to wash it against the smooth rocks at the river's edge. He was especially careful not to let his scabbard dip into the water, so the hilt rested uncomfortably against his side. He scrubbed the stains with salt from their supplies until he was satisfied and then draped the tunic over a tree branch. On his first long hunt, his father had taught him a spell for drying clothing, and he did not have time to wait for it to dry in the sun. He drew his wand and cast the spell and immediately noticed that the wand felt more powerful. His tunic dried in half the time he was expecting, and it sent a chill up his left arm. He quickly drew it back over his head and went to find Gus.

"Gus! The spell I just cast was twice as powerful as it should have been! There must be something going on with this wand."

"Boy, I want that wand to be as powerful as you say it is. The gold that I could make is... Well, you can imagine. However, there is nothing special about that wand! It is probably Bridgett's amulet that you are feeling, so let it go." Gus wrinkled his nose out of frustration and started to walk away.

Osric stepped in front of him. "Watch!" He aimed the wand at the wet hems of his breeches and cast the drying spell. To his surprise, it felt the same as it had in the security outpost. The power growth was gone. "I don't understand. It's not there anymore." Osric looked down at the wand in disappointment, unable to meet Gus's gaze.

Gus's ears twitched for a moment, and then his smug expression returned. "Maybe you need a new spell, eh, boy?" He walked around Osric, leaving him there with his head hanging in shame and confusion.

The rest of the morning went surprisingly smooth. They ate a quick breakfast and bathed in the cold river water before strapping the supplies on the dragon. Pebble amused everyone with his adorable ways, trying to get anyone to play a game he called "I see's somethin' you's don't." Gus, however, was not amused, and he reminded Pebble harshly that he couldn't play it with people who don't have the gift. Bridgett, Osric, and Kenneth took turns trying to humor him and play anyway. Pebble's response to their dreadful guesses was always, "You's gotsta look, silly." They would just laugh at his childish logic and try to guess his next target.

After a short time, they were flying again, their spirits high. Each time they stopped, they took turns keeping an eye on Pebble to ensure he didn't go with Kenneth anytime he left the camp. The only way they knew to avoid the horrific carnage of the vision was to prevent the events leading up to it from occurring.

The next four days passed uneventfully, and they occupied their time combing through everything Gus knew on the subject of wand-making. Osric entertained them with stories of the eagle-filled dreams he was having. Pebble kept them all guessing at his game, and Osric and Kenneth practiced their swordplay and marksmanship in the evenings. They would run through their drills meticulously, then swap weapons to maintain proficiency with both Osric's short sword and the heavier long sword Kenneth carried. They were both surprised at how quickly Osric was improving with his bow. Truthfully, he had never been bad at it, but Kenneth had to utilize his Hunter gift just to outshoot him.

As they traveled further east, the scenery passing beneath them changed progressively. The dense trees thinned as they approached the Diutinus River and left them crossing the immense stretch of plains on the far side of its eastern bank. After two days of monotonous grasslands, they came within sight of snowcapped mountain peaks, and the terrain became rockier, the vegetation more varied. They veered south, skirting the edge of the mountain range and avoiding the mountain troll tribes known to reside there, preying on careless travelers and poorly defended trade caravans. Each night, Greyback would locate a suitable campsite, and they would make their descent back to solid ground. They had covered a great distance, making good time, and Osric expected that they would have enough supplies to reach Barlington. He and Kenneth hunted regularly in the evenings to supplement their foodstuffs, and from Osric's calculations they would reach the coastal city to resupply within the week.

Their long days in the air were filled mostly with Gus telling stories of his travels over the years. They were still hoping he would think of something from his experiences that would bring light to the mysteries of the prophecy. Every now and then, he would get sidetracked on some explanation of how he had gained certain knowledge and techniques of wand-making, such as where to put the point of constriction, or how thick to make the magical shaft.

On a particularly off-topic day, he had said something that made Osric curious as to why he had such a bad relationship with Eni. Gus was sitting at the base of Greyback's neck, straddling the area between the spikes, where Osric and Kenneth secured their swords. He used the position often during conversations. It provided him with just enough height to be seen and heard, and Gus loved to be the center of attention.

"So, what caused you two to have such hatred toward each other?" Osric's curiosity got the better of him.

Angry and bitter, Gus growled, "Eni is an old dimwit. He is a couple years older than I and thinks that makes him wiser." Gus waggled his claw in the air, punctuating the absurdity of this assumption. "He fails to explore the craft of wand-making and insists that the theory he has been taught is the only way." He shook his head to express his distaste for such a narrow-minded way of thinking.

"So there are different theories to wand-making?" Bridgett inquired while Pebble snuggled in her arms, more interested in her attention than the conversation.

"Oh, yes. Many different thoughts and theories on that particular subject," Gus said. "And that is where our differences started."

"Your hatred is because of wand theory?" Osric probed.

"Yes, and over a specific wand theory as well," Gus stated with a serious expression. "The most highly debated Wand-Maker's theory, to be honest."

"I heard about that," Kenneth jumped in excitedly. "That's where some Wand-Makers think you can make a wand do its own magic, right?"

"Well, yes and no," Gus said. "But that is the common belief. So I will have to forgive your doltishness for now," he said in a jab, not just at Kenneth but at all who spread that story. "It is, in fact, a belief among many of us Wand-Makers that you can"—he paused, searching for the right words—"bind different abilities to the magical structure of a wand, without the presence of a stone or amulet. This would then endow that ability to the carrier of the wand."

"That's it!" Osric shouted.

"No, it is not," Gus replied with such vehemence that it silenced Osric mid-sentence. "Now, I am a believer in this line of thought, but as much as I want it to be true, there has not been a breakthrough in this area. If I had made such a wand, I would most definitely be able to see it in the wand's magical structure." Gus motioned at the wand Osric held in his hand. "Believe me, I would love to see it."

The pleading tone of his voice made Osric furrow his brow with frustration. He looked to the faces of everyone on board for help, but each one seemed to be battling their own confusion. They each knew that there had to be a connection, even though he had not noticed anything except the power growth from Bridgett's amulet. Somehow, the controversial theory must explain the wand in the prophecy. Pebble was the only one who did not seem to be searching his memory for a way to tie it all together.

"Is there any way that it could just be hidden from you?" Osric begged Gus to give him some kind of hope—an answer, anything to help resolve the mystery. Gus raised an eyebrow.

"That is another yes *and* no," he said, holding up his finger to silence Osric. "That is where the unicorns come into this conversation," he said, nodding in Bridgett's direction.

"What do the unicorns have to do with wand-making?" she asked, sitting up straighter in her seat.

"That's the thing, I have no idea," Gus stated unapologetically. "I am convinced that they hold the key, and their involvement so far is what has me believing you are right, Osric." Osric and Bridgett exchanged intrigued looks, wondering where Gus might take the conversation next. "I have told you that Wand-Makers can observe the magical strands within us all, right?" They nodded, not wanting to interrupt. "Well, with the unicorns, it's different."

"Different?" Kenneth asked. "How so?"

"When I look within one of you, I can see your gift like an orb, much the same as I see within your amulet." He motioned towards Bridgett. "When a Wand-Maker looks within a unicorn, the strands, the orbs, they're all cloudy," Gus replied with a pained look on his face. "And not like fog on water. It's like it was deliberately distorted."

"Are you suggesting that the unicorns purposely deceive us?" Bridgett's eyes narrowed at the offensive nature of Gus' comment, though she spoke softly, as Pebble was fast asleep in her arms.

"Not at all, my dear. Concealing something is very different from deceiving," Gus said with a shrug. "After all, they may be concealing things from us for good reason."

"So, what makes you think they conceal things?" Kenneth asked. "Isn't it possible that their magic is just beyond the abilities of Wand-Makers to view?"

"This is the point where our story comes full circle. I traveled to the village of Er'amar when I was young and still learning my craft." Gus smiled at Kenneth. "That is where all who are serious in their pursuit of crafting wands go to study. I was gathering sticks in a small field"—as he grew excited, his paws waved about frantically—"when I saw a small group of unicorns. I had heard stories from one of my instructors about the unicorns, stories of secrets she thought they held within them, and I wanted to discover them all for myself. So, I activated my gift and slowly made my way toward them. From such a great distance, I could make out very little, but I could tell that there was something within them that I had never seen. I crept slowly and quietly. The closer I got, the better I could see. There were tremendous wonders inside of them, still just out of sight. They possessed magical abilities that I just had to catch a glimpse of. Then, when I was within a stride or two of being able to make everything out, they each clouded up, just like that!" he said, clapping his paws together, obviously frustrated. "Then they all turned and looked directly at me, as if to ask if I enjoyed the show!"

Osric's jaw hung slack as he wondered what the unicorns could be hiding from the other races. Bridgett held Pebble a little tighter, disturbed by what she had heard but unable to deny that the unicorns were often secretive.

Gus sighed and continued with a somber tone, "I shared what I saw with my fellow Wand-Makers, and Eni was among them." His pitch rose steadily. "He called me crazy. Said that I made the whole thing up to make myself out to be better than the rest of them. Ever since then, he has done everything in his power to oppose me." Gus clenched his paw into a fist and his face grew angry. "I think he hunted my wife just to deprive me of the old wench's company!"

"Oh's neat! Look's at the birdies!" Pebble had roused from his nap, and he spoke with such innocent enthusiasm that it cut through the tension as he giggled. They all found themselves laughing with him until the levity fell from Osric's face. His pupils dilated, his muscles tensed, and he felt as though his skin were boiling without heat.

"Greyback! Dive!" Osric shouted and reached toward his sword.

Greyback looked up and spotted an eagle diving toward them. Bridgett grasped Pebble tightly, and Gus grabbed for the nearest spike to hold onto.

As Greyback began to bank to the left and dive, Osric stretched as far as he could, but the straps holding him in his seat were too tight, and his fingers could only brush the hilt of his sword. Just then, a large black eagle collided with Greyback's right wing as it swooped down toward them out of the clouds, sending them spinning toward the ground. Greyback fought to regain control, but her wing had been badly injured by the collision.

"No! You fool!" a voice shouted from high above them. Seconds stretched into an eternity in their uncontrollable fall.

Suddenly, they were right-side up again. Osric twisted in his seat to be sure everyone was accounted for. Pebble was giggling in Bridgett's arms, asking if they could do it again. He turned back and looked with fear at the spot where Gus had been standing; he was not there.

"Don't you dare eat him!" came the voice again, but closer and from the right. "Bring him right back up here this instant! Don't you ever listen? We don't hunt walkers, and we never hunt anyone on a dragon!" The voice came from a large eagle, roughly the same size as Greyback. He was gliding on huge black wings, and white feathers crowned his head. He had stabilized their flight somehow, and he was supporting Greyback's right wing with his left one.

"I hate to trouble you, feathered friend, but I must land. I am afraid my wing is broken," Greyback said with surprising politeness. Short, pained gasps of air could be heard as she spoke to the eagle, "I would be grateful for any assistance, if my passengers would allow me to land?"

"Of course you can land," Bridgett spoke quickly. Osric was amazed that she would feel the need to ask.

"Our aerie is just at the top of that mountain. Can you climb?" asked the eagle, motioning to the east. A dark shadow covered them, slightly smaller than the body of the dragon, causing them all to duck in fear of another attack. Osric breathed a sigh of relief as Gus was dropped in his lap.

"No. My injury is too great. I cannot climb. I am afraid I cannot stay in the air for long." Gus struggled out of Osric's hands, yelling insults at the smaller eagle for not eating him. "I could make it to the clearing ahead,

70

next to the tall oak and stream. I think that will be a large enough area to land in, don't you?" No one wanted to interrupt their conversation. Although he had just injured her, Greyback spoke to the eagle with great respect, and he seemed to reciprocate the emotion.

"But we were supposed to be hunting!" protested the younger eagle, whining in frustration.

"Silence is your best option right now. We will talk later!" shouted the bigger of the two birds. They began their short descent to the ground, landing awkwardly in a large field surrounded by oak trees.

Chapter 9
The Caves of D'pareth

The landing caused Greyback even more pain. What at first had been a typical break became two protruding bones, yet there was very little blood. The larger of the two eagles began to examine Greyback's wounds. Osric and Kenneth gently removed the equipment from her back.

"You need to go get help! Bring her transport and aid to carry her passengers!" the large eagle bellowed to the smaller one. The younger eagle let out a frustrated squawk and flew northeast toward their home. "I am sorry, but I must insist. We have Healers experienced in these types of wounds."

"Oh? You try to hunt passengers often, do you?" puffed Gus, glowering at the eagle. "Some kind of sport for you eagles, is it?"

"What is your name, friend?" the eagle asked Greyback, completely ignoring Gus.

"Greyback."

"I am known as Ero," he replied with a bow. "I have help on the way. Do not worry. We will take care of your passengers," Ero stated, looking at each of them with his large golden eyes, and motioning toward them with his head, to tell her that they would be all right. "We will have you all brought to our aerie. Our Healers can have you mended as soon as possible."

"So's we can see more birdies?" Pebble was bouncing with excitement.

"Yes, we will see more birds," Gus barked. "If you're lucky, they won't just eat you!"

While they waited, Bridgett and Ero tended to the broken wing, and Gus soothed and distracted Greyback. Kenneth and Osric organized their gear to be transported by the eagles. Osric checked the crates and let out a slow whistle.

"We have a problem." Osric sat down on top of the box. "All of our supplies are gone."

"Yes, of course they are. We were upside down twice before I fell off of the dragon, you idiot!" shouted Gus. "What did you expect?"

"Osric, it's Toby. Do you have a minute?"

Osric was startled by the voice emanating from his wand. He took it out of its leather pouch and held it up in front of him, and he could see his Profice's miniature figure standing in midair above it.

"Toby, do you have any news?" Osric was eager to hear of more survivors, and he hoped that some of his superiors were among them. It would make him feel better to at least have one of them tell him he was doing what they would have asked.

"We have uncovered another twelve survivors in the last week, but we still cannot get to the throne room. We are finding less and less whole walls as we uncover more, and we are having a hard time preventing cave-ins. It is making the whole rescue process slow and labor intensive. Our stabilizing spells can only do so much," Toby said apologetically.

They continued their conversation for a time, as Toby explained the issues they were encountering with the removal of the rubble from above the throne room. Soon, Osric could see eagles arriving to take them to their aerie, so Osric ended their conversation, but he asked him to contact him again when they uncovered more. Kenneth and Bridgett assisted him as he loaded their gear on one eagle, then they all climbed aboard another and watched as Greyback was ferried off by four more.

They watched the large oak trees fade into the distance as they gained altitude. Soon they could see that they were approaching cliffs with several thousand large nests nestled in the crags of the rocky ledges. The nests were woven from branches and vines. Osric got the impression that a single gust of wind would topple them from their precarious perch on the rocks, but the varying signs of weathering and wear on the branches showed they had been in place for a very long time.

The eagles landed on a wide ledge in the center of the nesting colony. The space had looked a lot smaller from the air, but upon landing they were awestruck by its spacious width. The eagles unloaded the passengers and their gear and flew off in silence. They were only a few strides below the tree line, and the temperature had decreased dramatically. Osric watched his breath float away in the bitterly cold air. One thing was certain: they could not sleep outside without cover. Osric could see the same thought in the eyes of his friends. Even Pebble and Gus, with their fur pelts, seemed to feel it as much as the rest. Osric decided he would have to do something about it, since their escort had seemingly abandoned them.

He informed the group of his intentions and set out to locate Ero, but it was no easy task. There were thousands of eagles about, none of whom looked happy to see a man walking among them. It was an odd thing for Osric to see. He had encountered many different species in Stanton, but the eagles were colder toward them than the mountain air. After all of the recent efforts to bring the world to the brink of unification, it was unnerving to experience their negativity at such a crucial point in history. He continued cautiously around several nests that would be large enough for Greyback to coil up in. He had to climb over sharp rocks to reach adjacent ledges and was quickly feeling the effects of the thin air at such a high altitude.

"Hold still, my cousin." Osric could hear Ero's voice from somewhere nearby, and he heard Greyback moaning as well, but he could see neither of them. "We need to set the bone or it will not heal properly."

Osric crossed to the next ledge and came up behind a large gathering of eagles. Their attention was focused on Ero and Greyback, and it did not take long to get around them. Osric arrived just in time to watch them set the bone, with the aid of some very thick leather straps. He looked on with curiosity as Healers wrapped her wing in a fibrous material. When they were done, Ero knelt down and touched the material, and it instantly became like stone.

"Osric, what can I do for you?" Greyback asked, attempting to stand to address him, worried that he would be upset with her.

"Don't get up. You could hurt yourself." Osric motioned her to stay down as he approached rapidly. "I'm here to speak to Ero." He was thankful that Greyback was there to witness the conversation. He had a strong feeling that he would get better results talking to Ero in the presence of the dragon. The intense gazes of the eagles gathered around them put him on edge. Greyback's proximity helped to ease his anxiety about the tense situation.

"What makes you think that you can interrupt her healing?!" Ero was clearly annoyed by the disturbance. "What do you want?"

"No disrespect intended. We just got dropped off on the side of a mountain after being attacked. We would be grateful for shelter or supplies. All of ours were lost when Greyback was injured, and we will freeze to death without them." Osric tried to sound respectful but assertive.

The expression on Ero's face went from anger and frustration to understanding, and then rapidly back to anger. It was as though he realized the responsibility he had, and he wanted to resolve it without speaking to Osric.

"Oh yes, I need to make sure my passengers survive." Greyback tried to get up again.

"No, beautiful." Osric tried to show the dragon the same respect that Gus had. Hopefully it would curry some favor with the eagles. "The eagles are responsible for the trouble we all face, as well as your injury. We will never hold you at fault for this. We will find a way to offer you more for your troubles, as well."

It was evidently the wrong approach, as several eagles cried out in anger and charged toward him. They separated him from Greyback, who screeched in protest. Osric gripped his sword hilt, prepared to draw it if the eagles provoked him. He drew his wand defensively and erected a shield charm around himself. The shield would not last long if it came to an attack of talons and beaks, but it would give him a chance to react. Power surged through Osric as he stared into the eyes of his would-be attackers. It was the same intense power he had felt when he cast the spell to dry his tunic. He thought quickly. It must have something to do with necessity, as he had needed his clothing to dry quickly, and he obviously needed to defend himself from the eagles. That was something he would have to explore later, as right then he needed to focus on fending off an attack.

"How dare you treat a creature of the air like that?!" Ero raged.

"What? With respect and concern?" Osric said, baffled.

"Ha! You are trying to prostitute her!"

"Prostitute her? Is that what you think?

"You offered her money in front of us! How could you deny it?"

"Extra gold for saving our lives? You are all fools if that is what you saw." Osric let out a nervous laugh.

"We witnessed it with our own eyes!"

"What you saw was me offering my friend a gift for saving my life! Are you the authority on what friends she can have as well?" Osric had begun to sense where their anger had come from. They thought it shameful to fly for payment. If he wanted the eagles to understand and respect them, Osric would need to take the moral high ground for now.

"Friends? Ha! You call your slaves friends? We have never lowered ourselves to service of another species! We are the authority in the air!"

"Because you separate yourselves from the rest of the world! You think yourselves better?" Osric turned slowly, looking each of them in the eyes. Power was coursing through him. The hair on the back of his neck stood up, and chills ran over his skin. "We offered her what she wanted in exchange for what we wanted, and now we offer her more in thanks. What is wrong with that arrangement?"

"How dare you?!" The angry eagles began to close in on him. He could hear Greyback protesting. The entire crowd seemed ready to attack. Resentment filled their eyes as the gap between them and Osric narrowed to only a light toss of a stone.

Then, from somewhere deep within, Osric felt a calming sensation as well as a certainty of movement. His vision seemed to cloud and get clearer at the same time. The eagles noticed a change in him as well, as he sheathed his sword and wand on instinct. Osric completed his last rotation, taking time to stare into each of their eyes. Then he walked directly to Ero, who looked terrified, and timidly backed away. The spectators gasped, their eyes wide. Osric placed his palms on each of Ero's feathered cheeks.

Hoarsely, he said, *"Ero of the majestic ones, from the time of the beginning, your species has watched, but those below do not see what you see. They do not know what your species knows. Share with them what you know of what has passed. Your aid is essential to their success. Look to the one who grasps your sight, for your future lies with him."*

Osric's vision began to return to normal, as his hands fell slowly back to his sides. His muscles began to tense again, and he was uncertain what had just occurred. The memory of the moment rapidly faded, drifting through his thoughts like sand in the wind. *What did I just say?* he thought in confusion.

He maintained his gaze into Ero's eyes, as he had a strong feeling that Ero was the only reason he remained unharmed. The last thing he wanted to do was reach for his sword or wand. He stayed poised to draw them if the situation called for it, but he resisted arming himself out of fear.

"You are a strange man," Ero said cautiously. "But yours is the only kind trusted by eagles. Follow me and we will find you cover, then we will show you things of interest."

Ero flew slowly toward his friends, following as quickly as he could. The events that had occurred just moments before still drifted through Osric's mind. Why could he not remember what had happened? The thought that he could do something and then not remember it troubled him. Ero had said he would show them things of interest, but what did that mean? *What did he mean about how 'my kind' is the only one trusted by eagles?* From behind the crowd of spectating eagles, as he skirted around them, he heard a giggle.

"We's got's a magic wand.
They's got's to figure's it out.
Riddles and rhymes, 'til we run's outta time.
We's got's a magic wand."

Pebble sang as he wove his way through the eagles' legs. Osric was surprised to see him there, but he laughed at the childish nature of the song. It was cute to watch him skip along, singing it aloud for all to hear, and it was refreshing to have it put in such a lighthearted, simple way. The pressure of the mystery was growing daily. He took advantage of the moment to smile and watch childishness at its finest.

Pebble continued humming the tune for a time, until he noticed a rather fierce-looking eagle. With some help from Osric, he climbed up onto his shoulder for protection.

"Wanna play 'I's see somethin' you's don't?'" Pebble cheerfully inquired once they were out of sight of the eagle that had scared him.

"Sure. Why not?" Osric couldn't help but laugh. Things had just taken a turn for the better, and he was growing attached to the pup, even if his game was impossible to win.

"I see's somethin' you's don't," Pebble initiated the game, looking around with an intense gaze. "And they's are two's green circles."

Osric laughed again. Pebble had ended his gaze at his face before announcing his discovery, so it would be an easy guess. Osric pretended to look around in concentration before he replied.

"My eyes?" Osric guessed with a smile.

"You's look'sed!" Pebble bounced up and down on Osric's shoulder. "Now it's you's turn," he said with a giggle.

They continued with their game until they reached the cold, scared group of travelers. Osric hadn't guessed any more correct answers by the time they arrived.

"Archana's bones!" Gus shouted. "How dare you run off without telling someone! We looked everywhere for you!" He ran to Osric's feet and glowered up at Pebble from the ground.

Bridgett came running to Osric. Pebble jumped into her hands for protection from Gus. He burrowed into her warm, folded arms and stuck his head out cautiously to look around. Bridgett's eyes were rimmed in red, as though she had been crying. Osric felt a twinge of nervousness as he stepped up and put an arm around her shoulders to comfort her.

"It's all right, everyone. He was in no danger that I witnessed. He was just curious," stated Osric, directing his gaze at Pebble. "You should tell somebody next time." Osric rubbed his head, lightly ruffling his fur. "The eagles have agreed to shelter us." Osric took note of the fact that Ero was standing close by, watching them and waiting for them to be ready to move.

"They have?" Gus looked a bit confused. "Now, how did you get them to do that? They haven't so much as acknowledged our existence," he argued, directing his glare toward Ero.

"Right now, the important thing is that we will have shelter. We can leave the hows and whys for another time. Pack up. We need to move quickly. It's getting colder out here," Osric said, as he headed toward their gear.

"We will have your things brought to you. Now come. You need to start a fire for warmth," Ero stated with an air of impatience.

"We will need food and blankets brought to us immediately!" Gus walked right up in front of Ero. "Your kind has cost us everything in the attack." Then he spat on the ground in front of the eagle. "Now, are you going to take us to shelter or just stand there like a bloody statue?"

Ero merely looked down and appeared to contemplate Gus, as he stood there in defiance of the eagle's size. Osric saw significant irony in Gus's confrontation with the large bird. Ero must have been pondering the same question he was. Why would a creature that size be so brash toward his natural predators? Osric almost wished that Ero would eat Gus and save him the nuisance of his attitude. Osric stole a glance at Bridgett. She had an amused yet contemplative expression on her face. After a brief moment, Ero turned away from the arrogant prairie dog and took flight, leading them slowly along the hazardous mountain ledges.

They each gathered what dry wood they could as they followed the eagle's measured flight. Ero guided them along narrow ledges to the opening of a large cave. He led them inside and indicated that they should enter the chamber immediately to the left of the opening. It would provide the best shelter from wind, as a cold breeze could be felt flowing toward the other three chambers. They piled the wood they had gathered against the wall on the right and Kenneth set to making a firepit in the center of the chamber. Kenneth had a blaze started quickly, and Ero left them in the cave, warming themselves by the fire.

They stood rubbing their hands together over the flames, huddled as close to its heat as possible without getting burned. Osric was starting to feel warmth returning to his hands, and he attempted to relate the tale of his encounter with the eagles and Greyback. He told them of the confrontation and how the eagles had grown more and more upset with every word he spoke. His apprehension grew as he recounted his memory loss.

"Then I did something, but I can't remember what it was. Ero told me I was strange, and he looked shocked at my behavior. Then he told me that my *kind* was the only one the eagles trusted." Osric shrugged and shook his head in bewilderment.

"Wait. You don't remember any of it?" Kenneth asked, confused.

"Well, I remember that I felt confidence in what I was doing. I think I said something, and I tried to remember the words, but they slipped away too fast."

"Did you eat any wild mushrooms, boy?" Gus shouted.

"Gus, I think that is quite enough of that for today," Bridgett came to his defense as Osric glared at Gus. "This is serious, can't you see? What if it has to do with the wand and the prophecy?" She spoke calmly, but her tone conveyed the importance of her questions.

"I'm sorry. You are right," Gus conceded quickly, shaking his head, and turned toward Pebble. "Pebble was with you. What did you hear, son?"

"I's no hears nothin'." Pebble was excited to be included in the conversation, offering his information with youthful enthusiasm. "I's just see's him," he said with a giggle.

"Cursed strands!" Gus swore. He put his paws on his head to think while growling low in his throat. Then he calmed and slowly raised his head and dropped his hands. "Were you using your gift?"

"Yeper's, Pa!"

"Smart boy. Well done. You see, everyone, what good parentage can do?" Gus said with pride. They all stared at Pebble, eagerly waiting to learn what he had seen. "Can you tell us anything interesting about what you saw?" Gus asked, smiling.

"Yep, he's is different now." Pebble pointed right at Osric.

"Different?" Gus said to himself, looking at Osric's stunned face and then back at his son.

"Look's at him," Pebble said, pointing again at Osric. Reluctantly, Gus raised his gaze to meet the hesitant expression on Osric's face.

Osric stood there in shock. He had been telling them all along that he had the wand. He knew it was the best opportunity to prove it to them, but he hated the idea of Gus peering within him with his gift. He steeled himself for the intrusive scrutiny.

Gus could sense the resistance in Osric from the expression on his face. Normally, he would never use his gift on someone who did not welcome it, but the situation called for drastic measures. He hesitated, knowing that if the boy were different, he would have to admit that the prophecy had been real, and they would all likely die on the journey. Gus's recent experience in the eagle's talons had reminded him of his own mortality, and even as he welcomed the thought of dying in a predator's grasp, he felt he still had much to learn. He glanced at his young son, thinking of Pebble's potential to carry on his legacy as Archana's greatest Wand-Maker, and he shivered at the idea of being torn limb from limb. As he braced himself to learn the truth and redirected his gaze back to Osric, his intended inspection was interrupted.

"If you are all warm enough, we would like to show you some things you may find interesting." Ero entered the cave and noted the awkward silence and uncomfortable stares between Osric and Gus. "Gentlemen, if you would, please come with me."

Kenneth tossed a few more logs on the fire so that heat would continue to build up in the cave while they were gone, and he lit the end of another to take along as a torch. Then he slapped Osric on the shoulder in quiet sympathy to his reservations at being inspected, before joining Bridgett at the mouth of their cave. Osric looked away from Gus uncomfortably, as they were both keenly aware that the examination must still take place. For the time being, they had gained a short respite from the inevitable magical probing. They joined the others, curious about what Ero had in store for them. Pebble tugged on Bridgett's skirt, and she lifted him up onto her shoulder with a smile as they set out.

Much to their surprise, they were not led back out onto the windswept rocky ledges from which they had arrived. Instead, Ero led them deeper into the main cave, winding their way into the heart of the mountain itself. After a few moments of walking along a smooth, narrow path the ground began to slope downward beneath their feet. They followed closely behind Ero, afraid that they could easily lose their way in the myriad of twisting tunnels. Osric attempted to keep track of the sequence of left and right turns, but soon he gave up and just focused on keeping the group together.

Ahead of him, Bridgett inhaled deeply. A warm breeze flowed through the tunnels from somewhere ahead of them. The passage had widened significantly as they descended deeper into the mountain. Ero took them around a final bend, and they got the impression that the tunnel ended abruptly in a cavern. The ceiling of the cave looked as though it had just broken away, and the walls swept outward, creating sheer rock cliffs to each side of the path they stood on. At first, they thought Ero had led them to a dead end, but he indicated that they should continue down a narrow stairway that had been carved into the cliff face to their right. As they approached the precipice to gain the stairs, they were able to look down into the massive cavern.

The sight that unfolded before them was beyond their imagining. They were still obviously within the network of caves, but the steep, crude stairway led down into a lush oasis. Osric could just make out the opposite wall of the cavern, thanks to the cloud of mist at the base of a waterfall cascading down the wall. They could see stars in the night sky through many voids in the cave ceiling. The light was too dim to make out the source of the water, but Osric could see the pool it formed on the rocks below and a river flowing away from it through the center of the space. The rocks were heavily blanketed by green moss, and the tops of trees were nearly even with their perch in the cavern wall. Their torchlight reflected off of massive crystalline stalactites hanging from the ceiling and from smaller crystals in the cliff face along the steps.

"You are the first outsiders to see these caves in a very long time." Ero stood at the top of the stairs, but not a single eye looked in his direction. They were stunned by the beauty before them. "Welcome to the Caves of D'pareth."

Chapter 10
Lessons Learned

The air smelled of sulfur, and steam rose from several small ponds scattered between the trees and rocks. The frigid cold they had been exposed to on the cliff ledge was easy to forget in the warm humidity of the subterranean paradise. From the base of the stairs, they followed a trail along the wall, ducking under hanging vines and sweeping large fronds of ferns from their path. A loud roaring could be heard as they walked, but Osric could not identify its source until water suddenly burst from a crevice high up in the wall ahead of them. The spray dampened their hair and clothing and lit on their eyelashes as the water cascaded down the wall and splashed upon the rocks at their feet. They jumped back in surprise, and Ero took flight to avoid wetting his feathers. They trekked into the heavy vegetation to cross the stream created by the newest waterfall, and then they veered back again.

Ero turned them from the path and guided them down a corridor to a smaller cavern. During the day, light would not penetrate beyond the first bend in the tunnel, and so the rocks near their feet were soon clear of the moss. Water dripped from the ceiling and pooled on the floor of the cave, creating massive stalactites, stalagmites, and limestone pillars where the older formations had met in the middle. Crystals lined the ceiling, walls, and floor, giving the space a surreal look. They passed under crystals that dominated them in both height and girth, jutting out in all directions. The light from their torch danced across the refractive surfaces, lighting the entire space with an orange glow.

They continued in silence, gazing around at the magnificent display. As they traveled deeper inside the caves, the air continued to grow warmer. Ero paused at the back of the cavern, waiting for each of them to take in the view. They could see an opening near the ceiling, and he indicated that they should follow him up to it. Crystals protruded from the wall, creating a natural stairway that they could climb without too much difficulty, but they each envied Ero's wings and his effortless ascent.

Joining him at the top, they found themselves facing the entrance to a small cave. He held out one wing to prevent them from stepping in front of him.

"Frigus Abscido," Ero muttered from outside the cave. The confused looks on his companion's faces assured Osric that none of them understood the language either. In response to Ero's words, a transparent, magical shield shimmered for an instant in the doorway of the cave, and then he dropped his wing to allow them to proceed. Warm, moist air rushed ahead of them into the room as they were led inside. Ero waited until they had all entered and turned, speaking the words, "Frigus Adaugeo," in the direction of the opening. They caught the momentary shimmer of the shield reforming, and it grew distinctively cooler in the room than it had been in the chamber outside.

"What was that you just did?" Gus inquired.

"Magic," Ero said in a disgusted tone. "You have all come a long way when it comes to magic, but you could learn a lot from the past. The past is why I have brought you here today."

"That is ridiculous! Magic has never been as well explored as it is today!" Gus was in the mood to argue, and when it came to the subject of magic, he refused to back down.

"By all means, wise one, tell us what you know of the spoken spell." Ero's voice dripped with sarcasm as he cocked his head to the side.

"Well," Gus stuttered over a few unintelligible words before he gave in. "Oh, go on then!"

"Or could you possibly inform us as to what magical techniques were being studied at the time when wands came to be?" Ero was pushing Gus to keep him quiet, Osric guessed, in case he intended to argue with him on another subject. "No?" Ero questioned, at Gus's grunt of displeasure. "Will you allow me to continue uninterrupted? I have much to teach that even you will find informative. My gift is not found among any of the walkers, and listening may serve you well."

"Go's on! You's don't gotsta be so mean!" Pebble came to the defense of his father and scrambled down off of Bridgett's shoulder to land unceremoniously on the floor. Gus looked even more uncomfortable about Pebble defending him.

"That's enough out of you, boy!" Gus barked at Pebble and then turned to Ero. "Teach us already, won't you!"

Pebble cowered down, looking over at Gus. Kenneth, Bridgett, and Osric looked at Pebble sympathetically.

"The first lesson is a short one," Ero stated, leaning toward Gus. "Never make your child think it is a mistake to love his father."

Gus growled irritatedly, while Pebble sat pouting at Bridgett's feet. Bridgett scooped him up and he snuggled into her arms for comfort, hiding his face from his father.

"Now, on to business," Ero said, assuming a proud stance. "To start this off properly, I should inform you that I am a Chronicleer."

"A what?" Osric and Gus spoke in unison.

"Ah." Looking a bit frustrated, Ero thought for a moment. "You are familiar with the gift of the See-ers, yes?" Ero gestured toward Osric and frowned at his confused expression.

"All too familiar!" Gus was grumpy again, and then he remembered his last lecture. "Well ah, I mean, of course we are. We encountered one the day we left on Greyback."

"Yes, well." Ero was baffled by Osric's reaction and Gus's reference, but he could ask them more about it later. "A Chronicleer is essentially the opposite." Ero glanced around at the questioning looks on their faces, growing ever more frustrated by their slow understanding, and adopted Gus's tendency for sarcasm. "You may be asking yourself what good it is to know what you had for dinner last week, but in fact, that is not what I mean. Recently, those of us with the gift have been having dreams and visions of the events surrounding the time of wand creation, and what we have learned from these insights is why I have brought you here today."

"Wait." Osric was bothered by the fact that he had somehow angered the eagles to the point of nearly killing him, and he wanted to know how. After observing Ero's interactions with Gus, he suspected that it was not hate with which the eagles looked at walkers, but superiority. He decided to play the role of an inferior, to learn from Ero how to avoid another confrontation with the eagles.

"Yes?" Ero questioned Osric.

"No disrespect intended, Ero, but I would like to understand something first, in order to prevent any future misunderstandings," Osric said in his most respectful voice, bowing slightly and awaiting permission before he continued.

"What is your question?"

"I am sure there are many differences in regards to walkers and fliers, and one of them nearly led to my death earlier today," Osric said, attempting to speak in a non-accusatory fashion. "I would like to know what it is that the eagles found offensive about my statements, if you could please."

Ero eyed him suspiciously as Osric knelt down before him, palms flat on the ground, waiting. As he looked upon the humble human, Ero's expression turned from suspicion to a deep sympathy.

"Has your knowledge of the past truly waned to this extent without our gift?" Ero said in a deep voice as he towered over Osric. There was a tenderness in his tone that none of them had heard from him before. "Rise and build me a fire, and I will tell you the story of those days first." A tear welled up in one of the eagle's golden eyes, rolled down his hooked beak, and dropped, landing in a salty splash on Osric's hand. He was shaken by Ero's display of emotion, and he was thankful that he had chosen to appeal to him in such a manner.

So Osric rose, wiping his hand on his tunic, and he and Kenneth collected wood from a nearby pile and lit a fire in the pit at the center of the cave. Pebble seemed to know it was time for a fire-telling, and he was antsy with excitement on Bridgett's lap as he waited. Gus sat off to the side, alternating glares at Ero and Osric for his humble display before the arrogant bird. Taken aback by the treatment he had received, he decided to keep to himself. After the fire was built, Ero began his story as everyone gathered to watch the flames.

"Three hundred and twenty-nine years ago, humans had just won their last war at great cost. The war they fought against the caldereth cost them dearly in crops, land, homes, and hunters to provide for families. Some areas had more than was needed, and others had none. Man needed to establish communication in order to ensure their survival, and the making of wands had not yet occurred." Figures could be seen coming to life in the fire in greater detail than any of them had ever witnessed. It was as though the story were occurring right before their eyes.

When Osric closed his eyes, he saw everything as though he were there. He could feel the dirt beneath his feet, smell the air, and touch the rubble that had once been homes and shops. *This eagle has an amazing gift for fire-telling,* he thought as he listened with his eyes closed.

"Our cousin flier, the dragon, was mighty at that time," Ero continued. "They had within them a deep love for all walkers, but they had a love for family which was even greater. Man used that love against them for fear that they would not help them in their time of need. Man fashioned steel cages strong enough to hold a dragon, fifty of them, and called to the dragon elders to come for a feast at the Braya Volcano.

"At this time, all dragons trusted humans and felt no danger in answering their call. So when they were told that their meals would have escaped without the cages, the dragons felt no need to question their methods. The trap was sprung, and the cages where sealed by magic.

"Their cries could be heard for miles as they tried to free themselves. Briefly, those in the air tried to come to the aid of their trapped kin, but the walkers killed the eldest dragon, Brinsop, who was one thousand nine hundred and thirty-two years old and the wisest and most loved of his kind.

"That act alone defeated the dragons. They cowered before walkers and submitted to their will. The walkers demanded to be flown about Archana for a small fee, and at all times, to aid any walker that needed travel. The freedom and joy that all dragons had at one time enjoyed was taken from them in violence and manipulation. They had to guarantee safe travel to any who needed flight to speed their journey. If the dragons kept to their part of the agreement, then no more of their elders would be killed, but they would be held there lest they should ever go back on their bargain. They sold themselves into slavery to keep their elders imprisoned but alive!"

Ero was visibly upset, and anger grew in his voice with every word as he spoke. As the images danced before his closed eyes, the sensation of bile rising in his throat caught Osric off guard. He felt physically ill. Each time Ero paused to let the narrative catch up with his words, he visualized the atrocities described as the cages slammed shut. Then he heard the cries of the eagles above rend the sky. He felt the horror as he watched along with them when the wings and tail were ripped off of Brinsop, and cried out at the defeat in every dragon's eyes with their eldest's demise.

There were many species that had participated in the slaughter. Irua, weasels, men, elves, groundhogs, and a few species that none of them had ever laid eyes on, could be seen in the abhorrent scene. Though sadness was apparent on some of their faces, none spoke a word in defense of the dragons.

"We were warned by a See-er not to interfere or to become slaves ourselves." Ero hung his head. "I have witnessed the vision he brought with him to our aerie. It is not a story I want to see transpire."

"You must understand, as commoners, we had no knowledge that these events even took place," Bridgett spoke through her tears as she comforted Pebble in his fear and confusion.

"Whether you had knowledge of it or not, you could not expect us to be happy to witness the slavery with our own eyes." Ero shook with restrained rage.

"And gifting us with this knowledge, instead of trying to slaughter the boy, was beyond you?" Gus gestured in Osric's direction. He was appalled that the eagles had withheld the information from the other races, in the interest of their own egos.

Ero looked at Gus in defiance and then looked away, hanging his head in shame. Kenneth, Gus, and Bridgett looked at each other in wonder. There was palpable tension in the air as they thought about what they had just witnessed in the flames. Bridgett looked with confusion at the tears streaming down Osric's face. He had sat near the fire and listened to the story, but he had never opened his eyes, yet Osric seemed to be more affected than the rest of them.

"My apologies to you all," Ero said slowly, lifting his head to address them. "It was wrong of us to hold you responsible for things you had no knowledge of." Ero gazed at Osric, who was shaking and drawing in deep, angry breaths.

"If there is enough power within me," Osric spoke softly into his chest, "I will see their slavery come to an end. I do not know if I can promise success, but I will die before what I just witnessed continues a day longer than it must." He raised his head to meet the gaze of Ero. "First, though, I must stop a war, and I…" he choked up.

"If any man can," Ero interjected in a soft respectful voice, "I believe it is you." He leaned in to embrace him, and Osric spoke a few words that none but Ero could hear. "Yes, you are," Ero replied to his whispered inquiry, and they exchanged a look of deeper understanding. "And I believe you are more than that. You may be the greatest wizard to ever walk this world."

Osric sat back down and shook his head, trying to process Ero's words. He held in the sobs that tightened his throat, and he ran his hands through his hair. This was not the life that he wanted for himself. He wanted his security post in Stanton. He wanted to live simply and to raise a family someday. Somehow, his life had been chosen for him, and the responsibility weighed greatly on his shoulders.

"Now, I know you all have absorbed much, but I must continue with what I brought you here to learn." Ero resumed his lesson after a short time, letting Osric regain his composure.

It was a fire-telling unlike any that Osric had ever witnessed. Only after Ero confirmed his suspicions did he understand why it was so different. He had been there in the story. He could smell the dragon blood and feel the tension in the air. It had shaken him to his core to see the desperation on the dragons' faces as they pled for Brinsop's safety. It took him several moments to regain control of his heaving chest. Though he had been hungry before the story began, his stomach was knotted into a twisted ball of anger and despair. He was thankful for the time Ero gave him to regain control, though he would have appreciated more. He realized that they did need to continue with their lesson. He closed his eyes and lost himself in the story once again.

"Shortly before wands were introduced to the world, there was a race to find a way to make magic usable for the masses. The two leaders in the field were a man named Er'amar, a human; and Argan, an ursidae. Both offered widely different ideas of how to go about it, but they promised to present their ideas at a meeting of the newly established Wizardly Union." Ero had regained his composure, as well as his lecturing tone, and the images once again danced in the flames. He paused at length to allow the pictures to play out.

The two figures of Er'amar and Argan were lifelike miniatures, as they presented their ideas side by side in the fire. Er'amar had the attention of the crowd, and he conducted himself with poise and charisma. He spoke with his whole body. The grand gestures of the young, enthusiastic man awed the spectators.

In contrast, Argan was a large, hairy ursidae who intimidated and scared the crowd with his large frame, claws, and sharp teeth. Every time he tried to imitate Er'amar's grand gestures, the people winced in fear of an attack. Argan stood on his hind legs, nearly half a body taller than the largest man there, and as wide as three combined. Neither the crowd nor those gathered from the Wizardly Union seemed inclined to listen to his ideas. Nor did his low, gravelly voice earn their trust." Pebble gasped in fear several times as the narrative played out in the fire.

"Both wizards went their separate ways to put together their plans for the Union. Months passed as they prepared. Er'amar spent his time with the unicorns in the plains far to the north, but where Argan resided during that time was unknown. Ursidae are extremely difficult to track, even for an eagle. They both slaved at their preparations—Er'amar attempting to make a wand, and Argan working with words. Soon, the time had come, and they appeared before the Wizardly Union in Rowain.

"Er'amar presented first and dazzled the Union with a wand! He demonstrated how, with sheer desire or willpower, he could make things occur. He levitated a cup across the room and into his hand with the wand. He constructed a chair out of a stack of wood sitting in the corner of the chamber. Then, to seal his proposal, he lit the chair on fire and while it burned, he roasted a pig over the flames for the feast after the presentations. The pig rotated in midair as the meeting proceeded through the other speakers.

"The final speaker to present his idea before the Union was Argan. He came to the podium with a thick, leatherbound book, and at first the officials were interested. However, when they realized that it only had two pages of spoken spells written inside, they frowned and whispered amongst themselves. The Wizardly Union did not take kindly to his haggard appearance or his crude communication skills. His presentation of the magic, however, was every bit as impressive as Er'amar's, but the Union officials did not like that the words he spoke were in an unknown tongue, or that his collection of spells was so incomplete. Argan cited that his gift was new to the world, and he had no one to teach him. In the months they had to prepare, he had muddled out that much on his own.

"The Union did not listen. They refused to hear anything further on spoken spells, and they dismissed him from the hall. Before he left the chamber, Argan swore to never take a mate. He would chronicle everything he learned in his life in seclusion and let his gift be buried with him in the grave. He swore that his gift had greater potential than anything brought forth in the hall by the others. He spoke of a See-er, telling him that his gift would save millions of lives, but he would see to it that never happened and their ignorance would be to blame. They disregarded his threats and had Er'amar escort him out with his wand. Angry and heartbroken, he made no attempt to resist them."

Ero's tale was interrupted by the sound of rustling feathers and the shimmer of the shield at the door. Osric opened his eyes as an eagle swept into the room with a satchel in her beak. She placed it on the floor next to him, and a wonderful aroma of fish and herbs renewed his appetite. The eager looks on his companion's faces told him they felt the same. Osric distributed the food to his friends, while Ero presented them with beverages. He whispered strange words under his breath, and a pitcher containing a red fruit juice and another of rulha levitated into the air and poured their contents into several steins. Osric welcomed the cup as it floated into his hands, and he savored the rich, robust flavor of the steaming, dark-colored liquid brewed from the bark of the rulha tree.

They enjoyed the simple meal while Ero continued his story. As there were no plates or silver, they held their food in their hands and ate at their leisure. The fish had a smoky flavor. Crisp on the edges and tender and moist within, it had a richness that both surprised and pleased them all. Osric had taken several bites before he realized he was watching the story in the fire again, rather than closing his eyes. Osric found the rulha to be well brewed. It had a satisfying, full flavor with a hint of bitterness that paired well with the fish.

The entire room erupted with laughter as Pebble dug face first into the fish Bridgett had set before him. He thoroughly enjoyed the fruit juice as well, giggling when it made bubbles in his nose as he lapped it from Bridgett's cupped hand. Gus sat apart from the group with a resentful look on his face, sipping rulha from the small mug Ero had sent his way. Osric offered him some fish, and after a moment of hesitation, he took a small piece and returned to sulking.

All the while, Ero kept talking, and though their attention was not entirely on him, his words stuck in their minds with surprising ease.

"Argan spent years traveling the mountains until, at last, he came to us. We shared his aversion to the rest of the walkers, and so we allowed him to take sanctuary among us. We provided him with the solitude he desired from the rest of the world, and he shared some of his knowledge of the spoken spell with us. He helped us transform these caves into what you see today. Even though we assured him that we would not share his teachings with walkers, he kept the majority of his discoveries to himself.

"Years went by as he lived among us and mastered his gift, but he kept his promise; not one eagle knew what his gift was. He was determined that it would die with him, and his book was charmed so that only those with his gift could read it. He had regular visits from the unicorns. He would barricade himself in this chamber with them each time they came, claiming that he was studying them for his craft and he needed privacy. The things he could do with mere words would have amazed the world. The true extent of his knowledge is not even known by those of us who lived with him.

"A See-er came to him one night while he worked on his book. The old weasel was only with him in this cave for moments, and then he was gone. Whatever had taken place in that short time had changed Argan completely. He was happier than I had ever seen him. He stated that his time was near an end and that he would one day be remembered by all who walked Archana. He said that no one in history would be born with his gift, and that fact filled him with joy. We inquired as to how he knew this, and his reply was, 'One never reveals what a See-er shows him.'

"Argan was busy over the next few days, stating that he must prepare for his death so he would be remembered. He locked himself in this cave for two weeks and finished the book. Then he left us for what he called 'a most important errand.' With a single silver coin in his paw, he vanished before our eyes, uttering words we could not understand with a wide smile on his face." Ero turned and motioned to a shelf full of relics. In the center of the shelf was a very dusty book that he nudged with his beak. "A few hours later he returned, beaming, and set this book here. Then he retired to his bed, and he died in his sleep. We have not moved the book since that day, but we have decided that it must leave with you." Ero was looking intently at Osric.

"So, indeed, we have no way to know if any of his spoken spells actually work then?" Gus barked. The hours he had sat silently by had yielded nothing that he considered proof, and his mood had not improved for it. "We are expected to leave this place with that book, and it could be nothing better than paper to wipe my nose on? How do we know that your story is even true, or if Argan really did write that book?" Ero looked at him with deep scorn and sympathy.

"Have you been paying attention to anything that has happened here?" Ero asked condescendingly. "Some of these things were done deliberately for your understanding of the nature of these spells."

"A fire-telling? Bah!" Gus was not impressed with Ero's tricks, and a fire-telling was poor proof in his eyes.

"When I brought you into this chamber, I uttered two different spells. If it were not for those words, all of you would have perished as you crossed the threshold of this room. Nor did I use a wand to serve you your beverage. If more proof is what you require, I will gladly provide you with it. Extollo!" Ero spoke with authority, and Gus rose up off the ground, struggling against the force that caused him to hang in midair, uncomfortable and spinning in every direction.

Gus pulled out his wand and cast a stabilizing spell to stop himself from spinning. He puffed out his chest and glowered down at Ero from his elevated position. "Put me down, you cloud-brained piece of paun vomit! Right now!" Gus shouted, above the gasps and giggles that filled the room.

"Demitto," Ero said, with a distinct look of satisfaction, and Gus was lowered gently back to the ground.

Chapter 11
The Road To Braya

Machai approached the elven ruins reluctantly. He felt much more secure on the solid expanse of stone that made up the mountain range he was entering than he had on the forsaken ship he had come south on. However, he felt a heavy sense of trepidation upon seeing the eerily quiet, crumbling structures that seemed to grow right out of the forest floor. He passed through a large archway and felt the remnants of a paved, stone road beneath his feet. Machai had traveled all over Archana, and he had never seen a place that looked as ancient as those ruins. He grumbled to the two horses pulling the creaky old wagon as he walked, kicking loose stones in front of him.

"Ye beasts be lucky to be waiting for me dockside. Ye did not have to wretch ye'r last meal into the sea. But ye could have warned me about this bloody heat. Rain would be better than this blasted humidity. I be boilin' in me breeches. Where be me guide, anyway?" He came to a sudden stop at the sight of a pair of booted feet propped up on a chunk of stone that had fallen away from the wall long ago. He heard a muffled voice from the other side of the stone.

"How am I supposed to sleep with you yammerin' to yourself. I thought these damn bugs buzzin' in my ears were bad." Machai reached up toward the heavy axe slung across his back as he signaled the horses to stop, and cautiously stepped around the broken stone.

A man was stretched out on the ground, one arm rested across his face, shielding his eyes from the dappled sunlight filtering down through the trees. The leather boots, dusty from the mountain trails, were the cleanest items of the man's attire. His faded tan breeches were patched in several places, and the right sleeve of his dingy tunic looked singed, as if he had gotten a little too close to his campfire. His shaggy hair was hard to distinguish from the mound of dirt he was using as a pillow. Machai pulled out his axe and hefted it easily in one hand.

"Tell me who ye be, or ye willn't have to worry about being awoken again." At the implied threat to his life, the young man lifted his arm and regarded the dwarf closely. A silly grin split his face, and he jumped up suddenly, causing Machai to take a step backward and to look up at the much taller man.

"I am Thom, your guide, and I think I will call you Shorty. They didn't tell me you would be a dwarf. I hear you guys are as feisty as you are short. Maybe this trip up the rock won't be as bad as I feared."

"It be in ye'r better interest to call me by Machai, or when ye be missing ye'r legs, ye'r friends will call ye Shorty." He held the axe menacingly and glowered up at the dirty young man. Thom laughed casually and hefted his pack up onto his shoulder, turning to head deeper into the ruins.

"All right. Machai it is, but it will be a long hike if you can't find your sense of humor." Machai slung his axe across his back and returned for the horses, then followed Thom with the wagon rolling noisily behind them.

The ruins stretched deeper into the forest than Machai would have guessed from his first impression, revealing it to be an abandoned city, rather than the minor outpost that he had first thought them. The further they traveled, the more overgrown the path became. What had initially been recognizable as a road became little more than a dirt trail between massive trees. The horses had to place their hoofs carefully to avoid overturning a stone on the side of the path. After an hour or so, the sunlight filtering down between the trees became the dim impression of daylight, as they traveled beneath a canopy of greenery so dense that no rays could break through. The ground beneath their feet progressed from soft soil to solid rock, and they were climbing as much as they were walking. Thom stopped and pulled a long white wand from his sleeve. He stepped around Machai and pointed it at the ground near the horses' hoofs. A soft puddle of light appeared around their pasterns and the wheels of the wagon. The horses didn't appear to notice, but as they continued up the steep rocky slope, their hoofs seemed to barely touch the ground, and they climbed effortlessly behind the two men.

Thom stepped off the path into a small clearing as the dim light faded rapidly into night. Machai unhitched the horses from the wagon to allow them to graze, while Thom gathered wood for a campfire. He pulled out his wand to light the fire, and Machai peered curiously at it. It was obviously carved from a long bone, bleached white by years of exposure to the sun, but in the firelight it seemed to glow with a reddish hue from within the bone. Machai could not think of any animal it could be from.

"What manner of beast did ye procure that bone from?" Machai sat on one of many fallen trees in the clearing, which looked to have been severed from their stumps by lightning or careless magic. He suspected someone had made the clearing as a convenient campsite, and they obviously had no regard for the life of the trees in the magnificent forest. He regarded Thom as he pulled a whetstone from his pack and began meticulously sharpening his axe.

Thom twirled the wand between his fingers and smiled savagely. "This is dragon's bone, my stubby friend. A gift, for my diligent work for mankind."

Machai glared at him for the disrespectful reference to his height, but he restrained himself from putting his axe to good use. "I wouldn't be letting a dragon see that. They would be picking you from betwixt their teeth with ye'r bones, lad."

Thom sneered at him from across the fire. "Nah. Those stupid beasts fear me all the more for having it." He slipped the wand back up his sleeve and walked off into the forest. Machai eyed him suspiciously as he watched him walk away. *Dragons fear that mangy human? Doubtful!* He would be surprised if he could *slay* them a rabbit for the spit.

Thom returned a while later, whistling as he came back into the camp, dangling a large hare from a noose over his shoulder. The animal was still alive, struggling against Thom's back with terror-filled eyes, and the young man smiled as he bashed its head with a rock before gutting and skinning it for the fire.

* * *

Machai was keeping watch from the lowered gate of the wagon, his axe resting across his knees, on a dark drizzly morning of their third day on the mountain. He trusted Thom less the more time he spent with him. The man was cruel and careless with animals and plants, tearing leaves from the trees they passed and throwing rocks at the creatures that scurried from their path. He had no respect for the various lives that surrounded him, and his carefree attitude grated on Machai's nerves. He was thankful that they would reach the volcano within the day, and he could make his delivery and return to his home. He was anxious to be away from that place, as beautiful as it was, and the boorish young man. He sat, listening to the last of the night's bird calls and the rain dripping from nearby trees, enjoying the peace afforded to him by Thom's quiet sleeping. It was the only time he was quiet. Machai sighed regretfully and jumped to the ground when Thom rolled from his blankets and immediately started whining about the rain. It would be a long day.

They had a quick breakfast of hard bread from Thom's pack and a juicy, green fruit plucked from a nearby tree, and they were back on the rocky trail shortly after it had lightened enough to see. The rocks were slick from the rain, and they had to be even more careful to avoid upsetting stones and tumbling back down the hill. The horses still seemed unperturbed by the unsure footing, and Machai considered asking Thom to cast the same spell on his travel-worn feet, but he would be damned if he would put himself in debt to a man he was despising more by the day.

As they got closer to the peak of the volcano, the trees began to thin out, and the hot sun broke through the heavy rain clouds. Thom dropped back to walk alongside the dwarf, twirling his dragonbone wand between his fingers. He stopped whistling, and his mood became more somber, slowing his pace to a casual walk on the ever-broadening path.

"I like you, Machai, so I am going to give you some advice." The dwarf let out a short, gruff laugh but held back his sarcastic retort at the serious look on Thom's face. "The entrance to the volcano is guarded by a dragon. He won't allow you inside. Don't challenge him, or he is ordered to eat you. Once you are paid for this shipment, I will lead you back to the trail and you can make your way back down the mountain. Don't ask any questions. My superiors don't like strangers. You must not make your camp any closer to the peak than this point, so you will need to travel quickly once you leave. I will recast the spell on the horses' hoofs, so you can ride one and lead the other. They will be less encumbered without the wagon, and you will make good time." Thom stared at Machai, trying to read his expression to see how he would accept his suggestions. He had gotten the impression that the dwarf was not apt to comply with rules he didn't understand or agree with. Machai looked back at him, blank-faced, deciding which answers he wanted first from the infuriating man.

"It be sounding like me life may be threatened on this trip by more than sweltering heat. I do *not* like ye, Thom, and I think it be time ye answer some questions." Machai indicated a rock on the side of the trail. "If ye answer to me liking, I will complete the delivery."

"I was afraid you would say something like that. Unfortunately for you, I am not allowed to answer any of your questions. There are many hardships on this trail. It would be a terrible thing, indeed, if you were to be killed by a rockslide so close to our destination, though it would not be the first time an accident befell a traveler along this path." Thom sneered down at Machai, his dragonbone wand clutched in his grimy hand. "I suggest you just do as I say, and you may well make it back to wherever it is you came from." He pointed his wand at Machai's chest and grinned maliciously.

In a flurry of movement that belied his stocky stature, Machai whipped the axe from his back, and the flat side of the blade connected with Thom's hand, knocking his wand from his grasp. In the blink of an eye, Thom found himself being knocked backward. He landed roughly on the same rock Machai had invited him to sit upon, with the dwarf's wand pointed at his right eye and the blade of his axe at his throat.

"And I *suggest* ye sit down and answer me questions. I do not doubt that ye'r superiors would not be too disappointed if I had to complete me delivery without me guide." Thom cradled his injured hand against his chest and glared at Machai, sitting eye level with him, and very angry. He had apparently underestimated the dwarf. Never had he seen someone attack with both weapon and wand, and he didn't want to make the same mistake twice.

"All right. It is obvious that you have the upper hand. Allow me to retrieve my wand and heal my hand, and I will tell you what you want to know." Thom's voice was contrite and sullen, but Machai had no intention of trusting him. Keeping his blade pressed firmly against the flesh at Thom's throat, he pointed his wand at his rapidly swelling hand. Soon, Thom could feel the bones knitting themselves together, and the pain slowly eased as circulation returned to his fingers.

"Ye may get ye'r wand when I be satisfied ye have answered me with truth. Why do ye be stationed at Braya Volcano?" He fixed his wand on Thom's chest, and lowered the axe to his side.

"I serve as a guard."

"What do ye guard?"

"Captives."

"Braya be a prison, then?" Machai hefted his axe up and rested it on his left shoulder. The movement did not escape Thom's notice, and he swallowed harshly before he answered.

"Not exactly. I assure you, Machai, these questions are better left unanswered, for your sake and mine. They will kill us both for the telling." Machai saw true fear in the man's eyes, but this did not deter him from his interrogation. He waited with restrained patience for Thom to elaborate. Thom recognized the determination in Machai's expression, and his shoulders hunched as he explained. "The volcano serves as a prison, but not for criminals. It cages the eldest of the dragons."

"Dragons?" Machai looked shocked, and the hand holding his wand wavered slightly in his surprise. "What in stone's blood are ye talking about, man?" Thom sighed deeply, acknowledging that he could not avoid a detailed explanation.

"I arrived here seven years ago with two of my peers. We had been trained in security measures and were told that we were being given the opportunity to directly serve our Turgent. I started out butchering sheep, hundreds of them a day. After the first year, I finally saw what I had been preparing meals for: dragons. There are lots of them, held captive to force the rest of their race to serve the wealthy and empowered as a means of transportation. For the past six years I have been a guard. It's better than chopping up sheep, aside from the occasional fire blast from one of those bloody behemoths." He peered down at his singed sleeve in disgust.

Machai was shaken by the tale. He sat heavily down on the ground before Thom and summoned the discarded wand with his own. He stared soberly at the young man and handed him back his dragonbone wand. He did not doubt the truthfulness of his answer. No one would make up that story.

"Thom, ye'r tale be hard to swallow, but I believe ye." He stood up and started pacing back and forth before the rock Thom sat upon, his wand and axe still gripped in each hand. "Who is ye'r commander?"

"Just a gruff old man named Aron, but the chain of command goes much higher, not that I am privy to any of those names. I really can't tell you anything else, Machai. You already know enough to have us both tortured and killed."

"I may not like ye, Thom, but I willn't allow ye to suffer for ye'r compliance with me demands. Ye will answer me a bit more, and then we will be on our way. I willn't indicate that ye have told me a thing, but nor will I wander into the trap awaiting me. And ye *will* tell me what I need to know to ensure I leave this blasted mountain with me hide intact. Do we have an understanding?"

"Aye, Machai. Ask what you will." Thom replaced his wand in his sleeve and leaned back casually on the rock. Maybe having an alliance with the dwarf would be to his benefit. He certainly didn't want to provoke another encounter with that axe of his, nor the ire with which he wielded it.

"Wise choice, Thom. Tell me, who will be accepting me delivery upon our arrival?"

"I assume it will be Aron, although sometimes a few of the guards are sent in his place."

"And if I appear to be unknowing of the happenings at the volcano, he will pay me and send me on me way?"

"Sure, this may be a hazardous trail, but if no one ever returned from the volcano, sooner or later someone would come to find out why. It is in his better interest to keep you ignorant and intact."

Machai stopped pacing and scratched his beard with his wand. "Ye say the dragons are caged. What manner of bars would hold such beasts as those?"

Thom hung his head and ran his hands through his shaggy hair. "They are heavily barred and locked, but the true restraints are magical in nature. I am told it took twelve men with the best wands gold can buy to weave the spells. No man could counter those enchantments. Nothing can get out, and thus nothing can get in."

"Well, ye fed the dragons. Surely ye must be able to get them meat."

"The enchantments are on a timed cycle. There are momentary lapses in the spell, but only for one cage at a time. As one shield falls, we drop meat through a feeding shoot and then proceed to the next cage as the spell resumes. Once in a while, a dragon will have a well-timed spout of fire aimed at the feeding shoot. Some men have not been as agile as myself. I've only ever gotten my clothing singed. The reinforced metal is sufficient to contain them for the short amount of time the shield is down." Machai was disturbed by the conversational attitude Thom had adopted in describing the cruel containment of such enchanting creatures, but he wanted to know as much as he could.

"And a dragon be guarding the entrance? No doubt under duress that his kin will be injured if he does not be doing the bidding of this man, Aron."

"Yes, he is under orders to eat anyone who attempts to enter the volcano without an invitation, and he is an awful brute. I wouldn't cross him if I were you. He takes out all of his wrath on strangers who wander too close to the entrance." Thom looked inquisitively at his short companion. "What exactly are you planning to do, Machai? Rescue the beasts? I am starting to wonder where all these questions are leading."

"Do not be a fool! What could I possibly be doing to free them? I just be here to make me delivery, and I be no elven assassin! Get on with it then. Lead me to this entrance and let me be done with it. The sooner I can be getting away from this volcano and ye, the better, if ye ask me." Machai slung his axe across his back but kept his wand firmly in his grasp. He whistled sharply at the horses, and they ceased their grazing and regained the rocky path. Thom shook his head in disbelief, but he stood up from his perch on the rock and cleared his throat.

"This is where we leave the path, my angry friend. Tell your smelly companions to follow us." Thom took a few steps away from the trail and then stopped and turned back to Machai. "I answered your questions as best I could. Will you answer a few of mine?"

Machai grunted, but his demeanor was cordial as he responded, "I will consider it. What be ye'r question?"

"What are those horses hauling beneath that canvas? I have never seen a dwarf make a delivery to this mountain." Machai was silent as he considered his response, but he decided the man would see for himself soon enough, so it wouldn't hurt to answer him.

"Dwarven blades." He noticed the spark of interest in Thom's eyes. "The finest steel weapons, forged in the fires of me mountain home and imbued with bloodstones. It seems ye'r superiors have need of arms." Machai inclined his head at Thom. "For an army, perhaps?"

"I wouldn't know anything about an army, but Aron has been drilling us harder than ever. I assumed he was just being cruel, punishing us for allowing a stranger to enter the volcano."

"What stranger?"

"A month or so before I left to meet you, a man arrived at the entrance to the volcano. He came on dragonback and spouted off something about being a Contege, summoned there by the Turgent himself to investigate the assignment of his Vigile recruits. I never saw him, but I heard about it from another guard. The guard who allowed him passage, rather than having him be eaten, was killed by Aron the next day as an example for disregarding his orders. He has been relentless in our training drills ever since." Thom indicated that they should keep walking, but he still seemed to have something on his mind. "Machai, may I ask you another question?"

"Aye. What is it?"

"Where did you learn to fight like that?" He grinned over at the dwarf. "No one has ever knocked me on my ass so fast!"

Machai broke out in roaring laughter and looked up at Thom. "Ye never be fighting with a dwarf, then, eh? Ye stupid humans. Ye only ever learn to be using one hand at a time."

Chapter 12
Blood in the Water

Osric was frustrated by their situation. He hadn't found many answers, and he had been bombarded by new questions. The book they had been given was a new source of irritation. Ero assured him that it contained the complete collection of Argan's life's work, but upon opening it, he had found only blank pages, yellowed and worn with age.

Greyback was not healing as fast as Ero thought she would, and there was no way to know when they would be able to continue. He spent the majority of his time staring at a book with no words, trying to figure out what was happening to him and waiting for Toby to contact him again. He had expected to hear from him a few days before, but nearly seven days had passed with no word. With ample time on his hands and the inability to pursue other answers, he distracted himself by studying the book.

They had passed Argan's book around their fire at night, taking turns examining the cover for anything that would hint at the contents. They had each flipped through the pages, squinted, and held it up to the sun and firelight—vain attempts to find something that the others had missed. The only worthwhile discovery had been the vial lashed across the pages, resting between the tops of the front and back covers for over one hundred years. Osric held it in his hand, studying it intently.

On its own, the vial was rather unremarkable. The contents of the small bottle, however, had piqued his interest. Whatever liquid it had once held had solidified and appeared almost black in the poor light of the caves. Osric had removed the small stopper and scraped out a bit of the substance. He sprinkled it on the book in the hope that it would make the words visible, but the attempt yielded no results. Despite the failure, he still felt as though the vial held the key to deciphering the book's mystery.

Osric had explored the caves extensively. The first few days after the book was gifted to them, his companions had accompanied him. As the week wore on, they joined him less frequently, and the fifth day of gazing at its pages found him in solitude with the blank book and vial. The circumstances that had led to his departure from Stanton, and the events of the previous weeks, had given him an overwhelming number of questions to ponder. Sitting alone on the cave floor, he tried to put the questions aside for a moment and to focus on the beauty of his surroundings, but his mind kept circling back to the book.

He was a bit uncomfortable with the cryptic explanation for the gift of Argan's book, to say the least. "Time has chosen you to carry the book," was the only answer Ero would give him. He also felt disturbed by the eagles showing him so much respect after their strange encounter. He still had no idea what had taken place during the confrontation about Greyback. He was perplexed by his apparent acquisition of the Chronicleer ability. He had a hard time believing that he had the gift. Ero's words resounded in his head: *You may be the most powerful wizard to ever walk Archana.* Osric couldn't help but wonder, *Why me?*

When Osric informed his friends of his newfound ability while sitting around the fire that night, Gus had gone crazy in an attempt to use his gift to look within him, but Osric had refused. Gus would not back down, and when he looked as though he was about to try anyway, Osric spoke the word, "Extollo," in an effort to mimic Ero's magic. Gus did not simply rise up and hang in midair. He was knocked unconscious when his head hit the ceiling of their cave. Osric quickly uttered the counter spell, and Gus dropped to the ground.

Several fear-filled moments followed while Bridgett made sure Gus would survive the incident. Osric decided not to attempt another spoken spell—on any being, at least—until he understood more about how they worked. It had been a truly sobering experience for Osric. *The spoken spells must rely on skill, just as wands do,* he thought, and he spent the next few days attempting to avoid the very angry Gus.

When he was not occupied with the vial and book, Osric was uttering the spells at rocks by a nearby pond. Each time he tried, the rock would simply keep rising until it clambered against the high ceiling of the cave or until he spoke the counter spell. It was frustrating that he could not master something that seemed so simple, but he practiced dutifully like he had during his early days of swordplay with his father. The only difference was the lack of instruction. Each time he attempted the spell, he saw the picture of Gus being smashed on the chamber ceiling, and the rocks played the same scene out over and over.

Osric had spent several hours looking for Ero on one occasion. He was tired of trying to learn the spell on his own, and he felt like asking would be the best approach—a sentiment that Gus shared. If he was going to be tossed around like a toy, it should be done, in his words, by someone who knew what they were doing. He had asked after Ero's whereabouts of several eagles with no results, but finally an old female by the name of Juniper informed him that Ero had gone on a hunt and might not return for weeks. He would have to continue practicing on his own.

Kenneth found Osric sitting on a rock, considering the book and the vial. He had been concerned for his friend, with all the pressure he had been under for the past few weeks. They had not had much time alone to talk, and Osric had been so distracted and serious lately. If he could get him to lower his guard for a time, he felt there was a chance that they could gain some perspective on the latest events. Osric had been all business for over a month—even longer, if he took into account the planning time for the ratification ceremony. Hopefully, some time talking with an old friend could bring some repose from the torment he saw on Osric's face.

"So, this is where you have been hiding?" Kenneth said with a laugh, and Osric gave a start at his voice. "Sorry, I thought you heard me coming."

Osric shook his head and let out a sigh in exasperation.

"I never know what to expect these days." A deep worried crease worked its way across his forehead as Osric examined the pond at his feet. "I half expected you to be a See-er, an eagle attack, or Gus, out for revenge. With my luck, I could have unknowingly discovered where the paun live in the winter."

Kenneth stood in silence for a few moments, observing as Osric set the vial on the open book in his lap and stared down at the gaupers swimming in the pond. Several small, lizard-like creatures he didn't recognize lined the bank on the other side, complacently chewing on the moss that grew at the water's edge.

"Remember when magic was fun?" Smiling, Kenneth tried to bait him into a conversation of better times. Osric ignored him and kept his attention on the fish chasing around in the water. "Os, are you awake over there?" Kenneth nudged his shoulder in a friendly gesture of impatience.

"Sorry. I'm not very good company right now." Osric tilted his face in his friend's direction, his eyes closed, his head resting on the heel of his left hand.

Kenneth desperately searched for a pleasant memory, something to break the tension. One attempt after another just seemed like water thrown at a wall; it could not break it down.

"Feeling like a blacksmith today?" Kenneth teased.

Osric gave him a look that not only suggested confusion, but a simultaneous impression of annoyance. This was the opening Kenneth needed.

"I bet the blacksmith back home felt the same way when he refused to let you apologize." A broad grin crossed Kenneth's face.

"That wasn't my fault. You said you could teach me to use the Hunter's gift." The beginnings of a smile started to form on Osric's lips.

"I still hold to that statement. You were just a bad student."

"There is a reason they call it a gift. Don't you know you're born with it?" Osric was chuckling under his breath. "Oh, and bad student? I did exactly what you said!"

"I didn't tell you to shoot him in the ass!" Kenneth cut him off before he could continue.

"You told me how to aim."

"I told you to aim lower."

"Yeah, and to release when I felt the click."

"In your head, not the stick you were standing on!" Kenneth, with the Hunter's gift, felt a click, or groove, when the arrow was in the right place to be released. The fact that Osric mistook the snapping of a stick under his foot as the gift was an enduring joke between them.

"If I had only known! To think, I've been doing it wrong all these years!" They were both laughing so hard that they could barely breathe. "That poor man, minding his own business, shoeing a horse!"

"Scared the horse to death when he screamed, 'My arse!'" Kenneth said between gasps for air. "The horse nearly trampled him to death when it took off running!"

"And then it kicked the leg of the ladder," said Osric. "And the man with the whitewash…"

"Fell on top of him!" they said in unison, laughing.

Their chorus of laughter echoed around the cave. The gaupers swam to the opposite side of the pond, and the lizards vanished from sight. A cacophony of flapping wings was heard as bats filled the air near the ceiling, their sleep disturbed by the clamor of the merriment.

The conversation continued for some time, and both Kenneth and Osric felt better—a peace that only time among friends could create. No swordplay had been involved, no discoveries made—just two friends talking about good times in a cave, with darkness slowly surrounding them.

For a moment, they were kings at banquet, the victors of a noble battle, and children in their mother's arms.

Eventually, the conversation turned back to the mysteries they had encountered. They spoke of the events in Stanton, the decision to set out for Angmar, the encounter with the See-er, Pebble's sudden appearance, the eagle attack, and then the book and the vile.

"I'll never forget watching you use that spell on Gus," Kenneth stated jovially, miming Gus being smashed on the ceiling with a laugh.

"I felt so bad about that." Osric felt good making light of the incident, and the laughter filtered its way in through his words. "I keep trying that spell, but I thought it safer to use rocks for now." They both chuckled. "Unless you want to volunteer yourself for an experiment?"

"No, um..." Kenneth looked around in feigned fear while laughing. "I've... I've got a date... Yeah, that's it!"

"Oh you do, do you?"

"Yes."

"Well, I'm sure you don't want to keep your eagle maiden waiting." Osric attempted a respectful tone, but laughter was getting the best of the both of them again.

"Yes, the eagle ladies find me irresistible!" Kenneth could barely speak through his laughter, but it was time to stop joking and see if his friend could see things in a new light.

Realization clouded Osric's eyes as he reached the same conclusion. Their uproarious laughter waned to soft chuckles as they savored the final moments of gaiety. For the first time since their conversation at the entrance to the palace in Stanton, he felt relaxed. As they quieted, the sounds of the bats diminished, and the gaupers settled back into their routine in the pond. The laughter ended, leaving in its wake a brief but important moment of silence.

"Still no word from Stanton?" Kenneth inquired.

"No," Osric spoke, after a quick exhaled breath, his only sign of disappointment that the light-hearted moment had passed. "Should be any time now. They were more than likely held up with questioning survivors. Don't worry. Toby always comes through."

"So, we can't do anything on that front right now, and we are stuck here until Greyback heals. What progress have you made with that book?" Kenneth quite easily summed up the concerns Osric had been wrestling with. The tone of his questioning was casual and unobtrusive.

"None whatsoever. I know it has something to do with this vial, but I can't bloody figure out what," Osric replied.

Kenneth took a few moments to think. Concern had not yet returned to Osric's face, but he did not want to push it to that point. *Maybe if I help him sort this out, it will keep that scowl off his face.* Spells with wands need only be done with the correct goal in mind. Maybe the same held true with spoken spells.

"So, walk me through the spells you have been practicing here. How do you go about casting them?" Kenneth was certain that they could figure those out, at least. That would surely give some hope to their journey.

"Well, I have no information to go off of, so I just... say it." Osric shrugged to emphasize how lost he really was on the subject.

"That's it? You just speak it?"

"Well, if I had any idea where to begin, I could try different approaches, but that is what Ero did, so that is where I started." Osric shrugged again.

"All right, let me ask you this. In the outpost in Stanton, when you summoned your sword belt, how did you do that?" Kenneth thought he was on to something, but he wanted to test the theory.

"I don't see what one has to do with the other. We are talking about spoken spells now; that is the wand technique you are asking about." Osric didn't know where Kenneth was going with his line of questioning, but he could see excitement in his eyes.

"Yes, but they are both *magic!*" Smiling broadly, Kenneth could barely contain his enthusiasm. "How do you summon an item with your wand?"

"I cast the spell by telling it where to go with my mind. How does that apply here? I'm not using a wand." Osric suspected Kenneth had an idea, but he was not catching on.

Kenneth arched an eyebrow. That was the answer he had been hoping for. That was the same process he used, and he imagined it was the same process for everyone. *Is it possible that all magic is that closely related?* Kenneth thought. *Only one way to find out!* Kenneth looked down at a large rock that lay beside the pond, but he was sure it would work and the nearest gauper was a much more tempting target.

"Extollo!" Kenneth spoke with authority.

A gauper rose slowly out of the water until it could look Kenneth in the eye. Anticipation flushed Osric's face as he waited with hope. The gauper held its place and did not move but for the thrashing of the tail and fins, its

107

gills seeking water to take a breath. Kenneth sat with a smile on his face and watched as it tried to swim in midair. Osric's excitement could hardly be contained, but he gave Kenneth a moment to enjoy his victory.

"Demitto!" Kenneth spoke again, and the gauper dropped back into the water.

"How did you do that?!" Osric shouted with joy at a grinning Kenneth, as he slapped his hands hard on the open book in his lap.

Only Kenneth's fear-filled expression indicated his mistake. A glint of reflected light hit his eyes and he realized what he had done. Time seemed to slow as Osric frantically reached up to grab the vial from the air, as it spun out and away from his body. Through his panic, he felt his gift activate, forcing a calming sensation through him that told him something good was about to happen. He tried to ignore it as he grasped for the vial that was falling rapidly toward the ground.

It brushed his fingertips as it fell out of his reach. Out of desperation, Osric attempted to cushion the fall with his boot, and it arrived in time but much too quickly, sending the vial directly into a rock. The vial split in two and fell into the water a few strides away. Osric flung the book to the safe, dry ground to his right and ran into the water. *I have got to save some of it!* Osric thought, as he searched the bottom of the pond for signs of broken glass.

Kenneth joined him and began to help in the search. Rocks and sand were the only things their fingers were finding. Though it was not yet night, very little light penetrated the cave they occupied. Light was exactly what they needed right then.

"Ow!" Osric shouted, as he pulled a bloody hand out of the water, grasping a piece of broken glass. "I've got one. The other one is over here somewhere!" He indicated with his other hand the area where the second half had entered the water.

The search continued, but Osric kept the injured hand holding half of the vial out of the water so he could check it later. His gift still forced a calm upon him, but he was sure that would not help him right then, and he resisted. They searched on hands and knees for a few moments more, and it felt like an eternity.

"Got it!" Kenneth shouted, as he pulled his hands out slowly so as not to disturb any contents that may have remained inside.

They crawled out of the water carefully, as they cradled the broken halves of the vial in their hands and tried to gently dry them on their wet clothing without emptying the contents. Osric's Portentist gift began to subside.

"Grab the book. We need to get out into the light and hope we see the substance is still there!" Osric shouted, as he took the other half of the vial from Kenneth, who quickly grabbed the book.

They ran as swiftly as they could without spilling the contents of the vial. The wet rocks where water dripped down, and the stalagmites and columns that rose up from the ground, made them cautious to watch their footing. By the time they reached the small opening that led to the cavern with the waterfalls, they were fighting to catch their breath. Osric was glad to see that the sun was still sending shafts of light through the holes in the ceiling, but they needed direct light and couldn't stop there. Kenneth led the way up the steps, and they bolted down the corridor, startling two eagles who were headed toward them. Sunlight broke through the dark as they entered the chamber outside their quarters, and they slid to a stop on the ledge at the entrance to the caves.

It was even colder than when they had arrived, and snow covered the landscape below them. Winter had officially set in. The snow reflected the bright light, and they squinted as they examined the contents of the broken vial.

"I think I see some! Right there!" Kenneth pointed to a small formation that clung to the inside of the bottom half of the vial. "Pour the water out slowly! Quick, so it doesn't dissolve!"

"All right, Archana help me now!" To allow the water to drain without losing the soggy substance, Osric tipped the vial carefully. Once the water had flowed out through his fingers, he exhaled in relief. It was less than a quarter of its original mass, but it was there.

"Oh, thank Archana!" Kenneth exclaimed.

Kenneth and Osric exchanged nervous looks while they continued to examine the contents until they were satisfied that it was not just mud from the bottom of the pond. He shook the remnants from the side of the vial so that they settled back to the bottom of the glass.

"We should probably get back inside and dry this by the fire." Kenneth eyed the storm clouds that were rolling toward them over the top of the mountain peaks.

"Good idea. Come on, let's go." Osric agreed, with one quick look at the sky. The last thing they needed was more moisture added to that vial.

As they entered their sleeping chamber, it was clear that they had some explaining to do.

"Archana burn me! What have you two got yourselves into today?" Gus shouted with a grimace.

"Are you two all right?" Bridgett looked with concern at their wet, muddy clothes and at Osric's expression of anguish. "What happened to the pair of you?"

Osric stared into her eyes, afraid to admit the mistake he had made. He stood silently, trying to find a way to explain. Kenneth, however, did not hesitate to launch into the tale, but the story he told was one that Osric had not witnessed.

"We figured out the spell," Kenneth spoke in Gus's direction apologetically. "I gave it a try, and it worked. I lifted a huge boulder. Osric explained to me that he just had to hold a location in his head first and the object wouldn't bounce off the ceiling." He had a sorrowful look on his face as he continued. "But, I was so excited that I thought of Osric when I spoke the counter spell, and the boulder crashed into the rocks at his feet." He glanced at Osric for reinforcement, but he had no idea where Kenneth was going with his story." Osric was knocked into the water, and I jumped in to help him out. Only, I didn't realize he had dropped the vial when he fell, and I stepped on it." Kenneth hung his head shamefully.

All eyes in the chamber were locked on him. Even Pebble seemed shocked at the news and stopped playing with the eagle feathers he had collected to listen. Gus was scowling like a hungry drogma watching its dinner swim away. Nobody had a chance to speak before Kenneth continued without pause.

"Osric thought fast, and got me to help him find it, but it had split in half. Lucky for us, he managed to save some of the contents with his quick reaction," Kenneth spoke rapidly and then patted Osric on the shoulder.

Osric was stunned. Kenneth had taken his place in the fire. The story was essentially the same, but Kenneth had completely switched roles with him in the telling. He sent a silent look of gratitude towards his best friend. He wasn't sure how, but he would make it up to Kenneth.

"Oh, thank Archana you saved it!" Bridgett laid her hand on Osric's arm and gazed at the broken vial. She lifted it from his hand and looked within, amazement and concern in her eyes as she witnessed how much was left. "Let's hope it is enough."

"Fools do foolish things and you thank them for it? Would you like your unity ceremony now?" Gus shouted at the two of them. "Holding his hand like a little girl! They could have just ruined the chance of spoken spells being understood for the whole world and you get weak in the knees?"

"Don't need's it no more." Pebble giggled and began twirling the feathers in the air again. Nobody listened to the nonsense of his words; as they were too busy arguing amongst themselves.

"You want to be hunted that badly? I can take care of that right now." Kenneth shouted back at Gus.

Osric was furious that Gus was still attacking him, in spite of the story Kenneth had told.

"Why are you attacking me? Did you listen to what he said?" Osric demanded, stepping in between Gus and Kenneth.

"Makes no difference who is at fault, the teacher or the student. Obviously your instructions were not good enough!" Gus's anger intensified and he had no reservations about showing it.

"What is it that you have against me, old man?" Osric asked him, in as calm a voice as he could muster. He removed his sword belt and wand pouch. *If this is what I must do to get some decent treatment out of him, then I will do it.* "If you must examine me to be happy, then go ahead, you bitter fool. You would make better use of your time figuring out the wand and the prophecy."

Osric disrobed, evoking astonished gasps from Bridgett and Kenneth. He wanted no excuse for Gus to think he was hiding anything, so he piled his clothes and equipment in the corner. Then he stood in front of Gus, naked and without shame.

"There are better ways to impress a lady." Kenneth shot Bridgett an exaggerated smile.

"Well?" Osric asked, as Kenneth scooped up Pebble and ushered Bridgett out of the chamber. "Are you just going to stare, or can we get this over with?"

Gus stood in shock as he thought about all the times they had quarreled about the inevitable. Was the boy really giving up so easily? Gus had expected to feel triumphant when he was finally able to inspect Osric with his gift, but seeing Osric standing naked before him in anger and defiance, he felt hollow and a little guilty for his behavior.

Gus activated his gift as he began to walk around Osric. From the side, he could see his Portentist gift at the back of his head just above his neck, the bright purple glow of that orb was one he had witnessed on many occasions. Just as he had expected, there were more gifts as well. What looked like the beginnings of the Empath gift hovered in yellow crescent shapes near his ears. *That is Bridgett's gift!* he thought. Toward the back of his head was a red orb that he had only witnessed in the eagles. *That must be the Chronicleer gift.* Beside it sat one small blue sphere, which he recognized as the See-er gift. Two orange orbs in his shoulders linked with a third and fourth in the back of his head, above and below the Portentist gift. They were joined by thin strands of magic fibers that wove their way through his body. *The Hunter gift?* Gus was shocked to see two green orbs in Osric's eyes that were fully developed. *The boy has the Wand-Maker gift as well!*

As if things were not already as far from normal as he had ever seen, Gus stood gaping at Osric's forehead. Even through his gift he could see that Osric was beginning to shift uncomfortably at the length of the stare. *I have never seen this gift!* Gus looked at it with a rare intensity. A large silver sphere hovered behind his eyes. It was strange, but there had to be a way to reason it out.

"Happy yet? Or should I sleep naked for you as well?" Osric had had about as much of the cold air as he could handle, and he walked away. "Any more examining you want to do, you can do with my clothes on."

Osric pulled his clothes back on and called out to Kenneth and Bridgett that it was safe to enter. Kenneth peered around the corner tentatively and then led Bridgett and Pebble back into the chamber. Gus stood in awe, and Osric regarded him with a cool stare. He hoped that Gus would stop attacking him and start actually trying to help him.

"Well?" Kenneth probed and Bridgett looked at Gus with anticipation.

Gus stood still, watching Osric as he set to making a fire for the evening. Dinner would be brought to them soon, and he would prefer to be warm while he ate. Gus could not take his eyes off of him, and he was not sure how to tell them what he had found.

"I am sure he saw what I told you," Osric answered Kenneth, tired of Gus silently staring at him. "I have the Chronicleer gift, as well as my Portentist gift, but he doesn't know how and neither do I."

"So much more than just those two. He has every gift in this room," Gus finally said, with a grave look upon his face. "In fact, he has a gift I have never seen before."

Everyone's eyes settled on Osric as he dropped the log he was about to add to the fire and his head jerked up at Gus' last statement.

"One you have never seen?" Bridgett inquired.

"Yes," Gus confirmed, the look of awe still on his face. "He really is the most powerful wizard to ever walk Archana."

Silence filled the room, and they each gazed around at the others, trying to make sense of what Gus had seen, or think of an explanation for the new gift.

Kenneth suddenly shouted out, startling everyone, "The book!" He ran and grabbed the book from under Osric's sword and wand, still lying on the ground. "Osric, open it!" he spoke excitedly as he handed the book to Osric.

"The book is blank, Kenneth! You were looking at it with me by the pond," Osric exclaimed.

"Os, trust me. I think I know what the gift that Gus has never seen before must be. Just open it." He knew he was right, and he needed Osric to see it too.

"All right, but I'm telling you, it's still bla..." Osric's voice trailed off as he opened the book. Words were scrawled in careless handwriting across every page. The age and dust that had worn the cover and the edges of the pages did not touch the writing.

Chapter 13
Rubble and Rumors

Toby glanced up from the papers he was signing and noticed light behind the curtains of the one small window in the room. He couldn't believe it was morning; he had worked through the night, and he felt like he had accomplished nothing. Toby threw his quill down on the desk and ran his hands over his smooth head. *Two weeks!* He had been supervising the cleanup and rescue efforts on the palace for over two weeks! They had found a few more survivors, but no leads or evidence to support Osric in his case against the irua. He had suffered a pounding headache for days, and there didn't seem to be any relief in sight. The Wizardly Union had sent a few men to assist him in his efforts. *What a farce!* All they had done was heap piles of paperwork on the Contege's desk that required *his* immediate attention, courteously remind him that there was nothing more he could do at the palace grounds, and suggesting that perhaps he should get some rest. He had spent more time bottled up in the Contege's temporary office in the barracks over the past two weeks than he had spent at the palace itself. Toby wanted nothing more than to go home and spend time with his family. He hadn't tucked his son into bed in days, and he knew his wife was worried. That was exactly why he had never wanted the position, but with Osric off flying around on dragons, he was left to clean up the mess.

He was sure if he had to sign another Requisition for Labor and Supplies Approval, or fill out one more Ledger of Use of Union Magical Abilities, he would tear out his mustache. Out of frustration, Toby stood up quickly, pushing away from the desk hard enough that his chair tumbled over into the bookshelf behind him. He bent down to retrieve the toppled books, anxious to get back to the palace, as they must be getting close to uncovering the majority of the throne room. The familiar handwriting scrawled across an open page caught his eye. He had worked closely with Thamas for seven years. He would recognize his writing anywhere, but he had never seen the man write in a journal. Toby picked up the tattered, leatherbound book and sat heavily back in his chair. *Why would Contege Thamas have a journal in the Records Room of the barracks?*

Toby thumbed through the book and realized that it was not exactly a personal journal. There were lists of various items and names, followed by a few sentences or paragraphs of Thamas's thoughts on the following pages. Some of the entries were merely a few weeks apart, and others had a span of two years between their neatly written dates at the top of each page. Toby flipped back to the first page in the journal:

Seventeenth day ~ Third month ~ Twenty-second year of Turgent Bartholo's Rule

I, Thamas, Contege of the Stanton Vigiles, have noticed an irregularity in the practices and procedures regarding new Vigile recruits. These irregularities have occurred over the past two years while I have occupied the position of Contege, and I can only assume, prior to my promotion. I feel it is necessary to document these discrepancies to assure my memory is complete and accurate, in the event I am ever questioned about them. As I cannot recall in detail the dates and names of those involved leading up to today, I will record events as they occur in the future. Archana willing, this will be my last entry...

Toby wasn't sure if he should even keep reading. He had known that Thamas was a careful man, but he had always thought him logical. *Conspiracy?* Toby couldn't believe that Thamas, in the seven years they had worked together, had been concerned enough to document it without saying anything to him. He turned the page to a list of supplies. They were the type of standard items typically issued to transferred recruits. The page was dated just over two months after the first entry. Below the list of inventory, Thamas had listed the names and some information of three recruits; Toby remembered two of them. They had been in the recruit class seven years earlier, the same year that Toby had accepted the promotion to Profice, but neither of them had completed their training to join the Vigile ranks. Thinking back, Toby couldn't recall what had happened to them. He had just assumed that the training had been too much for them and they had quit and gone back home.

— *Standard-issue tan tunic:*
  two sz three, one sz two.

— *Standard-issue tan breeches:*

two sz two, one sz three.

— Boots
three pair.

— Short sword:
three, with scabbards.

— Travel rations:
three packages, six days each.

— Shawn ~ Hometown:
Stanton. Parents deceased.

— Grayson ~ Hometown:
Rowain. Unknown family line.

— Thom ~ Hometown:
Unknown. Mother deceased, Father imprisoned.

Toby had only seen Shawn a few times during his training. He remembered him as a quiet boy, tall for his age and not very intelligent. He had no idea who Grayson was, but there were a lot of recruits every spring, and Toby didn't always have a hand in training each of them. Thom, however, he remembered well. He had joined the recruit class his nineteenth spring, several years later than most boys. He was an angry and antagonistic young man, often picking fights with other recruits or taunting vendors in the market district. Multiple complaints had been filed about his antics, and Thamas had told Toby that he was expelling him from the training. Paperwork for the expulsion had never come across Toby's desk to sign, so he had assumed that Thom had just left. The journal seemed to indicate something else entirely. The next page confirmed Toby's suspicions.

Twenty-first day ~ Fifth month ~ Twenty-second year of Turgent Bartholo's Rule

Contacted by Konsult for three more recruits. Each has been issued gear and signed transfer papers to Braya. Transfer papers filed in blue box and merchant wagon contracted for travel.

Toby had never heard of recruits with incomplete training being transferred, and he had no idea what a blue box was, but he was fairly certain that Braya must refer to the Braya Volcano. It was a remote volcanic area on the northern peninsula of the Elven Realm, surrounded by a large mountain range and dense tropical vegetation. As far as Toby knew, the area wasn't populated by anything other than tree sprites and elementals. The merchant wagon didn't make sense either. To reach the Elven Realm, you had to either cross by ship or dragon. *Why would the recruits travel with a merchant wagon when they could have contracted a dragon from Stanton?* Toby flipped through the journal, scanning page after page of inventory lists and groups of two to five missing recruits, followed by Thamas's brief explanations of their undocumented transfers.

The last entry was dated two days before Thamas had gone missing.

Twenty-sixth day ~ Sixth month ~ Twenty-ninth year of Turgent Bartholo's rule

I overheard a conversation between the Konsult and Domnal's scribe. I cannot stay and watch a corrupt system endanger innocent people. I will seek out an explanation where the fires burn hottest. Ahh, Archana... please let me place my trust in those who will not abuse it.

Letting the mysterious book drop heavily onto the desk, Toby laced his fingers behind his aching head and leaned back in his chair in contemplation. *What now?* He certainly couldn't show the journal to anyone. It seemed that Thamas had started asking questions, and he hadn't been seen since. He didn't think leaving it on the shelves in the records room was a very good idea either. How could Thamas leave something like that just tucked away on a bookshelf? In the wrong hands, it could be considered an assault on the Turgent himself. Accusing a Konsult, one of the inner circle of the Turgent's advisers, of corruption could have led to charges of treason. With few options presenting themselves, Toby stood and slipped the journal into the waistband of his breeches. Taking a deep, steadying breath, he strode out of the room and headed for the palace grounds. He would see the floor of the throne room by nightfall, or he would have someone's head!

Toby walked quickly and purposefully through the halls of the barracks. The plain stone corridor was a fitting visual for his frame of mind. He felt personally affronted by Contege Thamas. He had never wanted the responsibility of leading the Vigiles. Osric was a good man, but he wasn't experienced enough to handle the politics of his new position. If Thamas hadn't decided to start asking questions or to go looking for trouble with the Turgent's advisers, then he would still be there doing his job, and Toby would be at home with his family. Yet, Toby had to admit that if Thamas was right, and there were corrupt men advising the Turgent, then something had to be done about it. Toby had no idea what Thamas had overheard, and he couldn't even guess where he had ended up. For the moment, he would focus on unburying the rest of the palace, and he would leave intrigue and politics alone. He hoped that Osric was making good time on his trip, and as soon as he knew the status of the palace, Toby would contact him. Sometime before then, he would have to decide if he would tell him about the journal.

As he stepped through the doorway of the barracks, Toby cringed at the bright morning sunlight. He had spent far too much time in the dark office. The training grounds stretched out before him, an expanse of trampled ground bordered by the DuJok arena and a complicated and muddy obstacle course off to his left. A wide dirt path curved to his right, leading to the main road to the palace grounds. It felt good to stretch his legs, and he covered the distance to the palace in less time than he expected.

As he approached the palace grounds, he was pleased to see all of the activity that was taking place. Several groups of people surrounded the palace ruins, all working diligently together to lift slabs of fallen stone with their wands and dropping them into large piles scattered between the trees around the palace. At the nearest pile of rubble, a giant was working alongside a stonemason. The giant was sorting through the pile, pulling out large slabs of stone and placing them side by side in front of the craftsman. Toby watched, intrigued, as the man used his wand to meld the slabs of stone together into a seamless wall, preparing for the reconstruction of the palace. Several men were loading wagons with items recovered from the palace rooms. Obviously they had recently discovered the pantries, as Toby could see casks of spices and bags of flour in the closest wagon. At least not all of the palace supplies had been destroyed.

Toby veered off of the road and crossed over to a group working along the southern edge of the palace. The men saw him approaching as they placed a large piece of stone on a nearby pile. They bowed slightly in respect and returned to their work. Gordyn was overseeing the group, and he stepped away from the others to greet the Profice.

"Profice Toby, we're makin' good progress."

"I am glad to hear that, Gordyn. What have you found so far?"

"Well, we 'ave been working on clearing this section of wall all mornin', but it be awful deep. About an hour ago, we sent in a few o' the prairie dog scouts to see what we're up against. They scampered back an' said that the throne room is just beyond this layer, but the damned roof collapsed on top of it, so it's difficult to remove pieces without causing another cave-in. Those two cave-ins yesterday were bad enough. You don't want to have to do the paperwork on a bloodied ambassador." He grinned mischievously, but Toby knew the cave-ins had scared everyone into being more cautious.

"Did the scouts report finding any survivors?" Toby asked, hoping for some good news.

"Yes, a few lucky bastards between the wall and the head table were trapped but not injured. It's gonna take more work than brushing a magrog's teeth to create an opening for them. Those little imps squeezed through a crack in the stone and got to 'em. They 'ave enough food and water, but it might be a day or two before we get 'em out."

"Good work. I am sure they would like to get out of there soon. I will see if I can get you some more men to help out. Work quickly, but carefully. Let's get them out in one piece." Toby nodded at the rest of the workers and turned back to the road. He was sure that there must be more people available to work than what he saw there. If the Union agents had his men doing menial paperwork like they had tied him up with, they would find that he wasn't as easy to deal with as they had thought.

A large tent had been erected near what had been the entrance to the palace, a command center for the recovery operation. Toby could see the large oak doors, still intact, leaning against a nearby tree. Several voices were coming from within the tent, none of which sounded pleased. Toby recognized the deep timbre of James's voice, and his cart was parked just outside the tent entrance. Just as he reached out to pull the tent flap aside, James came storming through the door and almost knocked him to the ground. Toby sidestepped at the last moment and reached out to steady the angry man before he toppled over.

"Whoa, James. Easy, man! What's going on in there?" Both men were solid on their feet, but the expression on James's face made him look as though he might knock over a tree, or the tent.

"How can such an incompetent man rise to such a high position? I've spoken with men of limited intelligence before, but none with his arrogance! If I never have to deal with that man, it will be too soon. Where is Osric, anyway?" James continued to rant as he stomped over to his cart and began wheeling it down the hill, in total disregard for Toby and his questions. Toby could only shake his head. He thought he knew who had caused the vendor such distress. He sighed to himself, pulled the tent flap aside, and stepped inside.

A lantern on a small table dimly lit the inside of the tent. The three men standing inside looked up, startled by his entrance. Toby knew the two irritating Wizardly Union agents all too well, but he didn't recognize the third man. The stranger was very tall, his head nearly brushing the angled roof of the tent. Long silver hair hung down his back in a tight braid, in stark contrast to the black robes draped over his heavily muscled frame.

"Ah, Profice Toby, I am glad you are here," the small wiry official spoke with a nasally drone. Toby doubted very much that he was happy to see him, but he kept a pleasant expression on his face.

"I need to know where the rest of the Vigiles that are supposed to be working on the palace are. They need more men to help excavate the survivors." He noticed that the younger agent had turned away from him and was fumbling with a stack of paperwork on a desk at the back of the tent.

"Yes, er, all of the available workers have been assigned to their respective tasks, but I will look into reassigning some more men to assist them on that." He pushed his spectacles up higher on his crooked nose and stepped closer to Toby. "I would like to introduce you to the Turgent's Konsult, Dredek," he said, indicating the tall stranger on his left. "He has come from Rowain with good news."

"Good news is always welcome." Toby shifted to his right in an attempt to get a better view of what the other agent was doing. "Konsult Dredek, allow me to thank you for coming, I regret to say that I was not informed of your impending arrival or I would have greeted you sooner." He glared at the Wizardly Union official, bowing slightly to the Konsult and sweeping his arm gracefully before him.

120

Konsult Dredek acknowledged his gesture with a nod and stepped forward, his height causing him to hunch slightly in the confines of the tent. His eyes were a pale grey, closely set above a sharp nose and a thin down-turned mouth.

"Profice, I have come to inform you that we have in custody the culprit responsible for the tragic attack on the peace ratification signing." There was a strange inflection to his voice that Toby couldn't place. "The Turgent will deal with him personally."

"Well, that is good news. How did you apprehend the suspect so quickly?" Toby was amazed that they were able to find the person responsible before they had even arrived at the palace where the attack had taken place.

Konsult Dredek stepped around Toby to the door of the tent without his intense gaze ever leaving Toby's face. "Walk with me, Profice, and perhaps we will find these men you need to assist you on the palace." He stepped outside the tent, and Toby had no choice but to follow him. The Konsult moved slowly, and his long heavy robes created the illusion that he was gliding over the ground. They crossed in front of the palace, observing the work still in progress, and veered off into the dense trees that bordered the eastern wall.

Toby stayed a pace or two behind the Turgent's advisor, not sure where they were headed and not getting the impression that the strange man planned on answering any questions. They had been headed northeast into the forest for several moments, further from town with each step, when the Konsult suddenly stopped. Toby knew that there were men in the trees around them. He had too much experience from his years with the Vigiles and hunting with his men to miss the distinct sounds of footsteps on the soft carpet of pine needles nearby. For a moment, he wished he had Osric's ability to sense danger. It was an ideal situation for an ambush, and Toby was starting to wonder what exactly the powerful man had planned for him.

"I apologize if it seemed like I disregarded your question. We have men whose objective is to locate criminals. They are good at their job." It was not exactly an answer, but Toby understood it was the best one he would get. "How many of your recruits are surrounding us, Profice Toby? The ones you are aware of will be reassigned to assist you on the palace walls. Those that are beyond your perception will be assigned elsewhere." Toby could feel Contege Thamas's journal rubbing uncomfortably against his lower back. All of those recruits had been "assigned elsewhere." He

121

suddenly trusted the man much less than he had when they were introduced. The Turgent's Konsults were men of great power and persuasion. They advised the Turgent on all matters of running his realm, from the allocation of treasury funds to the succession of Ryhains. One of them was responsible for secretly transferring dozens of incompletely trained Vigile recruits out of Stanton, and Toby didn't need Osric's ability to suspect which one. Fortunately, Konsult Dredek would have no way of knowing that the journal existed, nor that Toby had read it and had reason to mistrust him.

"Elsewhere, Konsult Dredek?" Toby was focusing all of his senses on the forest around him, seeking any sign of his men. He had no intention of allowing Dredek to reassign any of his recruits. He didn't want to miss anything.

"The Turgent's personal guard is always looking for good men. The ability to conceal themselves from you will earn them the opportunity for further training. They will return with me to Rowain." The Konsult's pale eyes were boring into Toby's, daring him to challenge his explanation. Toby briefly wondered what the adviser's magical ability was, afraid that he could read his thoughts about the journal.

"We passed twelve recruits on our way here, but only eight of them are still south of us. Two of them joined five others in the woods to the east. There are four men on the ground to the west and another three north of us. Six are up in the trees above us, and two are concealed beneath the pine needles near your feet. I count thirty recruits in all." Toby made a silent plea to Archana that he hadn't missed anyone.

"I am impressed, Profice Toby. You are most perceptive. Those thirty recruits will return to the palace and assist your Vigiles. The two which you missed will be reassigned." Konsult Dredek called out to the recruits and ordered them back to the recovery efforts. They emerged gradually from all sides, seven men dropping silently from nearby trees and three rising from the humus at their feet.

"Andru and Belle, congratulations. You executed your concealment with efficiency and stealth. I was unaware of your presence, and your efforts will be rewarded. Report back to your unit leaders and await further instructions." Andru shot Belle a wide grin, which she returned excitedly as she shook dirt and pine needles out of her short-cropped red hair. Toby hoped that their excitement would not be short-lived when they arrived at their new assignment. He had no idea what was in store for them. He certainly felt like he had failed them, but he showed no sign of it as he turned back to Konsult Dredek.

"They are both good recruits. The Turgent would be lucky to have them in his guard."

"Yes, I am sure that he would." Toby was growing tired of the Konsult's cryptic responses, and he gestured that he should lead the way back to the palace. Dredek stayed where he was and regarded the Profice.

"We have been unsuccessful in contacting Contege Osric since the palace fell." Toby nodded in response.

"His wand was lost in the collapse of the castle. I would be happy to contact him on his new one." Konsult Dredek headed back through the trees towards the palace, not bothering to look back to issue the order.

"Tell him his investigation is no longer necessary and he should return immediately. I have responsibilities in Rowain that I would like to attend to as soon as possible."

* * *

Toby found himself staring once again at the stone walls of the small office in the barracks. His head was reeling from everything he had learned. He knew he had to contact Osric, but he had no idea what to tell him. He cradled his pounding head in his hands. He slipped the journal from his waistline and laid it before him on the desk. He hoped that Osric had good news, because he didn't expect to have any himself, with Konsult Dredek awaiting the Contege's return. He held his wand before him and focused on reaching out to Osric. A pale light started to emanate from the tip of his wand as he felt it link with Osric's. The image of a rocky mountainside appeared as the light became more defined. Toby could see Osric standing on a rock outcropping, and he couldn't imagine where he might be.

"Toby, I have been waiting to hear back from you. Did you uncover the rest of the palace yet?" Osric asked, smiling with excitement.

"We are making slow progress. Osric, where are you? And why are you grinning like a little boy at Harvest Festival?"

"Well." Osric grinned sheepishly at his surroundings. "It is a bit complicated. Are you alone?"

Toby checked the corridor outside the small office and closed the door. "Yes. What is going on?"

"We have discovered some interesting magical artifacts. One of them is a book that has all sorts of spoken spells in it, and I used one of them to come up here."

"Spoken spells? Osric, I don't know what you are up to, but the Turgent's Konsult arrived today and wants you back here immediately."

"I am in the middle of an investigation. There is no way we are coming back yet!"

"Supposedly, they have the culprit in custody, but there are some very suspicious things going on here." Toby wasn't even sure where to start in his explanation. "I found a journal written by Contege Thamas. It contained his suspicions that there is a corrupt Konsult transferring untrained Vigile recruits to Braya. I think I may have met him today."

"Contege Thamas? Braya? Wait, how could they have a suspect in custody already?" Osric's face twisted at the words.

"I thought that seemed impossible as well. Konsult Dredek must have left Rowain at least five days ago. That means that the Turgent's men had only ten days to hear of the attack and apprehend a suspect. They hadn't even seen the palace yet. As far as I can tell, the only information they had was coming from those incompetent twits the Wizardly Union sent up here to *help*. But the Konsult is cryptically insisting that your investigation is no longer necessary."

"Not necessary? Is he mad?! All of the suspects left Stanton after the collapse, and we still need to stop a war!"

"Actually, I think it may be worse than madness. The journal I found had a chronological log of dozens of recruits being transferred out of Stanton secretly over the years. The records are concealed somewhere, if they even exist. The transfer orders came from one of the Turgent's advisers. There could be a conspiracy in our own realm! That scares me more than the threat of a few weasels and irua trying to start a war. How close are you to the irua realm?"

"We were only a week out when our dragon was injured by an eagle attack. We are not even halfway yet, unfortunately. Are you sure the journal said Braya?" Osric appeared to be on to something.

"Yes, it said Braya. It didn't specifically say the Braya Volcano, but what else could it mean? Why?"

"It may surprise you, but dragons do not act as our transportation for their own enjoyment; they are enslaved by us. Their oldest and most loved are in cages at that volcano. We only just learned this ourselves, a few days ago."

Toby's mouth fell agape and his eyes went wide. How could that be true and no one know about it? "Osric, who told you this? Are you sure they were telling you the truth?"

"It is difficult to explain how I know the truth of the matter, but I assure you, it is true." Pain covered Osric's face and his voice trailed off.

"I believe you." Toby was confused by the apparent changes in the young Contege, but the blatant emotion in his eyes was enough to convince him that he had proof of the dragons' captivity. "If the leaders of our realm are transferring young, impressionable recruits to the volcano, chances are they are well aware of the enslavement. They must have the recruits working there, and they don't want anyone to know their destination, because no one knows there is work to do at Braya. No wonder they have kept the transfers secret."

Osric's mood seemed to brighten. "There may be a way to discover what they are doing and at least delay a war until we can figure out how to stop it, but we won't be flying back to Stanton. Where are you right now, this very moment?"

"Sitting in your temporary office in the barracks, the records room."

Suddenly, the image of Osric in the light of his wand vanished, but the mountain scenery never wavered. Toby squeezed his eyes closed. The stress of the past days was taking its toll on him. He opened his eyes, expecting to see that he had imagined it, and instead found himself sitting across the desk from the Contege. For the second time that day, he stood up so quickly that his chair went flying backward.

"Archana's bones! Where did you come from?"

"Half a realm away, my friend." Osric laughed at the look of dismay on the Profice's face.

"Maybe *how* would be a better question!"

"That book of spoken spells I mentioned—this was one of them. I am thinking of calling it the 'Toby Leap' after seeing how fast you can move." He grinned mischievously.

Toby righted his chair and sat back down slowly, never taking his eyes off of Osric. Suddenly, he laughed loudly and reached over and slapped Osric on the shoulder. "Can you teach me?"

"Of course, but if I were you, I would not let anyone see you do it." Osric winked slyly. "Until we have this mess sorted out, I do not want to give away our advantages."

"I agree. I will take any advantage I can get. That damned Konsult used me to select two more recruits. He says they will be returning to Rowain with him as soon as you arrive. I will tell him you need three days for your dragon to heal and another seven to make the journey back. I don't think I can stall him longer than that. That gives you ten days. You need to travel to the Braya Volcano and find out what is really going on." Toby leaned across the desk and looked intently at his Contege. "So, what's the plan?"

Chapter 14
A New Direction

"Look, it's right here in the book! We don't have to wait for Greyback to heal to keep traveling." Osric pointed at the page in excitement.

"I have to admit that you have been correct about things up to this point, but how many times do we have to tell you, boy, we can't see anything on the blasted page!" Gus eyed Osric with annoyance, yet there was a hint of respect that had not been present the day before.

"I've been reading the whole night. This is only the beginning of what we could do!" Osric paced with anxious energy as he spoke. "We do not have to be a part of the enslavement of the dragons anymore. All of Archana can *travel* as they please!"

"Although I am impressed with your level of enthusiasm, we still need proof that there are actual words in the book. Waking me first thing in the morning, before I eat, and pestering me is not a good start!" Gus's respect was wearing thin, and he glared at Osric.

"Eo ire itum!" Osric grinned with pride and disappeared.

"Blasted boy!" Gus rolled out of the small blanket he was sleeping in, walked through the opening of their chamber in the cave, and yelled, "Can we please get some food in here! A hot drink to wake me up would be great as well!" Then he returned to their chamber, muttering curses under his breath. Pebble giggled and jumped with excitement at Osric's disappearance.

"Where did he go?" Kenneth sprang to his feet, looking around in confusion. He sighed with relief when Osric reappeared in the same place he had been before he vanished. Osric held up a bunch of lavender-colored flowers in his hand with a smile.

"Where did you get those? Everything is covered with snow." Bridgett walked toward Osric and lifted the flowers to her nose. She inhaled deeply, their scent reminding her of the serenity and beauty of a sunny morning in a meadow of wildflowers with the unicorns.

"I went back to Stanton. They grow all over there this time of year."

"Stanton?!" Disbelief showed on Kenneth's face as he checked Osric for signs of wounds. "Try something closer the first time, Os! How would anyone be able to help if you appeared over the damned ocean?"

"It's not like that," Osric protested, after witnessing the look on their faces.

Bridgett reached out and touched Osric's arm in concern, "Kenneth is right. How do you know it is safe?"

"These are areas of magic that are yet unexplored." Gus's concerned tone contained no anger. "You must show more wisdom in your choices, boy. Who knows what could have happened. You must master these spells before you attempt such large actions with them."

"I know. I was up all night practicing this spell." Osric was trying his best to appeal to them. He had been careful, and he wanted them to see it. "Look." He took a deep breath and bowed his head in surrender. "I kept trying it throughout the night and *traveling* larger distances with each attempt. What is written in the book is a great start, but I can show you how to do it faster than if you could read it!"

"Boy, were you born an idiot or did you have to practice?" Gus stopped rubbing his temples, and he concentrated his gaze on Osric.

"What?" Osric didn't understand Gus's reaction, which, coupled with the looks he was receiving from Kenneth and Bridgett, made him feel rather nervous. He had just spent the night exploring a new magic that nobody knew, and the rush that he had experienced from it was astounding. Gus and the others acted as though he had been jumping off of mountains.

"Did you listen to the story Ero told us, or did you sleep through it?" Gus stood on his hind legs, his paws planted on his hips as he lectured Osric.

What does the story have to do with this argument? Osric shook his head. "Of course I heard it. What are you trying to say?"

"After the eagles witnessed that spell, Argan died that night! Are you sure you are all right?" Gus exclaimed.

"I am telling you, it is safe. You just have to picture where you want to go in your mind. It is easier if you have been there before, but the book says you can go to any location you can see. There was another reason for his death, I know it!" He could remember what he had seen as Ero told the story. Argan had looked sick when he returned, so Osric was sure he would have been sick already if it were due to the spell.

"There is a cost to magic, boy! It drains energy from you. Do you honestly think you could work all day, and dig a hole all night, without any ill effects? No, you can't, and you know it." Gus had lost his patience. He motioned to Kenneth to sit him down. "Check him over well, and if he is all right, I am going to examine him with my gift to see why he's not dead."

Bridgett placed her hand on Osric's shoulder, encouraging him to sit down. "We have no way of knowing why Argan became ill, but you are risking your life and your mission by practicing magic you do not understand." She looked him over carefully, checked his pulse, and pulled a few vials of herbs from her belt.

"I don't understand why you are making such a big deal out of this. If none of you believe me, then Gus should examine me now." Osric tried to sit still while Bridgett lifted his eyelids and examined his pupils.

"Don't you worry, boy. I am going to examine you whether you like it or not—just as soon as she makes sure you are going to survive. You can spare us the naked routine this time as well; that didn't impress anyone," Gus assured him.

Osric took Bridgett by the shoulders and gently moved her aside to address Gus. "It is my life on the line, so I can guarantee that I will be careful. I have no desire to die. She can tell you now that I am fine. Let's get this over with so I can teach you what I have learned."

Gus glared as Osric knelt down with a self-assured look on his face. Gus glanced up at Bridgett, and she shrugged. "As far as I can tell, there is nothing wrong with him." She sat and began pulling stoppers from the vials of herbs.

"You are too sure of yourself, boy! That will be your undoing if you are not careful," Gus said as he began his examination.

Osric sat still, patiently waiting to hear what Gus would find. It did not take long for Gus to locate what he had missed the first time.

"Incredible!" Gus pointed at Osric's back. "How did I miss those?"

"I told you I was fine," Osric said with a grin.

"What is it?" Bridgett asked.

"These little black orbs, here and here," Gus said, indicating two points between Osric's shoulder blades. "They are the dragons' gift of Endurism." Gus stood wide-eyed, shaking his head.

"What is Endurism?" Kenneth gazed at Osric with admiration.

Gus explained, staring at Osric. "A dragon flies by the use of magic. They are too heavy for their wings to carry them far without it, especially with passengers. This gift allows them great endurance with the use of magic. They would die without it, even after only a day of flight. Their gift directs the drain on the body away and casts it back to Archana."

"So, are you saying he can use magic with no physical effects of any kind?" Kenneth grinned widely at Osric.

"No. Even a dragon must rest after a day of flying, but I think he could use magic continuously for several days before he felt the drain on his body. He would still feel the natural drain of energy that humans feel, though, and there may be other effects that we haven't identified yet. With the amount of power you are able to use, Osric, there may be an even greater cost. You must still be careful!"

"I understand. So, can I show you how to use this spell now?" Osric stood excitedly.

Gus sat for moments, considering all of the information. "You were up all night. You must be exhausted?"

"Don't worry about me. I can get through another day on adrenaline alone." As Osric tried to assure Gus, an eagle entered the chamber with a tray of steaming mugs and fruit hovering in front of him.

"Perfect timing." Bridgett smiled and removed one of the mugs from the tray as it floated past her. "Osric, these herbs will prevent fatigue from setting in and give you the energy you need to fight off any illness that you may have contracted, even if you are not yet showing symptoms." She sprinkled the herbs into the mug and passed it to him.

Osric downed the contents as fast as he could, scalding his tongue with the hot liquid. The herbs had a slightly bitter flavor, and he reached for a piece of fruit to rid his mouth of the taste. Once he had finished eating, he looked at Gus questioningly.

"All right," Gus submitted. "But once this lesson is over, you will rest!" he yelled, as Osric led them outside. Enjoying the fruit from the tray, Pebble remained inside the cave chasing the small wormlike creatures that crawled along the edge of the cave floor, consuming moss from the rocks. The light-reflecting abilities of the moss caused the worms to glow in the dark, and Pebble loved following their luminescent forms.

Osric stood on the snowy ledge and pointed at the closest mountain's peak. "If I can see it, then I can go there. See that tree, with the big rock formation next to it? All I have to do is picture myself standing on it." He uttered the words, "Eo ire itum," and vanished.

They could see Osric standing on the distant rocks. He was waving at them, and he then turned away for a few moments, before disappearing.

* * *

Bridgett sat comforting Pebble as they watched Gus pace outside the entrance of their quarters. Kenneth was across the fire from them, sharpening his weapons, with a scowl on his face. They could hear Gus grumbling to himself, when he suddenly stopped pacing.

"Where have you been?!" Gus growled, as Osric appeared on the ledge outside the cave.

"We need to get ready to leave," Osric spoke excitedly, striding past Gus into the inner chamber.

Kenneth set his knife aside, rose up, and took deliberate steps toward Osric. He stared at him for a moment in silence and then swung his fist, connecting squarely with Osric's jaw.

"How dare you leave without telling us where you were going!" Kenneth shouted, while the others stared in surprise. "We looked for you for an hour!" He glared down at Osric, who was lying on the ground, recovering from the blow.

Gus recovered his composure rather quickly and joined Kenneth in the attack. "We used that spell of yours to take us up and down this mountain—rather successfully without your instruction, I might add—all in an attempt to find you!" He sighed with disgust. "Look at Pebble. Do you understand what these antics can do to people who care for you?"

Osric massaged his chin as he tried to recover his senses. "I guess I should have said something, but there was no time for that." He glared back at Kenneth. "Why didn't you let me speak first?" Osric looked over at Bridgett with pleading eyes, hoping he at least had her support.

Bridgett's cheeks flushed in anger. "How could you be so selfish, Osric?" She rose gracefully to her feet as Pebble climbed out of her lap. "I realize you are excited about the new magic and you want to explore its possibilities, but that is no excuse for being irresponsible. It was bad enough that you tested the spell without considering the consequences, but how dare you leave us here to think the worst!" She stood over him with flashing eyes, and he refrained from standing, for fear she might repeat Kenneth's assault.

Pebble scampered toward Osric and timidly poked at his arm. "I's was afraid you's dieded!" Then he buried his face in Osric's arm.

Osric ran his hands over Pebble's fur. He looked up at Bridgett's angry expression in disbelief. He had been sure that she would understand that he had not meant to concern them. "I am sorry that I caused you to worry. I know I left in a hurry, but you are all overreacting," he muttered, rubbing his sore jaw. "You need to understand that I am not here only to travel to the irua. We are trying to stop a war! My obligations are not just to this group; I am performing my duty as Contege of Stanton. The responsibilities of my position took me away for a time, that is all."

"What is so important that you would just take off like that?" Kenneth demanded.

"Look, this situation..." Osric sighed and paused to gather his thoughts. "We are dealing in magics never before explored. I was not asked to do this; it was forced upon me. I do not have to answer to anyone for the performance of my office—no one but the Ryhain of Stanton. It is reasonable to assume, with all we are learning, that situations may arise that demand my immediate attention. You deserve an explanation, but I did not deserve to be assaulted upon my return!" He considered each face as he finished speaking.

Pebble was the only one satisfied by his return alone, but his argument had struck a chord with his companions. Their faces softened, and Kenneth reached out and helped Osric to his feet.

"Toby contacted me almost the moment I arrived on that mountain," said Osric. "The information he shared with me changes everything. We need to prepare to leave. Now that we are all able to *travel* without Greyback, there is nothing preventing our departure, but we will not be journeying to the irua. You should all sit down. I will explain everything, and you will understand why I left so suddenly.

* * *

Osric climbed carefully over the jagged rocks to the next ledge. It had taken some convincing, but he had managed to persuade the others to go along with his plans. He had one more thing to do before they continued on with their journey. He needed to prepare the return trip that the Konsult would be expecting, but he had personal reasons for doing it as well. He wanted the dragons on his side, after all.

Greyback was lying with her good wing stretched out in the sun, the other still wrapped in poultices and bandages, and she started at the sound of his footsteps. As he approached her, Osric spoke softly, "Greyback, I know you have not completely healed, but we are preparing to leave today. You will remain here and the eagles will take care of you until you can fly again. I plan to rescue your ancestors."

Following his movements, her eyes narrowed and her nostrils flared at his words.

Osric walked slowly toward her, aware that if she did not believe him, she could easily kill him. He approached her head and spoke in soothing tones.

"I want you to know that before Ero shared your history with us, we knew nothing of your enslavement. We, as commoners, had no knowledge of the imprisonment of your kin. I truly believed that you flew for us for the payment, but now that I know the truth, I want to set you free. I want to set all of the dragons free! I have found a way to travel quickly without the aid of the dragons, and I can prove it to you." Osric stood near her head and pointed across to a nearby mountain. "Do you see that clearing between the tallest trees? Watch closely, and you will know that I speak the truth." Osric took a deep breath and vanished.

Greyback scrambled to her feet, and her eyes went wide with disbelief. She looked around the ledge and stepped forward nervously to the space where he had stood. When she failed to encounter his invisible form, she looked over to the clearing he had indicated. She could make out his small figure easily, standing on a large rock and waving. She sent a bout of flame up into the air so he would know that she had seen him.

Osric reappeared in a crouched position, and Greyback stepped backward quickly in surprise. He stood before her with a wide grin.

"I do still need your help, Greyback, but I will not demand that you obey me. You are free, and I am going to go and free the other dragons. Will you help me, please?" Osric pleaded with Greyback. He did not want anyone else to know that they could travel without her, so he would need the dragon's help getting back to Stanton.

Greyback leaned in and sniffed him, then craned her neck around to look behind him. She eyed him closely and said, "You are a walker, and you are not supposed to be able to fly. How did you do that?"

"I have unlocked the secret of a lost magic, and it allows me to travel long distances with great speed. So, I will not need you to fly us to our next destination: the Braya Volcano. I will free your kin, or I will die trying."

"I believe you, Osric," Greyback laid her head on the stone at his feet. "How is it you wish me to help you, if not to fly you there?" There was an edge of fear in her voice. "I cannot fight the walkers."

"The dragons will not have to fight, but I do not know who is involved, and so I cannot let anyone know about my new, um, abilities. When your wing has healed, will you meet me and take us into Stanton?" Osric knelt before her in supplication. "I will not force you to help us, but I am afraid that without you, we will be in grave danger upon our return. We need to know more to prevent the war, but by freeing the dragons, we can buy the time we need to investigate further."

"If you can free us, I will help you." Greyback lifted her injured wing and winced. "It is still very sore, but I will be able to fly soon. I will need to recover some of my strength before I can fly with passengers. How long will it be before you need me?"

"Nine days, maybe ten. I must get back to Stanton to prevent anyone involved from suspecting I know more than I should." Greyback nodded at him.

"I will be ready. Where should I meet you?"

"We flew over a small town, about two hours east of Stanton, remember?" Greyback nodded in acknowledgement. "Lothaine does not have a dragon platform, but there is a large clearing in the forest just south of the town. We will meet you there. Thank you, Greyback. After all of the wrongs done to your kind, I do not deserve your help, but I promise you I will see an end to the captivity of your elders." He stood and ran his hand along her neck, then turned to rejoin his companions in the cave. Before he could cross to the next ledge, Ero landed in front of him.

"Osric, I beg an audience." He bowed to show respect, and Osric felt rather uncomfortable with the display.

"Yes, of course, Ero." Osric was relieved when Ero straightened. "Please, tell me what you need, and then we must go."

"Go? Greyback is in no shape to fly. You cannot make her carry you with her injury!" Ero spoke rapidly, glaring angrily at Osric.

"Yes, I know. We will be traveling without her while she recovers. I have unlocked the secrets of Argan's magic."

"I knew you would be the one to fulfill the prophecies." Ero looked at him with pride and bowed low in reverence. "I bring you news. While on our hunt, I witnessed an army of walkers. Their numbers are greater than I have seen in all of my days. The dragons tell me that they are bound for Angmar and that they plan to exterminate the irua and the weasels. At least a hundred thousand will be on the move in two weeks.

"A hundred thousand!" Osric was astounded by the news, and Greyback looked terrified at hearing about the walker army. "Archana's bones! How could they have an army that size getting ready to leave already? It has only been a little over two weeks since the attack!"

Osric ran his hands through his hair and gathered his thoughts before he continued. "This changes nothing. We will still leave today to free the dragons. That will slow the army's movements until we can discover who is behind all of this."

Chapter 15
The Elven Realm

"Thank Archana your dad brought you to De'assartis that summer," Osric said. Their interactions were once again friendly and humorous, as he had forgiven Kenneth for his sore jaw. "It would have taken us much longer to make our way to the Elven Realm, if you weren't able to remember these woods!"

"You are lucky that you didn't have to come here the way I did. I was sick all seven days that we sailed." Kenneth set down his gear and sat on a fallen tree to recover from the trip. "I felt the effects of the spell this time. My head is spinning."

"Are you sure you are all right? Maybe you shouldn't have tried to take us this far so soon." Osric placed his roll of bedding and the book on the ground, concerned more for his friend's welfare than his sleeping arrangements.

"Yes, I just need a moment to adjust, but I will be fine." His breathing was coming easier.

"Should I stay here for a few minutes?" Osric sat next to him on the tree.

"No," Kenneth smiled. "Gus is probably running around swearing with the amount of time you've been gone already. Before you go, though…" He stood and walked a few feet away, drawing a large circle on the ground with his foot. "Appear in this area. The last thing I want is for one of you to land on me when you return. That I may not recover from."

"All right, but you sit down and wait until I get back." Osric stood and walked to the center of the circle to get a sense of the area and to make sure he could arrive in the same spot. Kenneth sat back down and grinned at Osric.

"If Gus gives you a hard time, just levitate him for a minute or two; that should shut him up."

"Yeah, that would make the rest of this trip pleasant!" Osric grinned back, closed his eyes, spoke his spell, and vanished.

When Osric opened his eyes again, the relieved faces of Gus and Bridgett greeted him.

"Thank Archana you are in good shape, boy." Gus walked around Osric, inspecting him closely for signs of injury. "Did Kenneth manage to get you two there with all of your limbs intact?"

"Kenneth was tired from the experience, but we arrived safely. I needed to make sure he was all right. Sorry for the delay." Osric helped Gus climb onto his shoulder. Bridgett had already collected Pebble in her hands and was standing close by.

"I know you haven't slept yet, but for my sake, I hope you have washed your shaggy hair lately or this will be a miserable trip!" Gus huffed as he climbed up Osric's shirtsleeve.

"At least you don't have to carry an overgrown, filthy rat on your shoulder. Imagine how I feel." Osric jabbed back at him.

"Keep talking, boy," Gus spouted back. "But try to say something useful and get us to our destination in one piece."

Osric took Bridgett's hand with a smile and spoke the words he had been practicing for over a day.

"Eo ire itum." There was only the slightest sensation of falling and forward movement, and then it was over. Osric had landed right where he was supposed to, and Kenneth sat smiling in the same place he had been when Osric left.

"How long was I gone, Kenneth?" Osric looked up for an indication of what time it was, but the dense tree cover obscured the sun's location in the sky.

"Not long at all. As far as I can tell, it didn't take any longer than when we were using the spell to look for you on the mountainside. Distance does not seem to matter. We *traveled* almost straight south and slightly west, across the ocean and deep into this forest. Technically, it may even be earlier here than it was in the caves!" Kenneth chuckled.

"Across an ocean! Boy, are you mad? You really need to start being more careful. You could get one of us killed." Gus began gathering leaves to place his blanket on. "The only bright spot of all of this is that it is not winter here."

"I hope you like rain, because we will get some tonight if my experience holds true." Kenneth started piling wood in the center of their clearing to establish a campsite. "It rains in this forest all year, and the insects are relentless. I will teach you all the spell my dad taught me to keep them away from the camp."

137

"Kenneth, in that case, can you scare us up something to eat before it gets too dark and wet?" Osric asked.

"Yes, I seem to remember these woods crawling with animal life. I won't be long." Kenneth grabbed his bow from where it was leaning on a nearby tree and took off into the forest.

"Don't get too comfortable, Gus. You and I are going to figure out this wand, even if it kills me." Osric could feel the effects of two days without sleep, but he needed to understand why Gus could see no difference in it before he slept.

"If you two are going to work together, you had better learn to get along. The last thing I want for dinner is prairie dog meat," Bridgett said, digging in her pack for a pot and some bread to go with their meal, and then she started a fire with her wand. She shot them a playful smile as she sat down on the fallen tree that Kenneth had waited on for their arrival.

"What makes you think it wouldn't be human we eat?" Gus looked at her with an arched eyebrow, and his chest puffed out. Bridgett giggled at his attempt at a joke and then laughed harder at the scowl that appeared on Gus's face.

"You need to focus on this." Osric tossed him his wand. "And leave the jokes to us."

"I could tell you all day that there is nothing different about this wand, and you would not listen." Gus shook his head. "But since you have the gift as well now, I guess I can show you."

Osric was grateful to see Bridgett smiling, and he found himself staring at her.

"Stop gawking at the pretty lady and get over here. We have studying to do!" Gus was still upset, though not at anyone in particular. He did not like having his understanding of magic challenged, and this had been happening far too frequently of late.

Osric blushed as he turned to face Gus, and he changed the subject quickly. "All right, you are going to have to run through the gift activation with me again. Let's try to do this without being rude today. I haven't slept in a while and would hate to accidentally hurt you."

Gus looked at him with disdain and then began the lesson. "You have to look past the wand." He laid the wand on the ground before him as Osric nodded in agreement. "And you have to look right at it, as well."

"What? Those are two completely different things. You might as well ask me to swim in water and walk on it at the same time."

Gus hung his head with a sigh. "I can see this is going to take some time." He looked up at Osric with impatience. "You need to learn to think differently. I am asking you to look, not only with your eyes but with the gift as well. You must look directly at it with your eyes, but into it with your gift."

"Ah, but how do I activate the gift so that I can *look into it*?" Osric's mocking tone emphasized the irony of the statement. Osric looked over at Bridgett, who shook her head and smiled at him, but Gus puffed out his chest and scowled at him.

"Extollo!" Gus shouted, and the spell turned Osric upside down.

Rage filled every inch of his being while he hung in midair, humiliated. He imagined several ways to kill a prairie dog, as he waited for Gus to drop him.

"You need to focus, boy! Can I have your attention long enough to teach you this or not?" Gus thrust his chin up and propped his paws on his hips.

Defiantly, Osric crossed his arms nonchalantly. "I can do this all day, but can you teach me while I hang here?"

"Demitto!"

Osric was lowered gently down. His face was tense as his feet rested back on the ground.

"Now, if I can direct your attention to the wand." Gus turned abruptly back to the object of their study. "Try to focus on this"—he pointed at the wand—"instead of where your desires take you."

"It's is like lookin' at da fishies in da waters," Pebble answered, pulling worms out from under a rock behind a nearby tree, obviously hungry.

Both Osric and Gus looked confused for a moment. Pebble peeked around at them with a grin as the light from the campfire grew in the coming night.

"When you's is lookin' for fishies, you's can'ts just looks at da waters. You's gotsta looks behinds it." He shrugged as if it were simple and he had no idea why they did not think of it first.

Osric smirked derisively at Gus. "Why can't you be as wise as your son?" Osric crouched next to Gus and attempted to do as Pebble had instructed.

Almost instantly, the vivid nature of the strands became visible with the insight Pebble had provided. The fibers within shone with all the colors

139

of a rainbow; a complex weave of dozens of them twisted throughout the wood.

"This is amazing!" Osric marveled at the sight.

"Don't get too carried away, boy. We are working here." Gus laid his wand on the ground next to Osric's.

"It's beautiful." Osric stopped looking long enough to steal a fleeting glace at Bridgett and smile.

"Focus, boy!" Gus barked

Osric returned his attention to the wands, and a thought occurred to him: *What do the magical fibers within someone look like?* Then, without thinking, he turned his gaze toward Gus, only to be greeted with a shower of dirt thrown at his face.

"Ah!" He fell to his side, rubbing grit from his closed eyes, completely caught off guard by the attack.

"You don't look at another with the gift, unless they are infants or they give you permission, boy!"

"Why didn't you just say that?!"

Gus smirked menacingly at a very angry Osric. "I could tell you all day, but will you ever forget now?" He turned toward Bridgett and added, "This is more fun, anyway."

"Gus! What is wrong with you?" Bridgett demanded, as she watched Pebble from her perch on the fallen tree.

Once the pain had eased and his eyes were clear of enough debris to open them, Osric stood up. Overcoming his desire to do bodily harm to Gus, he brought his attention back to the wands.

"Look at them." Gus indicated the two wands lying side by side. "They are virtually identical. The weave is the same. The constriction is at the same point, and they are even made from the same wood. There is nothing remarkable about your wand!"

He was right. Other than Osric's wand being slightly longer, they looked exactly the same. Osric stood there, peering within the wands for what felt like an eternity. He lost himself within the gift, but no matter how hard he looked, he could not find the answer. Osric couldn't understand it; there had to be something different about his wand. It didn't make any sense. He had heard the prophecy. He knew that it was special; he just couldn't see it. He glanced up at Bridgett, which seemed to ease some of his frustration. She had an introspective look on her face.

"Maybe it isn't the wand that is different, Osric. Maybe it is you." She smiled sadly at him, glad the tension seemed to have broken between him and Gus, at least for the moment.

Gus interrupted, drawing Osric's attention away from her once again. "That can't be it. I examined him, remember? He's strange, but I don't know why everyone thinks he is so special. You are beautiful, my dear, but it would be nice if he could keep his eyes off of you for one moment, and maybe we could actually accomplish something!"

Osric was so sick of the insulting little rodent making comments about him and Bridgett. Gus had no right to treat them that way. He cared more for her than he was willing to admit, and he couldn't stand there and listen to Gus embarrass her. Rather than kick him into the woods, Osric quickly backed away.

He could see Kenneth walking back. *At least we will be able to eat soon. I am starving.* Then realization and horror filled Osric as he noticed the rabbit in his hand. *The vision!* Kenneth noticed the look on his face and reached for his bow. He had an arrow notched by the time Osric had his left hand on his sword. Osric dove right and swung up with all of his might, letting the swing draw the blade from its scabbard. He felt the blade slice through something he could not see. The force of the swing sent him spinning in the air, and he heard Kenneth's arrow hit its mark, but he wasn't sure if they had killed it. Osric fell awkwardly, face down in the dirt, and scrambled to get up as he heard Bridgett scream.

Osric stood and swung around with his sword, ready to strike, but the thing lay dead on the ground. His blade had severed the head at the neck, yet Kenneth's bowshot must have arrived at the same time, as the shaft of the arrow had pinned the head in its original place on the creature's neck. Its right arm lay a few feet from Kenneth, separated from its body by Osric's sword. It was a beast he had never seen before. Thick muscles wrapped tightly around its body, and its pale-grey skin shone with sweat. Sparse patches of dark-grey fur were scattered along its body, thickest on the long, thin limbs. Claws the length of his wand came from the hands and feet and looked as sharp as his sword blade, and the creature's teeth were like small, jagged daggers. Whatever it was, it was a predator.

He crouched low to make himself less visible and crept slowly toward his companions. The last thing he wanted was to be spotted by another one of those creatures. He stopped suddenly as Gus and Bridgett gasped in surprise. They were staring at the ground behind him, with looks of astonishment. *Another one?!* Osric turned around, swinging his sword in a graceful arc and crying out to put as much force behind his swing as possible. His blade only encountered air, and he turned back to them, breathing heavily.

"Where did you go, boy?" Gus's ears twitched wildly as he looked around in confusion.

"What you are talking about?" Osric looked at him questioningly and stepped toward Gus quickly. Gus scrambled back, staring at the leaves at Osric's feet. "Gus, what's wrong with you?"

"Boy, either you are invisible or there is a ghost here with an unnerving ability to mimic your voice." Osric looked down the length of his body in surprise, as his eyes took in only the wet leaves and twigs upon which he stood. Being unable to see himself was decidedly odd, and he felt a nervous flutter in his stomach. Just as the thought that he needed to be visible to lead the group passed through his mind, his form came back into view. Gus rushed over to him, as Bridgett scooped Pebble up into her arms and ran toward them.

"Osric, how did you do that?" Bridgett asked.

"I have no idea! But I don't want to be standing here discussing it when another one of those things show up." Osric indicated the ugly creature at their feet. "We need to leave, now!" He hurriedly started collecting his pack and motioned for the others to do the same. "Hurry, grab ahold of me and I will take us as far as I can tonight before it is too dark to see. Have any of you seen a creature like that before?"

"I don't think anyone has, but I am pretty sure I know what it is." Gus stared at the beast in shock.

"What is it?" Kenneth picked up his gear and stood beside Osric, ready to leave.

"I've seen the aftermath of these creatures before. The claws and those teeth! I believe we are the first to witness one die."

"What is it?!" Osric was not in the mood for one of Gus's lengthy explanations.

"I think it's a paun, and you are right, boy, we must leave fast. Who knows if those things travel alone or in packs!" Kenneth picked Gus up quickly and hoisted him onto his shoulder.

Osric grabbed Bridgett and Kenneth's hands, looking around in fear. "Eo ire itum!"

Chapter 16
Braya Volcano

As they came around a final curve, Machai saw a huge tree hugging the face of the mountain. Its trunk was so big it would have taken eight of him to encircle it with his arms. Its massive roots had broken off chunks of stone from the volcano, and they lay scattered at its base like bones at an altar. Out of the corner of his eye, he caught movement off to the left. What he had thought was a large boulder sitting next to the tree revealed itself to be the dragon Thom had warned him about. Its tail was wrapped about the trunk, and tangled among the loose stones like the horrible aftermath of a giant sea serpent amongst the wreckage of a ship dashed upon the rocks. The dragon had the same sorrel hue as the volcano, and it difficult to discern unless he moved. His long, sinuous neck terminated in a head nearly as large as the wagon, and the horses snorted and pawed at the ground, refusing to traverse any closer to the vast predator.

Machai halted with the horses and stared, enchanted, as the dragon swung its head around to watch him with one swirling gold eye. He was sure that if the order were given, the massive beast would thoroughly enjoy devouring him. Yet, looking into the dragon's eye gave him such an impression of sorrow and solitude that his heart ached for the creature. He felt so much empathy for the beast that he had to look away, lest he wander unwittingly within its reach.

Machai turned away and busied himself with calming the horses, while Thom walked right past the dragon and disappeared into the rock wall behind the tree, twirling his bone wand in his hand and whistling. A few moments later, Thom returned, accompanied by an older man and carrying two large canvas sacks. He dropped the bags near the cart, with the noticeable sound of clinking coin, and leaned one hip against the rear wheel. He obviously did not want to miss the unveiling of Machai's load of weapons.

"Thank you, Thom." Aron was a tall man, the lines of his age and profession etched clearly on his face. His steel grey hair was cropped close to his head and faded into a short beard on his square jaw. Machai guessed him to be in his early sixties, but his broad shoulders and straight posture indicated he might be younger. "You are dismissed. I am sure you have duties to attend to elsewhere." Aron arched one eyebrow at the sullen pout on Thom's face as he eyed the wagon, and Thom straightened quickly and headed back to the entrance, kicking a stone at the dragon as he passed and then breaking into a run to avoid a swipe of its massive tail. Aron glared at Thom's back as he watched him disappear behind the tree trunk, and then he turned his eyes upon Machai. "I expected your delivery four days ago. Did you run into trouble?" His keen gaze was disconcerting, and Machai busied himself unlashing the ties on the canvas tarp covering the wagon.

"Aye, an ugly storm three days into a forsaken sail, and more rain an' mud than I ever expected to slog through. Ye'r lucky I be only four days behind." He pulled the canvas back, revealing saddlebags half emptied of their supplies and two hundred of the finest dwarven blades ever crafted. He heard Aron's sharp intake of breath as he pulled one of the blades from the wagon and handed it to him. He held the blade out before him, testing its perfect weight and balance, and carved an arc through the air. Aron was relishing the feel of the sword in his grip, but he looked perplexed when Machai glanced back up at him.

"How do you activate it?" Machai was tempted to tell him to figure it out himself, but the edge of the blade was sharp enough to take his head off with ease, even without utilizing the sword's magical properties imbued by the metal masters who had forged them. As much as he hated delivering dwarven weapons into the hands of humans, he decided it would be best to keep the meeting short and pleasant.

"You be using it by focused intent, similar to ye'r wand. The bloodstones be forged into the hilts. Focus on the feel of the metal in ye'r hand, and *intend* to ignite the blade." Aron scrutinized him with doubt, but as he focused his attention back on the sword, the blade began to glow red. Machai could feel the heat radiating from the metal, and he stepped back several paces. The red glow brightened slowly, and soon the edge of the blade was white hot. Aron stepped away from the wagon, walked slowly and deliberately toward the massive tree, and raised the sword up over his right shoulder. Machai thought he intended to sever a low branch from the tree, but he turned suddenly and brought the sword down at an angle, dropping low and sweeping his left leg out to his side in a graceful motion. The blade bit deep into the tough hide of the dragon's foreleg, and he screamed with fury and pain. A huge gout of flame poured forth from his throat, directed into the air rather than at his cruel captor. Aron stood for a moment, as if testing the beast to see if he would retaliate and give him an excuse to punish the other dragons. The angry dragon growled low and menacingly, but he did not make a move against his attacker. Aron walked back to Machai and the wagon, mentally withdrawing his attention from the sword and grinning widely as the blade rapidly cooled to a high metallic sheen, giving no indication it was any different than the short sword at his hip.

"Very impressive, dwarf. It is rare to find a blade which so easily penetrates dragon hide." Machai grunted in disgust at the look of pleasure plastered on the man's face after seeing the destructive potential of the two hundred weapons he had just acquired. Machai gritted his teeth against the rage building within him, and tore his eyes from the temptation of the swords in the wagon. Any man who would be so cruel to another creature deserved to die an agonizing death, but Machai could not be sure how many men would swarm from the volcano for vengeance the moment the blade touched Aron's throat, and another would surely take his place to torture the dragons.

"Aye," he said, managing to rein in his tongue. Climbing up onto the wagon hitch, Machai took a mental inventory as he emptied the supplies from one set of saddlebags into the other to make room for the payment. Attempting to control his temper, he changed the subject. "Can I be getting more supplies from ye? That dockside market smelled worse than a drogma's breath after munchin' on fish guts."

"I have many mouths to feed, but I can sell you enough rations to get you by. You are taking a hefty bit of coin off my hands for these weapons, though. I won't be inclined to give you a good price."

"I need only some mash for the horses to regain strength, and ten days or so of rations for meself to make up for the time I be losing."

"I will have what you need brought out, and horses brought around to move this wagon. Make yourself comfortable. Just don't wander too close to the dragon." He placed the blade gently back into the wagon with the others and walked away. Machai unhitched the horses from the wagon. It was apparent that he was not going to be let anywhere near the inside of the volcano. Not even his horses would be allowed in to complete the delivery. He opened the heavy sacks that Thom had dropped on the ground. Satisfied that there was a sufficient amount of gold, he threw them in with his supplies and the swords. He led the horses around to the back of the wagon, dropped the gate, and pulled himself up. Standing on the open gate, he hoisted the saddlebags onto their backs to prepare for his return journey.

* * *

Machai led the horses, rather than ride one as Thom had suggested. He was well supplied and had enough time to reach a campsite as far away from the volcano as Thom had advised him. He had not excited the anger of Aron, nor the abused dragon guarding his post. He should have felt elated to be returning to his home, but the things he had learned plagued his mind and slowed his pace. He couldn't get the pain swirling in the dragon's eyes out of his thoughts, knowing that the majestic creature was impelled by invisible bonds to accept any torture, guarding his own kin caged behind a layer of stone. Suddenly, he veered off of the path and turned the horses back toward the volcano. He had no idea what he would do, but he couldn't leave without learning more.

He wove his way between the trees, keeping a sharp lookout for guards from the volcano. He hoped that having a dragon guarding their door would make them overconfident and lax in patrolling the forest. When he reached the point where the trees thinned, he paused and tied the horses to a branch. He walked carefully over the damp ground, thankful the rain had ceased, increasingly wary of encountering someone as he approached the volcano. He reached a large rock formation on the border of the open expanse near the base of the mountain, and he climbed to its apex to get a better view. From his perch he could see the enormous tree that hid the entrance to the volcano, and looking closely, he thought he could pick out the outline of a massive head resting on clawed forelegs. He didn't doubt that the dragon was aware of his presence as well.

He saw two men come around from either side of the mountain, pause for a moment in brief conversation, and then walk again in opposite directions along the base of the volcano. They would be the patrolmen he had feared running into on his way there. He crouched patiently on the hard stone, observing the patterns of the guards. Twice more, he saw patrolmen return to the entrance and then part again to cover their rounds. Estimating how long it took them to complete their pass, he decided he had a large enough window of time to learn more about the situation. He knew he could not get past the dragon to get into the volcano, but nothing was stopping him from asking the beast itself a few questions—well, nothing but the teeth, which were nearly half as long as he was tall.

When next the guards were out of sight, he climbed down the rocks and crept toward the entrance. He stopped just out of the dragon's reach and knelt down before him, casting a shield to prevent the men within from hearing him speak.

"Greetings, wise guardian. I am aware ye have been ordered to eat me, but I beseech ye to hold off on ye'r meal until we talk. I be appalled at the treatment of ye and ye'r kin. Will ye allow me to ease ye'r wound and then conceal meself between ye and this tree and speak to ye?" The giant dragon peered down at him, and a thin line of smoke trailed up from his nostrils. Machai realized that he might prefer his meals roasted, and the short distance between them would not protect him from dragon fire. Just when he was starting to doubt the wisdom of the conversation, the dragon spoke.

"Why would you offer to ease my pain. Do you not fear the men who reside within this mountain?"

"Aye, guardian, I fear them. They be causing great harm to ye, and I fear they will threaten others soon." Machai pulled a small wooden box from his pack and opened the lid. "This be a salve of strong magic, willow bark, and fairie tears. It will ease ye'r pain and heal ye faster than any wand." After a moment's hesitation, the dragon shifted his weight and positioned his foreleg within reach of Machai and his healing salve.

"I suppose there is no harm in conversing with you before I consume you. I do relish the opportunity to hide something from these abhorrent humans. I will permit you to hide, dwarf, assuming your fairie paste is helpful." Machai could not help but keep one eye on the dragon's head while he gently smeared the salve across the angry, cauterized wound. He sighed in relief when the dragon's breathing slowed. He tested his weight on the leg and then crouched down between the great trunk of the tree and the dragon's bulk. The dragon curled up and rested his head on the ground where he could see Machai and better conceal him. "What is it you would like to discuss, stone dweller?"

"I am aware of the atrocious wrongs being done to ye and y'er kin by the men in this mountain. I am wondering if there be any way I may help ye. Can ye tell me how many men be here?"

"Why should I believe that you want to help, when you come bearing a load of weaponry for these men?"

"I did not know when I set out to deliver the swords that they might be used to punish ye and keep such majestic creatures enslaved. I cannot retrieve the wagon, but if there be another thing that would benefit ye, I will do it gladly." Machai could see fear in the dragon's eyes. "I know ye be having no reason to trust me, and if these humans suspect ye be plotting with me, it could lead to more devastation for ye'rself and the others kept here, but change willn't come without risk." The dragon eyed him wearily, but he held his head proudly and answered Machai's question.

"Fourteen, including Aron. Four are currently on patrol. One lies idle from an injury."

"I be a capable fighter, but I willn't be able to take on nine men by meself. I apologize, but I cannot storm the volcano."

"If killing these men was all it would take to free us, we would not be kept here by the likes of these humans. Killing them will not disrupt the magic keeping them caged. There is nothing you can do to help us, dwarf. Begone. I will not eat you."

"How can the spell be interrupted?"

"The magic is strong and well planned. I do not believe that one man can free us, even an honorable dwarf such as you. Thank you for your concern, but you should leave before you are discovered. I do not want to see another join us in these cages."

"Another? These men be holding others besides y'er kin?"

"There is a human caged as well. He has not been here long, and I am not sure why he is in a cage rather than providing me with a meal. I believe Aron fears him; he keeps him hidden away from the guards so he may not speak to them, but he speaks to the dragons. He has compassion for us as you do, but from behind the magical shield, he can do nothing to help us."

"How does he speak to the dragons? Be there a way for me to speak to them?"

"He speaks to us within our minds, but the spell prevents me from communicating with him while he is caged. Is this something you can also do?"

"Nay, I do not have that ability. I be sorry there is naught that I can do for ye."

"You are forgiven, stone dweller. Be safe on your journeys. The guards will return soon. You must leave now if you wish to escape from here." Machai stepped out from the shadows and bowed before the dragon.

"Farewell, wise guardian. If I find a way to release ye, I will return." He ran back to the cover of the trees and regained his horses, anxious to be away from Aron's men yet heartsick that he could do nothing to help the dragons. It would be a long journey home, knowing of the savagery taking place in the Elven Realm and being unable to stop it.

He kept up a steady pace and quickly traveled far from the volcano entrance. Before it became too dark to see, he stopped and set up a crude camp far enough from the trail that passing travelers would not see him. He was gathering wood for a small fire and casting detection spells so he would be awakened if someone neared his camp, when he stopped suddenly and crouched behind a nearby rock. He rubbed his eyes to clear them and to be sure he was not delirious. Near the trees, across a small clearing, two men and a woman had appeared out of thin air. Machai pulled his axe from his back and crept toward them for a better look.

Chapter 17
Chance Encounter

Osric looked exhausted by the time they reached their destination. He almost collapsed from the strain of the magic. With Kenneth and Bridgett's help, he stayed on his feet long enough to stumble over to the base of a tree. He was asleep almost as soon as he hit the ground, and Bridgett checked him over, making sure weariness and not injury had caused his fatigue.

"I believe he will be fine. The best thing for him now is sleep." She pulled a vial from her belt and removed the stopper. She sprinkled a fine powder into her hand and gently blew it into Osric's face. "It will help him regain some of his energy. He has been through so much, I am not sure that sleep will be enough to restore him," she explained.

"Huh." Gus shook his head. "Seems your beauty is the least of your charms."

Kenneth had set to gathering wood from the small clearing, and Pebble curled up in Osric's lap. He soon began snoring contently, sharing the warmth of his body.

"That fool would be dead now if not for the dragon's gift he developed by chance, but I think he should be fine after a night of sleep. The Endurism gift he has may recharge his body faster than any amount of sleep would do for us. If you are going to be a fool, you had better be a lucky fool, and he has luck in abundance. We will need it if we are going to free the dragons." Gus rubbed his temples and growled. "I am growing tired of things I once thought impossible happening before my very eyes!"

Kenneth had stacked the wood for a fire, but when he went to reach for his wand, he could barely move. It felt as though his limbs were stuck in stone. He could breathe easily, but his arms and legs were rooted in place. He was about to call out when he heard Bridgett squeal and Gus swear behind him. He could not turn around to see what was going on, and terror gripped him as he realized magic was the source of his immobility.

"Os, wake up!" Kenneth felt helpless, frustrated that he could not overcome the spell. Osric and Pebble did not stir from their sleep, and Kenneth wondered if they were spelled as well. "Bridgett, are you all right? What's happening?" From his right, he heard twigs snapping and saw Gus backing up, slowly moving in front of Kenneth, his eyes locked on something behind him. "Gus, I can't move!" Gus stopped on the other side of the firepit and glanced over at Osric and Pebble with concern. Suddenly, Kenneth felt the restraint ease slightly from his legs. He still could not reach for his wand or his weapons, but his legs felt as though he were thigh-deep in mud rather than locked into stone. He turned around as quickly as he was able, terrified of what he might see and powerless to stop it.

Bridgett was crouched down near their packs, and the dried meat and hard bread that was to be their meal were scattered on the ground at her knees. A dwarf stood behind her, and Kenneth could see that he was holding an axe to her throat. In his other hand, he pointed a wand directly at Kenneth. How could they have been so careless? With all that had happened, they had overlooked such obvious safety measures as posting a guard in their camp or casting detection spells. *This is all my fault! I should have been protecting them, and all I could think about was getting a fire going so we could eat and rolling up in my sack to get some sleep,* Kenneth berated himself. Their recent adventure had taken its toll on him, and now they were all suffering for his weakness. He was not sure Osric would ever forgive him for putting Bridgett in that situation.

The dwarf glanced over at Osric and Pebble sleeping against the tree, keeping Kenneth restrained both by the spell he had cast and the threat to Bridgett should he attempt to move, but he directed his question at Gus.

"What did ye say about freeing dragons?"

"Uh, you must have misunderstood me. Let the girl go. She has no bad intentions toward anyone." Gus was very slowly inching toward Osric and his son.

"The man and his mouse will be awakening when I counter the spell. Stop moving. Tell me who ye be and what ye be doing here, and I will let her go. And do not be lying to me." Kenneth was furious that he had not been able to escape from the dwarf's spell, but he was terrified that something would happen to Bridgett. He interrupted before Gus could respond in his typical way to the insult of calling Pebble a mouse.

"We are from the human realm, a city called Stanton. We are accompanying the Contege"—he nodded toward Osric—"to an outpost near Braya Volcano." Kenneth hoped that by giving him something close to the truth, he would be inclined to believe his story without asking for more information.

"Contege?" Machai looked contemplative, as if he had heard the word before.

"Yes, the leader of the Vigiles, the city's security force. He is a very important man. The consequences for attacking his party will be severe." It was a risk. The threat might anger their assailant, but it might deter him from doing any actual damage. The dwarf seemed to come to a realization, and he moved the axe blade slightly so Bridgett could breathe easier. Kenneth exhaled a deep breath he had not realized he was holding.

"I do think we be on the same side, but I have spoken to the dragons on the volcano, and y'er Conteges are not being welcomed with graces. I suspect he will be either eaten or slain. If he be as lucky as one, he will only be imprisoned." Gus had stepped up to Kenneth's side and was staring accusingly at their attacker.

"What do you mean?" said Gus. "You have talked to the dragons? And who are you, anyway, to come and attack us and then demand all these answers. Same side, huh? What side are you on exactly?"

Kenneth cleared his throat to stop Gus's tirade before he insulted the dwarf enough to cause harm. He feared that Bridgett might pay the price for Gus's brash personality, but surprisingly the dwarf moved the axe away from her neck and allowed her to rush to Osric's side. He looked meaningfully at Kenneth and then lowered his wand. Instantly, Kenneth felt control of his limbs return.

"Me name is Machai. Y'er Contege should be hearing this also. Ye may awaken him now." Bridgett gently shook Osric awake without disturbing Pebble in his lap. He smiled when he awoke to see her face so close, and he traced his thumb down her cheek.

"Bridgett? Why are you crying?" Osric glanced up at Kenneth and Gus, and his expression turned to one of dread.

"Osric, you need to wake up now. We have a, um, visitor." Bridgett's voice was steadier than Kenneth expected it would be, but she had obviously been badly shaken by having a sharp blade pressed to her neck. Osric gently lifted Pebble from his lap and placed him on the ground without waking him. He stood stiffly and brushed the dirt from his pants. Osric locked eyes with his best friend and read a multitude of information from his expression. He looked over at the dwarf standing near their gear and at the food scattered all over the ground.

"What's going on?" Osric asked, and Gus jumped in front of him and started ranting about dragons and axes. Kenneth plucked him up by the scruff of his neck and carried him to the other side of the camp, lecturing him about waking sleeping children. He sat on a tree stump, one boot pinning Gus's tail to the ground, forcing him to listen patiently. Osric addressed the dwarf, "Who are you?"

"Me name is Machai, of the FireFalls Clan in the mountain region far north of y'er home. I have been to the Braya Volcano, and I be thinking ye may want to be hearing what I know."

"What makes you think you have anything to offer us? We can do quite well on our own." Kenneth could tell by Osric's tone that he was a bit put off by the assured way that Machai was speaking to him.

"I overheard the angry squirrel say ye are to be freeing the dragons. If that be true, I will help ye. If the big brute be telling the truth and ye are a Contege on business to the volcano, ye shall meet y'er death in the maw of the dragon that be guarding the door. Either way, ye be needing me help."

Osric looked him up and down, trying to decide if he could believe—or rather, understand—anything the dwarf was saying. "I promise you, if we want in there, we can make it in, with or without you. What else can you offer to prove your worth?"

"I willn't prove a thing to ye. The lass has her head, ye awakened from ye'r sleep, and I be the only one here that has been speaking to the dragons. I wish ye luck; ye will need it." Osric wasn't sure what the dwarf was referring to, but it seemed he had missed a lot while he was sleeping.

"If I were to try to save the dragons, why should I believe you would not try to stop me? Why should I trust a stranger in the woods with information that could lead to our capture? *If* that is why we are here." Osric felt something; he was unsure what it was, but since he had gained the Empath gift he had never attempted to discern whether or not someone was telling him the truth. His Portentist gift seemed to be working, in a different way than he was used to, but he knew Machai was being honest with him. The hesitation came from his desire to keep the true extent of his abilities a secret from the stranger.

"I swore an oath to the dragon that guards the entrance to the volcano. If I be finding a way to free them, I must be returning. I need to be knowing y'er intent. Do ye be for the dragons or no?"

"It is a bit more complicated than that." Osric hesitated slightly. "But we do intend to free the dragons." Osric's statement was greeted by shocked looks from his companions, yet somehow he knew he could trust Machai. "How did you come to know they were enslaved?"

"Ye be having no idea how complicated. I traveled to the volcano to make a delivery. Me guide, the rotten gib, informed me of the dragons' enslavement. I can be very persuasive when the need be arising. If ye want to free them, I will help ye. Seems to me ye need it." Machai crossed his arms defiantly at his chest and stared at Osric.

Osric felt within him, trying to discern Machai's intentions more clearly. He took slow, deep breaths, trying to tune out his own emotions and feel what the dwarf was feeling. It was not a great shift from his own desires. He felt Machai's strong need for help in freeing the dragons, and his nervousness about the risk of trusting a misfit troupe of travelers. Osric sensed that Machai wasn't sure that they would be able to pull it off, but he had an intense desire to correct the wrongs taking place at the volcano. Osric could only hope that Archana had brought them together for a purpose, and he felt that Machai had the same musings.

"What can you tell me about the volcano?" If Machai knew something that would help free the dragons, then Osric needed that knowledge as well.

"The description of the man in charge, the number of men, the patterns of patrols, the weapons they carry, and I be acquainted with the dragon that guards the entrance. I also know that there be a Contege held prisoner within the volcano, along with the dragons. Do ye be thinking I can help ye now?"

Osric stared at Machai in disbelief. Either the dwarf was involved with the captivity of the dragons and was trying to lure them into a trap or Archana had blessed their mission greatly. If Machai's intentions were malicious, then his Portentist gift would be triggering, so Osric had to believe that the dwarf had crossed their path for a reason. "I believe you can be of great benefit to us, and maybe we can be of use to you, as well."

"I should be telling ye, the men at the volcano be well armed with dwarven bloodstone swords." Machai looked around at the members of Osric's group with a scowl. "It would not be in our best interest to try and fight them."

"Of course, I wasn't planning on storming the place. You don't happen to know where the back door is, do you?" Osric wasn't sure if the dwarf was insulting him or not, but he sensed that Machai was much more comfortable with combat than with stealth.

"Nay, but I be thinking I can get us past the guards so ye can be finding us one."

"Well then, I invite you to join us for the night. I am afraid we must rest. It has been a long trip for us to get here."

"Aye, this camp could be using the extra eyes, eh?" He grinned at the glare that Kenneth directed his way. "I will be retrieving me gear, and I will stand the first watch."

Chapter 18
Training Day

Osric felt great after getting a few hours of sleep and eating the stew Bridgett had made from wild onions and the rabbits Kenneth had hunted the night before. Osric checked to be sure that their shields around the camp were holding, so no one would hear them and come to investigate, and he joined Kenneth with his sword drawn. Working through their fighting forms with their blades was a welcome exercise for them both. Kenneth was breathing hard a few minutes into it, but Osric felt great, given their turn of good luck lately. Kenneth swung his long sword with a grunt, and it glanced to the right off of Osric's sword.

"What's wrong, Kenneth?"

"Wrong? Nothing is wrong. I'm just a bit nervous that we may be eating prairie dog in a day or so."

"I don't like prairie dog. Too stringy," Osric answered. "What makes you think we would eat him anyway?"

"Well, Gus is going to want to examine you after the run-in with the paun." Kenneth's muscles tensed, as he prepared to strike at Osric again. The sun made his bronze skin shine with the sweat that ran over his body. "You were invisible! You know he is going to want to figure out how you did that."

"Well, I have no idea why I am able to be invisible, but..." Osric was about to demonstrate that he had discovered how to control the ability, when he noticed Machai approaching them. Kenneth used the moment of distraction to strike at Osric with renewed vigor.

Osric deflected the blow with ease. His short sword was much lighter, thus his breathing was more controlled, and his muscles had not yet begun to ache. He smiled as Kenneth turned aside his return strike, and Machai began to laugh.

"Would you mind sharing the joke?" Kenneth sheathed his sword and turned to look at the dwarf. Osric trusted him, but he was still hesitant to let Machai see all that he was capable of.

"Ye tire too quickly, because ye do not breathe." Machai stood up from the rock he had sat upon to watch them duel and walked over to them. "Kenneth, it be true that ye have the Hunter's gift, yes?"

"Yes, it be true, dwarf," Kenneth mocked.

"Then why do ye not use it?"

"What are you talking about?"

"Ye swing ye'r sword with ye'r arm," Machai stated, as if it were an obvious mistake. Osric looked at him in confusion.

"What do you suggest he use instead, Machai?"

"If he be using his gift and not his arm, he would not be tiring so soon. Nor would ye be able to best him so easily." He turned his attention to Kenneth. "What do it be feeling like when ye shoot ye'r bow with ye'r gift?"

Kenneth thought for a moment. "It feels like the arrow finds a groove in the air that will carry it along my intended path." He shrugged. "And then I release it."

"Aye, ye'r sword has such a groove as well, ye need only find it. Rather than the straight path ye seek for ye'r arrow, find the arc which will be getting past ye'r opponent's defenses." Machai stood back and motioned for them to return to their forms. They began exchanging blows once more, and Osric could see both concentration and doubt on Kenneth's face. After many swings with no better results, Kenneth was showing signs of fatigue. "Breathe, Hunter! Ye must be controlling ye'r breath. Do not be controlled by it."

Kenneth glared over at Machai, and Osric slapped his shoulder with the flat of his blade.

"Focus on my sword or I may accidentally take your arm off next time." Osric laughed, but he was paying attention to the directions Machai was giving Kenneth. He wanted to see if he could use it the same way.

"What makes you think you know anything about how the Hunter's gift works, Machai?" Kenneth looked a bit perturbed.

"Ye do not be the first Hunter I have instructed in the proper use of a sword." Machai sat back down on the rock. "Not that ye have a proper sword, but if ye are going to be swinging steel, ye should be swinging it with efficiency."

"Let's go again." Kenneth looked at Osric with a sardonic grin, then grasped the sword in both hands, taking a deep controlled breath. As they circled each other, the formal movements of their training forgotten for the thrill of the competition, an expression of determination settled on Kenneth's face. Osric raised his sword and understanding lit Kenneth's eyes. He brought his sword up swiftly, stepping close to Osric and preventing his attack, and laid the edge of his blade gently against Osric's throat.

Machai jumped up. "Ye found it! Aye, the only difference between a hunter and a warrior be their prey, but ye still be breathing poorly."

"Oh yes, I found it!" Kenneth backed away and began circling Osric again.

"Well, do you think you can teach me without endangering any blacksmiths?" Gus had said that he had the Hunter's gift, so he might as well learn how it worked.

"Just take a deep breath, feel the resistance of the air against the blade until you sense that the angle is correct, and then follow through." Kenneth grinned widely and advanced toward Osric.

"Osric, ye have the Hunter's gift?" Machai asked in surprise.

"So I have been told, Machai. It's a long story." To discourage any more questions, Osric turned his attention toward Kenneth. He focused on the Hunter's gift as they circled each other. He paid attention to the sensation of the air filling his lungs, and the weight of the sword in his hand. Kenneth seemed to be pacing with a purpose. The only other time Osric had seen this look on his friend's face was during a hunt; it was a bit disconcerting. Osric ran through his hunting skills in his mind, trying to decipher a way to use the newfound gift.

As Kenneth lunged, it occurred to him, and he managed to deflect the blow at the last second. A calm sense of purpose filled him as he looked at his childhood friend in a way he never thought possible. He felt the surge of the gift ignite within him as he lunged at Kenneth as if he were his prey. Each of them, with a new motivation, was able to find weaknesses in the other's defenses, and each of them was equally able to react before the strike could land. The clash of metal on metal filled the air. Gus and Bridgett were awakened by the noise, and they stood and watched in awe as perfect attacks were miraculously turned aside, time and again. Osric could see that Kenneth's breath was as controlled as his, and they both wore the same elated expression.

"Aye, very good, Osric. Now ye need an advantage or ye will be exchanging blows with ye'r friend for eternity. Take out ye'r wand." Machai stood off to the side with his arms crossed at his chest and an amused look upon his face. "Defend with ye'r sword; attack with ye'r wand."

Osric glanced over at him quickly in disbelief and nearly reacted too late to Kenneth's strike. He recovered swiftly and adjusted his stance, reaching for his wand with his right hand, but the stretch threw his timing off and Kenneth struck him with the butt of his sword, knocking him to the ground. Kenneth stood over him with a grin, and Machai roared with laughter.

"This would be a whole lot easier if you were not spouting nonsense, dwarf!" Kenneth glared at Machai. Practicing the new combat method was an amazing experience, and the dwarf's instructions had caused it to end too abruptly. Osric stood and brushed the dirt and twigs from his clothing and shook his head as Machai continued to laugh.

"You have a lot to say, but I would like to see you do better. Show us how it's done, Machai," Osric challenged him. With the Hunter's gift to aid in the fight, there was no way the dwarf could be a match for either of them, no matter how good he thought he was.

Machai reached for his axe and strode between the two of them, gazing at them as if he intended to fight them both. With a wicked smile, he growled quietly in excitement. "Heft ye'r blades, gentlemen, and I will show ye what I be saying." He twirled his axe in one hand and held his wand lightly in the other.

"You want to fight us both? Are you crazy?" Kenneth asked.

"Are ye scared, Hunter?"

"No, I am not scared." Kenneth held his sword high and adjusted his stance. "I just had not really planned on killing a dwarf today." Kenneth looked at Osric with a nod, and they took several cautious steps toward Machai. As they moved in close to him, fire sprung up in a closed ring around them, isolating the three of them from the rest of the group. Osric gasped, as the flames burned close to his heels, but he felt no heat radiating from the fire.

Bridgett lifted Gus up onto her shoulder for a better view and watched with a worried expression. Her fingers traced along her throat where Machai's blade had been the night before. "Ah, Gus, I hope he knows what he is doing." She whispered quietly as they circled the dwarf.

"That little bastard can conjure fire!" Kenneth exclaimed, looking at Machai in surprise.

"Aye, Hunter, I can do more than that. Scared yet?"

Kenneth scowled and began to circle again, and Osric joined him. Osric could feel his breath, controlled and invigorating as he looked at

Machai and the hungry expression on his face. He felt the blade slide into its channel and brought a strike down, as Kenneth lunged with his sword tip toward Machai.

Machai spun and hooked Kenneth's sword with the edge of his axe blade, dragging it up and around to block Osric's blow. Kenneth and Osric exchanged worried looks as they withdrew. If he could use one attack to block another then they needed to be wiser in their approach.

Machai chuckled low in his throat, more of a growl than a laugh. As Osric held back, waiting for him to be distracted by Kenneth's next attack, he realized his feet were rooted in place. He did not notice the wand was pointed at him until it was too late. Kenneth's assault came at the same time, with a storm of rapid strikes. Machai moved swiftly as he turned each of them aside and then hooked the blade again in his last attack, using the momentum to throw Kenneth through the air directly at Osric.

Osric tried to brace himself against the weight of his friend, but he could not move a muscle. Kenneth crashed into him, and they tumbled to the ground through the flames, as Machai dropped the hand directing his wand at Osric. Osric stood quickly, expecting the dwarf to be right behind them. Machai had not moved, and he stood in the center of the dwindling flames with an amused look on his face.

"Now, if ye do not be too embarrassed, come over here and I will teach ye to defend ye'rself and maybe even to be attacking with more than ye'r anger."

Kenneth stalked toward the dwarf, rage in his eyes and his sword raised, and halted at the sound of Osric laughing behind him. He turned and looked at Osric with dismay. Osric walked up with a grin and slapped Kenneth on the back.

"If the two of us could fight like him, we would have a much better chance of freeing the dragons. I don't know about you, my friend, but I will put my pride aside and allow him to instruct me." Kenneth did not look ready to give up so easily, but Osric knew if the dwarf could turn aside their attacks, which were even more formidable with the aid of the Hunter's gift, it had to be worth learning. He was the better of the two with a sword, and Kenneth was his match with the new ability, so Machai deserved their respect. He stepped up to Machai. "Can you teach me?" Osric asked humbly.

"Aye, if ye are willing to learn." Machai held his axe easily in one hand and his wand up in the other. "Ye are good with ye'r sword, but ye focus on what ye are about to do with it. Ye should be thinking about what I will be doing next and allow ye'r experience to guide ye'r sword. Do not be thinking about ye'r wand as another sword, which demands ye'r attention. Be thinking of it as a shield. Ye can defend ye'rself with ye'r wand and use ye'r gift and instincts to be attacking with ye'r sword. Are ye ready?"

"I believe so." Osric grabbed his wand in his right hand and began to circle Machai. He wasn't sure how to start, but he had an idea, so he envisioned his wand as his shield and placed himself in the Hunter's mindset. He used his wand to raise a shield that would protect him against any spell Machai could use against him, and once again he was impressed with the resistance he felt from the wand. As much as he wanted to explore the mystery of his wand's varying strength, he did not want to be caught off guard, so he focused on the dwarf.

Osric felt his shield deflect a magical attack and hold strong. Machai was testing his defenses, but he was encouraged by the dwarf's failure to penetrate his shield. Machai grinned and launched his attack. Osric found that turning aside the heavy axe with his short sword was not as easy as he thought it would be. He forgot about the shield for only a moment, and it disappeared. Osric found himself held in invisible constraints again, with an axe blade pressed hard against his chest.

"Never be letting ye'r guard down." Machai stepped back and released Osric from the spell. "Again."

Osric was growing more and more frustrated as Machai repeatedly beat him with either axe or wand. He could not maintain his focus on defensive spells and still be effective with his sword. In a final attempt to thwart the dwarf, Osric attacked with his blade and intended to cast an offensive spell to take Machai by surprise. Machai sidestepped to avoid the slash of the sword and knocked the wand from Osric's hand with the flat of his axe. Osric yelled out in frustration, "Extollo!"

Machai grunted in displeasure as he was hoisted into the air by his feet. His enjoyment of their violent exchange had disappeared from his face as he dropped his axe and fought clumsily with his arms and legs to find some bearing. Laughter erupted from Kenneth and Bridgett. Only Gus seemed to be displeased at the sight of Osric gaining victory without his wand. It took only a few moments for Machai to calm down and gaze at Osric curiously as he folded his arms in surrender.

"Ye'r wand be on the ground, and I be dangling in midair. I must admit, it be perplexing."

Osric was a bit frustrated with himself for displaying the advantage of spoken spells. Though he had not yet told Machai about the new magic, he would no longer be able to conceal it. If Machai had not realized he had used a spoken spell when he lifted him up into the air, he would when he cast the counter spell. Unless he wanted to leave Machai dangling in midair, he had no choice but to cast it. "Demitto," Osric said, and Machai settled slowly back to the ground.

* * *

"Gus, stop pacing," Bridgett scolded. "I am sure they will be back soon."

"I don't know why I want them back. Osric is going to be even surer of himself if we succeed! He picked up on Machai's lessons quickly once he started using spoken spells. I still think it was a mistake to reveal our only advantage to a stranger." Gus shook his head.

"I sympathize with your concerns, but we just have to trust Osric. Once the dragons are free, we will see what happens with Machai, but if any race would be able to keep these new abilities a secret, it is the dwarves." Bridgett still had a hard time looking at Machai without recalling the memory of his blade pressed to her skin, but she knew that as a race they were honorable, and the dwarves rarely shared their secrets or techniques with outsiders. She had been very surprised that Machai had taught Kenneth and Osric to fight with both weapons and wands.

"I agree, but that fool could have at least informed us of his intentions first. Osric behaves as though his life is the only one being risked in this venture."

"I do not believe he intends to endanger us. We were aware of the risks when we joined him. He is young and inexperienced, but there is much more to him than his foolhardy antics. He has the potential to be the greatest wizard ever born, and there is much at stake in his learning to use his new abilities. We need to support him, Gus, not degrade him."

Gus looked toward the peak of the Volcano and kicked a rock. "Somebody needs to keep him in line or he will think he can do *anything* by sunset."

"Perhaps he can." Bridgett looked at Gus and smiled at the pout on his face. He was cloaked in anxiety, but knowing someone's emotions did not always make it easier to engage them in conversation. She sensed his fear that they would fail and that his home and family would suffer for it, as well as his pride about how Osric had come so far since they left Stanton, but she could also feel something akin to jealousy from Gus. She knew that was what kept him from encouraging Osric when he needed it most. "Who are we to say what the limits of his powers are?" Gus turned and gazed at her with displeasure.

"My interest is only for the purpose of learning. We have been at this campsite for three days and Osric has not let me examine him yet. I need to know why he disappeared when he killed that paun. Just because he has figured out how to become invisible, doesn't mean we shouldn't learn why he has the ability in the first place! He has been gone for nearly half a day scouting that bloody volcano, and if he gets caught, my opportunity to study him will have gone as well!" Gus's expression brightened, and Bridgett laughed out loud as his ears began to twitch, an indication of his intense curiosity. "Unless you want to tell me of the magic you witnessed with the unicorns?"

"I doubt very much that I will be able to answer your questions, Gus, for your curiosity is insatiable, but I will try. What would you like to know?" Bridgett honestly did not think she knew the secrets of the unicorns that Gus was so determined to learn, but humoring him was better than listening to him rant about Osric. She dug through her pack to find something for them to eat, waiting for Gus's inevitable questions.

"Well, tell me why you believe their magic is intentional, rather than instinctive." Gus sat forward, eyes wide and ears perked. Bridgett thought for a moment while she sorted through their supplies. Then she stood and began her story.

"The unicorns perform magic the way an artist sculpts clay: with a delicate precision that takes your breath away. One winter, I saw a unicorn bury a rotten plum with his hoof and then cast a spell to cause a new tree to grow. When the tree had matured to bear fruit, he sat by and watched as a hungry family of squirrels collected enough food to feed them until spring. Then he caused the tree to age, fall, and decay, returning its nutrients to Archana. The entire event took a single afternoon, and he provided for the animals without allowing the unnatural tree to interrupt the natural process of growth which takes place on Archana." A wistful smile graced her lips as she described the scene, and Gus sat speechless before her. "The unicorns do nothing without reason, my friend."

Gus stared at her intensely, and Bridgett was amused by his interest in the unicorns. The way he sat in silence, without interrupting her, was a welcome relief from his normal behavior. She sat down near the fire where Pebble was playing, and he grinned up at her with childlike joy. "I's likes that story! Those plums sound's yummy."

"I do not have any plums, dear, but I do have some dried apples." She handed him the fruit and smiled at his delight. In favor of a mid'day meal, he seemed to forget all about the game he was playing with colored stones he had collected around the campsite.

"Have you ever witnessed a unicorn bless a newborn? Can you tell me about that?" Gus's tail was twitching along with his ears, but before she could respond, Osric appeared inside the large circle sketched in the dirt across the fire from her, holding the shoulders of Machai and Kenneth. He grinned and directed a satisfied wink at her and Gus. They must have had a successful day.

Chapter 19
Damsel In Distress

"Osric, for the last time, you will not be able to get past those guards without a distraction. Pebble can stay with me, and while I speak with the guards, you four can get up to the mouth of the volcano unseen. I appreciate your concern, but I assure you, they will not feed me to the dragon." Bridgett regarded him calmly. They had been arguing all morning, but the expression of defeat on his face told her he had finally seen the logic of her plan.

"I don't like it, Bridgett, but you're right. It may take all four of us to interrupt the spell holding the dragons, but from what Machai says of their policy with strangers, I fear for your safety." Bridgett could sense Osric's torn emotions. He was proud and grateful that she would risk her life for the success of their mission, but he was also afraid that she might be sacrificed for it. She laid the palm of her hand against his cheek and smiled sadly, touched that he felt so worried for her. She reached up and lifted the Aduro Amulet from her neck and placed it in his hand.

"Take this. You will need it to amplify your powers." She traced her fingers along his jaw and then looked away quickly. Turning to Machai, she asked, "You spoke to the dragon that guards the door. Is there something I can say that would indicate that I am working with you to fulfill your vow? Our chances of success will be much greater with the dragons' support."

"Aye, I cannot be assuring ye the dragon will not eat ye, but since I still be alive, it be reasonable to assume he will allow ye to live as well. He called me stone dweller, so if ye use the same term, I imagine he will know who ye refer to." Machai reached into his pack and handed Bridgett the small wooden box. "I used this salve to be healing the dragon's leg." Rage and concern swept across his features. "It be willow bark and fairie tears. This the dragon will be remembering, and if he still be favoring his foreleg, apply what be left in the box. We may well be needing the dragon at full strength before this day be over."

Bridgett tucked the salve into a pouch on her belt and lifted Pebble up onto her shoulder. Gus had an uncharacteristic look of concern on his face, and she smiled at him reassuringly. "Do not worry, Gus. I will take good care of him." She knew his apprehension was not for Pebble alone, but he nodded and walked away. Kenneth and Machai checked their weapons and wands one more time and stepped toward the trail that led to the volcano. They would be performing a great deal of magic in the near future, so they would set out on foot to preserve their strength. Osric found a large tree that had been hollowed at the base by weather and insects, and he tucked the book and the rest of their belongings inside. Osric and Machai had erected a wide shield around the clearing they stood in, to contain the horses while they grazed and to keep anyone else from discovering their gear.

Osric took Bridgett's hand in his and managed a weak smile. "Please be careful, and if you get into trouble, call out. We should be able to hear you and we will come to you if you need us."

"Thank you, Osric, but I will be all right. Use caution, and work quickly, and we will all come out of this just fine." Bridgett squeezed his hand and walked away through the trees, to arrive at the volcano first and to buy them the time they needed to reach the peak unseen.

* * *

Bridgett sat on a rock formation near the tree line, calmly watching the dragon lying next to the massive tree Machai had described. She had not seen any guards patrolling, so it could be only a matter of moments before they arrived, and she needed to work quickly. She pulled several vials from her belt and began mixing and grinding herbs in a shallow bowl. "Pebble, come up here for a moment. I want to teach you a new game."

Pebble hopped up onto the rock with an excited grin. "What sort'sa game?"

"We are going to play a game with the men who work here. Do you remember that really scary thing that Osric killed in the woods?"

"Yep! Pa said's it was a paun!" Pebble held his claws up and bared his teeth in a comical impression of the beast.

"Yes, I want you to think about how scared you were when the paun came. We are going to pretend that one is chasing us, all right? Do you think you can be really scared when we go talk to the men?" Bridgett smiled at him and then donned an expression of terror to show him how she wanted him to act. Pebble rolled over onto his back, laughing at her expression. "Pebble, if you laugh, the men will know that you are not scared and we will lose the game. Can you look really scared?" At the mention of losing, Pebble stopped laughing and his face got very serious.

"I's can be scared, I's never loses at games!"

Catching a glimpse of a guard approaching, Bridgett poured the powdered herbs into her hand and closed her fist tight. She did not want Pebble breathing them in by mistake. "Pebble, are you ready to play the game? Pretend the paun is right behind us and we are going to run over to that man and ask him to save us, all right?" They climbed down from the rocks, and Bridgett took a deep breath. She said a silent prayer that Archana would help them succeed, and she ran out of the woods with Pebble close behind her.

The guard was whistling as he made his rounds and twirling his wand in his fingers. He stopped suddenly as he saw her burst from the forest and run toward him. She crashed into him, tears streaming down her face, crying out for help.

"Whoa, little lady. Where did you come from?" He looked around suspiciously, but he did not restrain her.

"The forest. It was terrible! Please help me!" Her words were vague and nearly unintelligible between sobs, and she wore an expression of sheer terror. "A beast attacked us. It killed everyone!" He stared at the tree line behind her and then glanced down at Pebble clinging to her dress.

"What sort of beast?" He drew his sword, but his attention was on the forest. The other guard had come around the corner, and was approaching them quickly to see what the trouble was. Bridgett cried hysterically, stalling until both men were close.

"It's was a paun!" Pebble said in a frightened voice, hiding in the folds of her skirt and whimpering. The second guard was close enough to hear Bridgett crying and ran the rest of the distance to them.

"What's the trouble?" he asked the first guard, drawing his own weapon and eyeing Bridgett.

"The lady says a paun attacked her."

The guard laughed. "A paun? They're just a legend used to frighten children." He stood next to the first guard and frowned at Bridgett. "Who are you?"

"Really, it is true. Look!" Bridgett raised her hand and both men looked intently at her closed fist. She opened her fingers and blew the powder into their faces. As they gasped in surprise, they inhaled the herbs. Bridgett danced backward, as both men attempted to lunge at her with blades raised. They staggered to their knees and their weapons clattered to the ground as they fell face first in the dirt.

Bridgett scooped Pebble up in her arms and walked quickly toward the final bend in the path that led to the entrance of the volcano. She slid to a stop as she came face to face with the largest dragon she had ever seen. Smoke curled up from the dragon's nostrils, and he looked past her at the guards lying unmoving on the ground. Before the dragon could decide to eat her, Bridgett pulled the small wooden box from her belt. "Your acquaintance, the stone dweller, bid me soothe your wound with a salve of willow bark and fairie tears. Does your foreleg still pain you, mighty dragon?"

He turned his large, swirling eyes back to her and regarded her with a cool stare. "No. The fairie paste did all the dwarf promised it would. Has he returned to make a foolish attempt to free us from our indentured existence?" A low, deep laugh rumbled from the dragon's chest, and his words dripped with sarcasm.

"Yes," Bridgett replied. "And he has brought help. Will you aid me in ridding this mountain of those guards and ease their task?" She nodded toward the two men. "They are unconscious, but they will wake soon, and then they will continue to pose a threat to you and your kin." The dragon stilled, all humor gone from his eyes, and glared at her.

"And what do the charitable dwarf, the pretty little Empath, and a pup think they can do to help us?" Bridgett was not surprised that the dragon was aware of her ability as an Empath. She sensed the great age and wisdom of the creature as easily as she sensed his doubt that Machai could free them. The dragon probably had more experience and intuition when it came to reading people than any Araseth Empath. If she had not given the Aduro Amulet to Osric, she suspected she would have been able to communicate with him telepathically.

"My role was to distract the guards and seek your aid. Machai has the power and magical abilities of many others with him, and they intend to interrupt the spell holding the dragons. The fewer men there are to stop them, the more likely they will succeed. Will you help us?" Bridgett had no doubt that the dragon would suspect her words were intentionally vague, but since they were true, she thought he might overlook it. Dragons were well known to be superstitious, and so she continued, "The man leading the incursion is prophesied as the greatest wizard to ever walk Archana. This may be your only chance at freedom." One of the guards behind her moaned, and she turned around quickly to see that they were both still lying on the ground.

Bridgett felt a wave of deep hatred radiate out from the dragon as it walked around her and stalked toward the guards. "These men will never wake." The dragon gripped each man with the sharp claws of his front legs and took flight. Bridgett watched as the dragon spiraled higher and higher into the air, and she quickly covered Pebble's eyes as their bodies plummeted toward the ground over the forest.

Pebble snuggled against her hand. "Did's we win's the game?"

"Yes, Pebble. You did wonderfully. Thank you so much for helping me win the game."

Chapter 20
Dragon Fire

Osric crouched down in the forest on the south side of the volcano. He saw the dragon rise up into the sky to the west and head for the forest with two men clutched in its claws. He gave Gus the signal to take his place in a bush up on the ridgeline of the volcano. Bridgett had cleared the guards for them. Osric just hoped that she and Pebble were all right and that the dragon had not harmed them. Only time would tell, and he had to focus to make sure the rest of them survived.

The long sprint up to the rim of the volcano was all that was left before they could survey the interior and make their move. Gus waved at them, signaling from his high perch that there were no patrolmen in sight.

"This is it," Osric whispered, as he looked at Kenneth and nodded, then glanced at Machai, who wore a disturbingly excited expression. They sprang out from behind the trees they were using for cover and jumped from boulder to boulder, quickly making their way up the side of the volcano. Kenneth arrived first, followed quickly by Osric and then Machai. Gus sat a short ways away, peering over the edge of a large rock, and they lowered themselves to their stomachs at the edge to look down at the interior of the volcano.

From his lofty position, Osric could see four guards: one manned a sentry tower that stood in the center of the hollowed crater, one stood near the entrance, and two sat at a large table near the tower playing a game of bones. A man in a bloody apron entered the chamber from an adjacent room, set a platter of meat and bread down on the table, and then left.

"I need to get a closer look. You three stay here and I will be right back," Osric whispered. Then he vanished, and a few small stones were disturbed as he stood. "Eo ire itum."

Kenneth grinned over at Gus. "Now that he actually gets to use the invisibility trick, maybe he will stop practicing it by sneaking up on us."

Osric was crouched down on the far side of the guard tower from the two men at the table. He knew the men could not see him, but he still felt exposed and feared they would hear him. He held as still as possible and tried to keep his breathing even and silent.

He estimated the main chamber to be about one hundred and fifty to two hundred paces across and fairly circular in shape. The fifty dragon cages were carved into the stone of the volcano, their metal doors making up about three quarters of the curved wall. Osric took note of the entrance, although the trunk of the massive tree that stood just beyond the only opening to the outside blocked most of the daylight. Four archways led off of the main chamber to the left of the entrance. Three of the rooms beyond were dim, and he had a hard time distinguishing what they contained, but Osric assumed the man with the food had come from the kitchen. The room closest to the entrance was obviously the armory, for he could see torchlight reflecting off of various weapons and equipment. A crude staircase, carved into the stone to the right of the entrance, led to what appeared to be small chambers on a second level above the cages. Osric could not risk climbing the stairs and attracting attention, but he was relatively sure that the rooms would be sleeping chambers for the men.

Five guards were unaccounted for, and assuming that they worked in shifts, they would most likely be asleep. Osric hoped that Machai's information was correct and that one of them was still recovering from an injury and would not pose a threat. They needed to move fast if they were going to have control of the volcano by the time the spell cycled for feeding. Osric intently pictured the ground he had been lying on when he *traveled* into the volcano, and he whispered as quietly as he could, "Eo ire itum."

Kenneth jumped slightly at the sound of a grunt and Osric appearing at his side. He had managed to *travel* to the correct location, but rather than lying on his stomach, he was still in the crouched position and his hands and knees had contacted the stone harder than he had intended. Osric drew his wand and cast a protective spell around them so that the guards would not hear them conversing.

"What did ye see?" Machai asked, staring down into the volcano.

"Not a whole lot more than what you can see from here, but there are several rooms carved into the wall over there," he said, pointing down and to the left. "And I assume the row of doors above the cages over there lead to sleeping chambers. Hopefully that's where the other five guards are."

Studying the layout, Kenneth said, "So, if anyone is going to surprise us, it will be from there."

"Ye see that arrogant brute that be cheating at bones? That be Aron, the leader. He be the one to watch out for." Machai clenched his fists as he regarded the men below. "Me guide, the pathetic arse, probably be in a dark room torturing a small animal. I be looking forward to seeing him again."

"So what is our best course of action?" Kenneth asked.

"I don't want to kill anyone if we don't have to," Osric stated. "Machai, can you handle Aron?"

"Aye! Just be giving me the chance." Machai grinned wickedly. "Gus, ye be a fine wizard, but ye may be better able to knock them from the walls upon waking than restraining an armed man."

"Well, I never had any intention of trying to match swords with a half-trained Vigile," Gus said dismissively. "I can knock a flea off a mouse's ass at this range, so I think a little target practice would be the perfect job for me!" He took out his wand and jabbed it in Machai's direction.

"Kenneth, that be leaving ye and Osric with two a piece. Do ye think ye be up to it?" Machai jested.

Kenneth ignored the dwarf and turned to Osric. "I'll take the guard by the door and the one at the table. You keep the one in the tower from picking us off. And could you grab me some lunch when you find the guy with the food?" Osric grinned at his friend's attempt to ease the tension.

"Spread out along the rim, but you will need to crawl to avoid detection, and I don't want to see either of you use magic until I give you the signal. The last thing we need is for you to wear out too soon." Osric gave the orders and they each nodded in agreement and began to move. Kenneth remained behind for a moment, and Osric looked at him curiously.

"Be careful, Os. You still owe me a stein of mead from last Harvest Festival. Like it or not, she kissed me and you lost the bet. Nothing short of death will get you out of paying up." Kenneth smiled. "By the way, when this is all over, you get Leisha to serve me that mead and we will call it even for me taking credit for breaking the vial."

"I could have sworn I bought you a stein or two to ease the pain of the smashed finger you got her to kiss, but if we manage to succeed today, I will buy you another one."

Kenneth winked and then began his silent journey to his post.

Osric waited patiently until they each reached their positions, and then he gave the signal. He saw Machai and Kenneth disappear from the rim of the volcano, and he looked down at the man in the sentry tower. Osric *traveled* to the tower; he wanted to keep the guard from loosing any arrows from his high perch. "Eo ire itum."

Osric appeared suddenly in the tower, and the guard activated an alarm as he spun around, dropping the bow and arrow in favor of a knife from his belt. Osric was much faster and knocked him in the head with the butt of his sword, catching him as he collapsed to keep him from falling from the tower. Then he dragged him quickly to the center of the platform and began binding his hands.

Osric heard a battle cry from the ground below him. He peered over the edge quickly and saw that Machai had Aron lying on the ground and was tying his hands. Kenneth had the guard near the door restrained, and the guard that had been playing bones with Aron had his hands held up in the air with Kenneth's sword tip pressed between his shoulders. Seeing movement from the corner of his eye, Osric glanced up to see the guard in the bloody apron running toward Kenneth with a cleaver raised high over his head. Kenneth was unaware of the advancing attack, and Osric had no time to *travel* the distance to save his friend. In a panic, Osric threw his sword with all of his might at the attacker, praying silently to Archana that it would hit its mark. Shock and relief filled his mind as the blade sunk deep into the man's chest. The guard's eyes went wide with surprise as he stopped his advance and stared down at the protruding sword. His mouth hung open in shock as he fell to his knees then awkwardly toppled to his side.

Osric lashed the sentry's ankles and grabbed his arm, *traveling* with him to the chamber below. He retrieved his sword, cleaning the blade on the guard's apron. Kenneth and Machai stood in front of him, having both secured their men. The cook was the only man who lay dead, though the sentry and the guard near the door were unconscious. Machai had managed to secure Aron awake, and he glared at each of them with hate-filled eyes. Osric looked up at the second-story rooms, as Gus appeared next to him.

"They're all sound asleep. Stop worrying, boy! Not a natural sleep either. They'll wake, but they'll have terrible headaches."

"We need to bring all of them down and tie them together so we can watch them," Osric said, as Machai looked around the volcano for signs of more guards. Kenneth vanished almost as soon as Osric completed the statement and reappeared crouched on the floor, holding the arm of a sleeping guard. He quickly tied the man's hands behind his back and left him sleeping on the ground while he went to retrieve another guard.

Both Kenneth and Gus *traveled* up to the small chambers, bringing back an unconscious guard with each trip, while Machai stood watch. Osric dragged the sleeping soldiers, two irua guards and three humans, over to the wall near the stairs and tied them to each other. The last man Kenneth brought down had his arm in a sling, and Osric carefully bound his torso and his ankles rather than his hands. At last, they had accounted for all nine men in the volcano, and Aron's glare grew more intense as they worked.

"You will never get away with this!" Aron spat at Machai with a disdainful snarl.

"Ye keep silent or I will be cutting out ye'r tongue. Or maybe I will be feeding ye to the dragon. I do not doubt he would love to be repaying ye for ye'r kindness," Machai said, lifting Aron's chin with the edge of his axe.

Osric was about to begin questioning Aron about the cycle of the spell when he heard a man's voice shouting from just outside the volcano. He quickly turned and stood shocked as two men stepped through the entrance and walked to opposite sides of the chamber. One held Bridgett before him with a dagger at her neck, and the other held a horrified Pebble in one hand with a small knife at his belly.

"Nobody move! You make a move toward one of us and the other will kill his hostage!" He was stepping to the right, holding Bridgett securely across her stomach, his head barely in view over her shoulder.

"Now, untie Aron or this little one is my next meal!" the second man said in a high, shrill tone that sent chills up Osric's spine.

"You harm him and I guarantee I will be eating your eyeballs for my dinner!" Gus stepped forward in a fearful rage. "You will still be alive and I assure you, I will enjoy your screams!"

"No! Gus, stop." Osric studied the men, looking for a way to free Bridgett and Pebble. He grudgingly admitted to himself that they could not move fast enough to stop both men before one of them killed their hostage.

"Ye be a lucky bastard." Machai seemingly came to the same conclusion, as he moved slowly toward Aron and began to untie the ropes binding his hands and feet.

Aron stood up, marched over to the unconscious men, bent over, and slapped one across the face. "Wake up, you fool!" He slapped him again and spat at Kenneth. "You, bronze-skinned ogre, untie these men, now!"

Osric cringed at the way Aron treated his men and hung his head as they were all untied. They were relieved of their weapons and wands, their hands and feet bound, and then forced to kneel on the ground in front of Aron as he paced back and forth in obvious frustration. The only relief in the tension was when Bridgett and Pebble were sat on the ground next to them.

"Did you think you would succeed, honestly? What did you want to do, anyway? Control dragon flight for yourselves?" Aron looked furiously at his men, shoving one of the irua guards to the ground.

"No. We intend to free them." Osric glared back up at him with pride.

"Free them? We need them!" Aron looked at Osric in confusion. "Your selfish ignorance would have isolated all of Archana's inhabitants if you had succeeded!"

"You don't know as much as you think you do," Osric argued.

"Ye have been deceived into thinking that dragons must be caged and controlled, but ye'r beliefs do not be justifying the cruelty you thrust upon them." Machai scowled up at him.

Aron kicked Machai in the face with a grin and watched as he fell over on the ground. "It takes extreme measures to contain these beasts! It calls for extreme men to do what is necessary to serve Archana's inhabitants." He grabbed Machai by the throat and spoke through gritted teeth. "And now, I will show you why I am in charge here!" He raised his dwarven blade over his head and a deep roar filled the air.

Osric looked up and saw the massive dragon sweeping down from the top of the volcano into the group of guards, accompanied by several eagles. Aron spun around and ducked just in time to avoid being grasped by the talons of one of the giant birds. Osric threw himself to the side, knocking Bridgett out of the way as the dragon landed and spewed flames at Aron's men. Several of the men's clothing caught fire, and they rolled on the ground screaming, trying to put out the flames. The dragon clutched two of the guards with his front claws and soared up out of the volcano, their screams echoing through the cavernous space. The guard who had taken the brunt of the dragon's flames writhed in agony on the ground and then stilled, his smoldering clothing and skin sending fetid smoke into the air.

Kenneth and Machai cheered as the eagles went after the eight remaining guards. Most of them ran for cover and were snatched up in the eagles' talons one at a time. Aron screamed in rage as he watched his men being caught and dropped unceremoniously in a pile. He swung his sword wildly in the air as three eagles swooped down at him in random patterns. One dove in fast from his right and dragged his talons along the length of his sword arm. He cried out in pain, dropping the sword, and another eagle grabbed him and dragged him to his men.

Osric looked up just in time to see Ero land before him. "Well met, my friend," the eagle said.

"It is good to see you, Ero!" Osric smiled and turned his back to him. "Can you free me of these bonds so I can help?" Ero sliced through the ropes with one sharp talon, and Osric rose swiftly to his feet. He surveyed the volcano interior as he helped Bridgett stand. "Are you all right?"

"Yes, I believe so." She was shaky but uninjured. "I am so terribly sorry that I failed you, Osric. The second patrol arrived much sooner than we expected, and they took me by surprise."

"You bought us the time we needed to get inside and convinced the dragon to aid us. That is no failure in my eyes." He wrapped his arm around her shoulders and asked, "Are you sure you aren't hurt?"

"I am growing very tired of having sharp blades pressed against my flesh, but I am uninjured. How can I help you open these cages?" She looked around in dismay. Ero's fire-telling had told them that nearly fifty dragons were held within the mountain, but his words had not prepared her for the sight.

Ero ruffled his feathers and addressed Osric, "Yes, how do you propose we free them?"

Osric turned and called out, "Machai, his blood will only tarnish your blade. Leave him, and let's go over this once more while there is time."

Machai held Aron by the hair with his axe at his throat. At Osric's call, he released him, landing a hard kick in his ribs, and walked away to join them.

Chapter 21
Chain Interrupted

Gus and Osric sat side by side at the table, observing the chain of spells that cycled across the cage doors with their Wand-Maker's gifts. "Do you see the difference between the layers in the spell, boy?" Gus asked.

"Yes, I see it. There are what, eleven... no... twelve different variations in the strands?"

"Yes, I see twelve," Gus said. "Oh, look. There is the interruption! That cage is unguarded!" he exclaimed with renewed excitement, pointing at the first cage to the right of the entrance. Then he continued in an exasperated tone, "That lapse doesn't last long enough to throw a rock at the door, let alone throw meat through the slot. How did the dwarf say they feed them?"

Osric stood up abruptly and stomped off in frustration. He located Machai outside the volcano, speaking with the dragon. "Machai, may I speak with you?" The dwarf turned excitedly at Osric's approach.

"Aye, Osric, I be glad ye are here. I be learning much from this majestic creature. Thom be not only cruel and ignorant, he be a liar." He directed his next question at the dragon. "Stargon, would ye please be telling me friend what ye just told me?"

Osric looked curiously up at the dragon. "I doubted that any would ever be capable of freeing us, but if you are truly a man of prophecy then perhaps there is yet hope. If you succeed, the dragons will forever be in your debt, and you will need only to ask for our aid." Stargon lowered his head gracefully to the ground before Osric in a gesture of respect. "I was speaking to Machai of the spell which contains my kin. There is a key of sorts that must be used to stall the cycle of the spell. That is how they may open a door or a feeding slot. You must find the key."

Osric was stunned. If there were a key that could interrupt the spell, they would have the dragons free in no time at all. "What sort of key, exactly, and where would I find it?"

"If I knew that, would I have allowed my kin to remain caged?" The dragon turned and stalked away. Osric turned to Machai with a look of despair.

"I be thinking the men will know where to find the key. Let's be asking one." He pulled his axe from his back and walked into the volcano. Osric followed him through the entrance and across the chamber toward where the eagles were guarding Aron and his remaining men.

Machai stopped before them and regarded them each with a harsh scowl. He watched them all silently and then walked slowly and deliberately around the group of guards, tapping the flat of his axe blade against his open palm. He paused and glared at Thom, but after a moment he continued on. One man sat cowering on Aron's left, and he was whimpering slightly as Machai eyed him closely. "Ye, come with me," Machai snarled, pointing at the man with his axe.

The man cringed, but he rose silently to his feet and hesitantly followed Machai to where Osric stood near the sentry tower. Osric pulled a chair over from the table and sat the man down roughly. Machai stood next to him and rested his axe blade on the man's shoulder, eliciting a scared whimper from the guard. He recognized him as the man who had stood in the tower with the bow before Osric had defeated him. Machai looked meaningfully at the doors of the dragon cages and then back at the scared man.

"I be thinking these dragons are growing mighty hungry. Where be the key to the doors, so we can be feeding them?" The guard's eyes widened in fear, and Machai leaned in close, putting ever more pressure on the blade near his neck.

"I don't know what you are talking about," the man whined. Several eagles cried out as Aron lunged toward Machai, screaming at the guard what he would do to him if he talked.

Osric yelled out, "Restrain him!" As the eagles were attempting to wrestle the unruly leader to the ground, Thom took advantage of the chaos and broke away from the group, sprinting across the room. He disappeared through the archway farthest from the entrance, and Osric tore after him. Osric slid to a stop outside the dim chamber and lit the tip of his wand, wary of the possibility that Thom was armed and waiting for him. He stepped through the doorway, sword drawn, and Thom stood just inside with a wide grin on his face.

"You will never free those filthy beasts!" He held a small, dark crystal in his hand, and as Osric lunged toward him, Thom threw it to the ground and crushed it beneath the heel of his boot. There was a sickening crack, and Osric saw thick black smoke rising from beneath Thom's foot. Just as

Osric grabbed Thom to thrust him back into the main chamber, he heard a startled yell from Gus.

"By the strands! Boy, what did you just do?! Get over here and look at this!" Osric knelt and picked up the broken shards of the crystal and ran over to see what Gus was yelling about, dragging Thom with him. "What happened? Look at the strands, boy!" Osric activated his gift and looked at the cage doors, immediately noticing what had caused Gus so much distress. Where there had been a simple yet impenetrable weave of twelve variations of strands, there was now an intricate, impossible weave of three times as many strands. Osric could distinguish the same twelve variations, but the pattern was significantly harder to follow and discern. He growled in frustration and punched Thom as hard as he could, splaying him out on the floor.

Bridgett had been sitting on the staircase, watching and waiting for an opportunity to assist them. At Osric's display of violence and defeat, she stood and walked over to him. She felt the conflicting emotions raging within him: fear and frustration, anger and purpose. She sensed his strong desire to free the dragons and an immense despair that their efforts seemed futile without the key.

She glared down at Thom and then raised her eyes and said, "Stop it, Osric!" He met her gaze with a stunned expression.

"What?" he asked, confused by her scolding tone.

"Stop feeling sorry for yourself. Stop thinking that someone else should solve the problem and let you go back to your small life in Stanton." He stared down at the ground, and she raised his chin so his eyes met hers. "Stop doubting yourself! You are the most powerful wizard who has ever lived. You do not have to like it, but you cannot deny it. That amount of power comes with responsibility, and these dragons are counting on you to find a way to free them. So stop thinking about yourself, all of the things that have gone wrong, and everything standing in the way of freeing them, and start thinking about what will open these doors!" Osric stood in surprised silence as he considered her words. He was distracted from his thoughts by Gus's laughter. He glanced down at him as he stood on the table chuckling.

"She's right, my boy. If twelve wizards could concoct this irritating mess of a spell, then surely our collective powers can unravel it. So, what are we going to do?"

Osric stared at them both in disbelief and then turned and walked out of the volcano without a word. Bridgett watched him walk away and was overwhelmed by sadness. She had believed that her words would sway him into action, but she had never imagined that he would abandon the mission altogether.

Gus stared intently at the doors for a moment before jumping down to a chair and then to the floor. "Come with me, my dear, and grab Kenneth and that crazy dwarf. I have an idea!" He scampered as quickly as he could toward the entrance. Bridgett shook her head and then swiftly went to retrieve Kenneth and Machai.

When they exited the volcano, they found Osric standing just outside glaring down at Gus.

"Stop pouting, boy, and focus!" Gus yelled at him.

"What are you doing?" Bridgett asked.

"I am instructing him on how to make a wand," Gus responded, glancing up at her.

"What?" Kenneth demanded. "He has the most powerful wand in existence, if that prophecy is to be believed. Why does he need another one?"

"He isn't making a wand; he is learning *how* to make a wand." Gus watched as Osric turned a small stick over in his hands. "That's it, boy! Do you think you can do it?"

"I don't know, Gus, but this just may be crazy enough to work." He looked up at his companions, as his expression changed from one of irritation to hope. "The four of you, form a circle around me. If I can't do it with you, I won't be able to do it with the spell." Bridgett exchanged a confused look with Kenneth and Machai, but they shifted to stand in a rough circle with Gus and Osric.

Osric held the stick out before him and activated his Wand-Maker gift. For a long moment, he stared at Gus, who stood immediately to his left, and a look of intense concentration crossed his features. He turned his gaze on Kenneth, standing next to Gus, and then at Bridgett. When he focused on Machai, a thin sheet of sweat broke out on his brow and his arms trembled slightly, but he kept the stick steady. After a moment, his shoulders sagged and he broke eye contact and handed the stick to Gus.

"You did it, boy! Four separate variations of strands! I can't believe I never thought of it before. Honestly, I'm not sure I could have done it." Gus looked up at him with awe and respect. "You truly are a wonder."

"Let's just hope it is enough. Let's go." Osric turned and walked back into the volcano with a renewed posture of pride and strength, and the others followed him inside.

They crossed the volcano to the first cage door and stood watching Osric expectantly.

"Do ye need me to be getting ye another stick?" Machai asked, breaking the heavy silence.

Osric laughed. "That won't be necessary, Machai. I have no intention of preserving the strands of this spell to be used against anyone else."

Osric lifted Gus to his shoulder, activated his gift, and looked once more at the intricate weave of the spell caging the dragons. He found the most obvious variation in the strands, indicating the power of the wizard that contributed to the spell, and followed the single strand with his eyes until it ended at a small indentation in the metal of the door. Walking closer to the door to get a better look, he realized that the indentation was exactly the same shape as the crystal that Thom had smashed.

"That must be where the key was placed to stall the spell," Gus mused.

Osric focused all of his power on the beginning of that single strand, and he drew it out from the spell, the same way Gus drew a strand from Archana to create a wand. The same way he had drawn specific strands from his friends when they stood outside. He felt resistance from the spell, which fought him to retain the strand and stay intact, but Osric was stronger and it finally gave way. He watched with his gift as the strand untangled itself from the weave of the spell and coiled into his open palm. Gus exhaled audibly as he watched Osric achieve what no Wand-Maker before him had ever even attempted.

Osric found a second strand with the same variation as the first. He wanted to eliminate the power of a wizard entirely before moving on to the next. He traced the path of the strand back to the indentation and again focused on drawing it out of the spell. He felt the same resistance, but it gave way much faster than the first, and as it coiled in his hand, it melded itself to the original strand as though they were actually only one. It took him a moment, but he was able to locate a third strand, and it too melded with the others as he drew it out of the spell. Osric looked down at the strand of power lying in his hand and then looked at Gus.

"Uh, what should I do with it?" Osric asked him. Gus laughed out loud and jumped onto Osric's outstretched arm, causing his hand to drop and the magical strand to fall to the ground. Osric watched, intrigued, as the power was absorbed into the stone at their feet.

"Give it back to Archana, my boy!" Gus exclaimed happily. "This is incredible! Do it again!" he shouted to looks of astonishment and confusion from their friends behind them. Osric grinned and turned back to the spell.

He had managed to withdraw all of the strands of seven of the wizards when he started feeling very fatigued, and his head began to pound terribly. Kenneth and Bridgett looked on with concern as he broke out in a sweat and his body began to shake.

"I don't know if I can finish this," Osric said through gritted teeth.

"Just a bit longer. You have to do this, Osric. No one else has the power," Gus responded.

Bridgett didn't know exactly what Osric was doing, but she could see the strain it was putting on him, and she could not stand back and watch him be destroyed by his own power. "Osric, where is my amulet?"

"Don't distract him now!" Gus exclaimed. Bridgett walked up beside Osric and reached into his tunic, pulling the amulet up and over his head. She ignored Gus's glare and motioned for Kenneth and Machai to join her at Osric's side.

"I want you two to focus on this amulet. Pour all of your energy and power into it that you can. Will your strength into the stone, for Osric's sake, and for the dragons' sake. He needs us now more than he ever has before. You must channel your desire to help him, and your will. Do you understand?" Machai gazed at her with a deep respect and nodded.

"I can't say I understand, but if it will help him, I will pour my soul into that damned stone!" Kenneth stated, and Bridgett smiled over at him.

"Good. Just focus on the amulet, and think about putting all of your strength and power into it so Osric can use it." They did as she asked, and she used a technique she had learned from the Araseth Empaths to channel their power from the stone to Osric.

Just when Osric thought he would collapse from the effort, he felt a surge of strength and power envelop him. He put everything he had into drawing out the strands, and suddenly the woven strands still feeding into the doors began to quiver in his vision. The structure of the spell had become so unstable that it could no longer sustain itself, and the remaining strands fell to the ground, disappearing back into Archana. Osric sat shakily on the ground, breathing heavily, and Gus jumped down from his perch on his arm. Bridgett dropped to her knees at Osric's side, and Gus climbed up onto her shoulder and kissed her cheek.

"Brilliant, girl! Just brilliant!" Gus jumped back to the ground and ran up to the door of the cage. "Somebody open this thing up!"

Kenneth stepped forward and braced his shoulder under the massive bar that crossed the door. He stood with a grunt and swung the bar out of its cradle. He hesitated a moment before opening the door.

"I think you should all step back, and someone should probably go get that dragon to tell his friends that we are the good guys." Kenneth waited for them to retreat, and as he caught sight of Stargon flying down from the mouth of the volcano, he heaved the door open and dived to the side. Fire came spewing out from the cage, and a green dragon much smaller than Stargon burst out into the chamber. The larger dragon leaped between it and the rest of the volcano's occupants.

"Be still, Treethorn! These men have freed us from our bondage!" Stargon roared, and the smaller dragon stopped and looked around in amazement. Treethorn let out an ear-piercing cry and then she shot up the vent of the volcano and into the open air, spreading her wings wide and streaking back and forth across the sky.

"Let's hope they are all that happy to see us," Kenneth said as he levitated the bar from the next cage with his wand.

"Stargon, with the spell disabled, can ye be telling ye'r kin that we be freeing them and not to be roasting us?" Machai asked the dragon.

"Already done, stone dweller. You should have no more resistance from us. Please, release them from these cages." Stargon's voice was thick with emotion.

Osric, Bridgett, Machai, and Gus aided him in unbarring the cages. As the doors were opened, the dragons flew up and out, joyously celebrating their freedom. Soon, all fifty cages stood open. When the last two doors were opened and nothing emerged, Osric approached the cages tentatively. He looked inside the first cage, and it stood empty, no doubt meant to hold Stargon. Upon peering into the last, he smiled in relief; it was occupied by a familiar face.

"Contege Thamas. We were wondering where you had gone off to."

Chapter 22
Homeward Bound

Machai took great pleasure in locking Aron and his seven remaining men in one of the cages, and he asked several of the eagles to stand guard outside the door. He left the volcano and went to find the others. They were standing outside speaking with Thamas, and Machai headed in their direction.

Thamas stood beside Osric shaking his head. "I can't believe you found a way to free the dragons! Don't misunderstand me; I am elated that they will no longer be held captive and tortured, but how will the people of Archana travel without them?"

"No single race should suffer for the convenience of the others," Osric replied. "We will just have to find a way to get along without forcing them to fly us around. Perhaps if we ask nicely they will still take us where we want to go." Osric winked over at his friends and walked toward Machai, leaving Thamas to ponder the repercussions of the day's events.

"The guards be secured. I be hoping they enjoy their time in the cage. They will be having a while to think about what the dragons have been going through all these years," Machai told Osric and inclined his head toward Thamas. "Ye be knowing the Contege they had caged?"

"Yes, I was promoted to replace him when he went missing. I am truly glad to find he is alive, and we have much to discuss, but we need to plan our next move. I don't think it would be wise to inform Thamas of all we have learned until we know if he intends to take back his position as Stanton's Contege." He glanced back over his shoulder. "Will you join me in speaking with the dragons before we go?"

"Aye." They walked over to Stargon and several other dragons where they were lying in the warm sunshine. They all stood and lowered their heads to the ground in a respectful bow as Osric approached.

"High Wizard, we are forever indebted to you for our freedom." Stargon gazed up at the sky. "The dragon elders have regained the skies, and our race will never be controlled and obligated to serve others again."

"What is a high wizard?" Osric asked.

"No wizard should ever have been able to unbind that spell. You have the power of a wizard of a higher capability than any other ever born. You are a high wizard, Osric—*the* High Wizard." Osric was shocked, but after all that had happened he could not argue with the dragon. He bowed slightly in acknowledgement.

"I am just grateful that we were able to free you, and I certainly did not accomplish it alone, but I would like to speak to you about the future of your race."

"Our race has a future, thanks to you. What would you like to discuss?"

"Well, actually, I have a favor to ask of you. Dragons should be free to decide where they fly and why. I hope that you never feel obligated to fly passengers against your will again." Osric took a deep, calming breath. "But I would like to request that you aid our cause in preventing a massive world war." With a hopeful expression, Osric looked up at the dragon towering above him.

"We may not be very sympathetic to the races that have held us here for so long, but a world war would be devastating for all of the races who have never caused us any harm. What is it that you need from us?"

"I believe that the men who have been overseeing your captivity are the same men who have amassed an army and intend to initiate the war. Without the dragons to fly the troops, the army will be forced to move slowly, and it may buy us enough time to find a way to stop them altogether."

The small, green dragon that Stargon had called Treethorn stepped forward and said, "Wait, you are asking us to do you a favor by *not* flying humans and their cruel sharp blades around on our backs? I love this High Wizard!" She leapt up into the air and twirled around with excitement.

Osric smiled at her antics, but his expression grew serious as he turned back to Stargon. "Actually, that is only part of my request. First, let me express that very few walkers were aware of your captivity and the threat to you which forced the other dragons to fly for us. The average person truly believes that dragons provide us with transport in exchange for payment."

"Osric, I am aware of the difference between our captors and our passengers. It may surprise you, but I have been in contact with a friend of yours. Greyback is anxious for your arrival to thank you in person." Stargon's eyes twinkled at Osric's shocked expression. "Ero has been a wealth of knowledge as well."

"You spoke with Greyback? How?" Osric asked in dismay.

Stargon laughed from deep in his chest. "You have much to learn about dragons, High Wizard, and I look forward to teaching you. All dragons have the ability to communicate telepathically. The spell created a barrier that prevented me from communicating with the other elders, but I have had contact with all of our descendants as long as I remained uncaged to stand guard for those wicked men."

"So her wing has healed then? She is all right?"

"She is doing well, impatiently awaiting your arrival at your agreed-upon rendezvous point. So, what is the rest of your request?"

"In order for us to learn what we must to stop this war, we need to avoid suspicion and fear from spreading among those who have the power to oppose us. If the dragons are no longer providing transportation to the masses, then the leaders of the various realms will feel isolated and threatened. They will be far more likely to be swayed by the vile men who would like to see the world's alliances torn apart. We need those leaders to trust in the security that the peace ratification would have assured them, rather than the false promises of a corrupt usurper."

"Ye be asking them to give up their freedom before they have even had a chance to be tasting it!" Machai objected passionately.

"No, Machai, I am asking them to help me prevent the most widespread panic and devastation to ever be visited upon Archana!" He spread his hands as he appealed to the dragons. "If you stop providing transportation to the entire world, all of our efforts to bring peace and unification to the realms of Archana will be wasted, and the men who have held you prisoners here for so long will have truly won! Please, I need your help, but I will not demand it. No one will ever be able to demand anything from you again. It has to be your choice." He dropped his hands and waited with bated breath for the reply.

The dragons stood in silence, and Osric began to think that he had asked too much of them and they would not be able to give up their newfound freedom. Then Stargon said, "We will not demand that our descendants serve, any more than you will demand the same of us." Osric's heart fell as he listened to the dragon's words. "However, we have as much to lose from a war as you. Though we will leave it up to each dragon to decide for themselves, I believe that most will choose to help you. Tell me more of this army and what has transpired that led you here to our mountain."

* * *

"Toby showed me your journal." Osric sat across the fire from Thamas, observing him closely. To Thamas's credit, he did not seem surprised, nor did he try to deny writing it.

"I had hoped that if anyone ever found it, it would be Toby." He met Osric's gaze with his head held high. "Will you charge me with treason, or will you help me to understand what is happening in our realm?"

Osric weighed his options, and erred on the side of caution. "I do not believe you capable of treason, and I am relatively certain that the Turgent is unaware of the degree of corruption surrounding him. I would like nothing more than to send you back to Stanton in my stead and to relinquish the title and responsibilities of your position, but I would more than likely be sending you to your death. I have not yet discovered how deep this goes, nor who is involved, so it would be wiser to send you elsewhere until we find out." He smiled over at the previous Contege. "Besides, you deserve some time away"—he laughed under his breath— "without the cage."

"Where would I go? Stanton is the only home I have ever known."

"There is a whole world to see. I think you may enjoy spending some time traveling, and Machai could use the extra sword on his journey home. How would you like to learn to fight with your sword and your wand?"

Thamas laughed, nearly choking on his rulha. "You can't be serious!"

"Oh, I am quite serious. It took me a while to master, but it is a very handy trick, and Machai seems to enjoy teaching us slow-witted humans to be better warriors."

Thamas shook his head and stared down into his mug. "I have always wondered what it would be like to leave my responsibilities behind and travel the world, but it never seemed realistic before now. I suppose if it will save my life then I can leave you to my duties for a while longer. After all, it would be beneficial to have the dwarves behind us if a war is unavoidable."

"Indeed," Osric said, rising to his feet. "I will speak with Machai and make the arrangements."

Osric entered the volcano and found Machai speaking with Ero. He approached them and waited respectfully for Ero to finish his explanation of how Argan had helped them sculpt the Caves of D'pareth with the spoken spell.

187

"I spoke with Thamas, and he has agreed to accompany you on your return journey. Have you spoken to the dragons?"

"Aye. That quick little 'un, Treethorn, has agreed to be flying us. Beats a sail on a forsaken ship."

"Good. We should leave in the morning, and you will need to depart with Thamas first. He is a good man, but he will be safer for now in his ignorance."

"Aye, I will be watching over him."

"Thank you, Machai. Let's link our wands so we can stay in contact." They established the link and Osric left them to continue their conversation. He climbed the stairs to the small sleeping chambers to find Bridgett. As he reached the landing at the top, he could hear Bridgett and Gus speaking, and he paused outside the door. He didn't want to interrupt them, and he almost turned and went back the way he had come when he heard his name.

"Yes, my dear, the way he unraveled the spell on those cages was incredible. You should have seen it! I must admit, I have grown to respect Osric greatly." Gus's voice drifted through the doorway. "But if you tell him I said so, I will never admit it." He heard Bridgett giggle, and he couldn't help but stay and listen.

"Gus, your secret is safe with me, so long as you can restrain yourself from insulting him every chance you get." Osric smiled at hearing her defend him. "He has truly grown into a powerful wizard. It will be hard to part ways with him tomorrow, but I must return to the unicorns." His smile faded. He had not considered the possibility that Bridgett would not return to Stanton with him.

"Ah, girl, I would give anything to spend time in that grove learning about the unicorns. Would you consider allowing me to accompany you?" Gus asked.

"What about your family and your home?"

"Most of my pups are grown, and my home will be there when I return. I couldn't leave Pebble behind, of course, but he is rather fond of you and would love to see more unicorns. Besides, there wouldn't be a better place on Archana for him to develop his wand-making abilities than in that enchanted grove."

"Well, I cannot guarantee the unicorns will allow you to study them, but you are welcome to join me and ask them." Osric heard Gus whoop with excitement, and he turned and crept silently back toward the stairs.

Osric made considerably more noise walking back to the door, and he called out to Bridgett as he approached. He entered the room to find them sitting comfortably on the small sleeping pallet. Bridgett smiled up at him, and gestured for him to join them.

"Bridgett, I'm glad I found you. We are making our final preparations for leaving tomorrow. Will you be returning with us to Stanton?"

She smiled knowingly at him and replied, "I must return to the Grove of Unicorns, Osric, and Gus will be joining me."

"Oh. I am sorry to hear that." Genuine disappointment filled his voice.

"I do not believe that the unicorns' interest in you has expired, but I need to return to them and tell them what we have learned. Perhaps they will be able, and willing, to help."

"Yes, you are right. You will be sure to stay in contact?" Osric asked.

"Yes, boy. You can't get rid of me that easily. You will be hearing from us regularly, if only to make sure you haven't gotten into any trouble." Bridgett cleared her throat at Gus's insulting tone, and he walked out of the room with a scowl. She waited until she was sure he was out of earshot.

"Osric, if you are going to stand outside of a doorway and listen to an Empath's conversations, you should learn to mask your emotions more effectively." She smiled as his cheeks flushed red, and she followed Gus from the room.

After waiting a moment for his embarrassment to fade, Osric descended the stairs. He found Kenneth shoving stale bread through the feeding slot of the cage that housed the guards.

"Why do you look like you just got caught stealing Miss Lidya's rhubarb?" Kenneth asked jokingly as Osric walked up.

"What? Oh, it's just been a long day." Osric waved dismissively. "What are we going to do with them?" he asked, nodding toward the cage.

"I say we just leave them locked up to rot," Kenneth replied.

"You know we can't do that. That's what they would do."

"Yeah, I know. We will strip this place of all forms of weapons and unbar the door before we leave in the morning. Did you figure out what to do about Thamas?"

"Yes. He is going to travel with Machai until we can sort out this mess."

"Good. Everything is in order then?"

189

"Looks that way. Gus and Bridgett are going to travel to the Grove of the Unicorns, and Pebble will go with them. So it's up to you and I to get back to Stanton and save the world." He smiled weakly at his friend.

"Ah, Os, I'm sorry. But you will see her again soon, I am sure of it." Osric was startled that his disappointment was so apparent, but Kenneth had always been able to read him. Before Osric could deny his attachment to Bridgett, Machai walked up.

"I be leaving now to retrieve our gear from the tree," he said. "I will be releasing the horses, unless ye would prefer I brought them back here."

"No, Machai," Osric replied. "That will be fine. That should give them time to be far enough away that they won't tempt the dragons, and they won't be of use to Aron's men either."

"Aye. Ye will be releasing them then?"

"Yes, in the morning before we leave. It is the right thing to do."

"Aye, but I do not have to be liking it." He stomped off toward the entrance, grumbling to himself.

Osric turned back to Kenneth. "We all need to get some sleep. Tomorrow will be another long day." He climbed the stairs, lay down on a pallet, and fell into a restless sleep.

* * *

Osric woke in the morning with a pounding headache and very stiff muscles. The immense amount of power he had expended the day before had taken its physical toll on his body. He walked stiffly down the stairs to find the volcano busy with activity. He gratefully accepted a steaming mug of rulha from Kenneth.

"What's going on?" Osric asked. A large wagon sat in the middle of the floor between the sentry tower and the entrance. "Where did that come from?"

"Machai is loading all of the weapons he can find into the wagon with the shipment of dwarven blades he delivered. He found a false wall in the back of one of the cages. It was bolted from the outside, and there was a tunnel leading to it from the kitchen. That's where Aron had stashed the wagon. Gus and Bridgett are packing rations from the kitchen, and I just finished collecting all of the spare gear from the guards' sleeping chambers and the storerooms. No sense in leaving it to make Aron and his men comfortable."

"Kenneth." Osric looked over at him suspiciously. "What are we going to do with the wagon once it is full?"

"I'm glad you asked." Kenneth grinned. "Do you remember that chamber in the eagle caves? The one you showed me the day before the vial broke, with the smooth reflective walls?" Osric nodded reluctantly. "Ero tells me that Argan originally designed that chamber as a stronghold. It is heavily shielded. Ero just hasn't activated the shields since there has been nothing inside to guard."

"Well, that sounds like the perfect place for all of these weapons." Osric waited for Kenneth's inevitable response.

"I thought so too. That's why you are going to take it there." Kenneth's grin widened.

"You want me to *travel* with a wagon full of weapons to a cave half a world away?"

"You are the only one who can do it, Os," he stated seriously. "I will have your breakfast waiting when you return."

Osric grinned over at him wryly, "I want honey cakes." He approached the wagon as Machai levitated the last dagger into the back and raised the gate.

"It be all ye'rs. That be every dwarven blade, poorly made sword, crooked blade, dull axe, and kitchen knife in the volcano. I willn't leave Aron and his men with a stick to pick their teeth if I can be helping it." Machai latched the gate on the wagon and walked outside to assist Thamas in rigging Treethorn for flight and loading their supplies.

Osric rested his hands on the side of the wagon and took a deep breath. He closed his eyes and envisioned the chamber in the caves. Gripping the wood tightly, he said, "Eo ire itum!"

He opened his eyes and sighed in relief to see that the wagon had *traveled* with him. There was nothing else in the chamber, and the smooth, reflective walls had an ethereal shine about them. The only entrance into the room was a narrow doorway, and Osric walked over to it slowly.

"Frigus Adaugeo," he said softly. His words echoed back to him, and he saw the shimmer of the shields as they activated. Osric turned his thoughts back to the volcano and spoke the words again, "Eo ire itum."

Osric stood where the wagon had rested, and Kenneth stepped up to him with a plate of honey cakes, saying, "Amazing! I barely had time to get these from the kitchen before you returned. Are you all right? I know that was quite a journey."

Osric took the plate and bit into a honey cake. "I'm fine, just hungry," he said with surprise, around a mouthful of the pastries. He finished his breakfast, and then he and Kenneth went to see Machai and Thamas off.

"We be ready to depart," Machai stated, as Osric approached.

"I wanted to see you off, my friend." Osric smiled at Treethorn's impatient excitement, as she danced around, ready to begin the long flight. "Are you sure those straps are snug? She is the fastest dragon I have ever seen, and I would hate to hear that you plummeted into the sea." Osric grinned as they climbed up onto her back.

"Aye, they be tight." The dwarf looked behind him and reassured himself that the saddlebags containing their supplies and the gold were securely strapped behind his seat. He lashed himself in just as tightly, and with a word that they were ready, Treethorn launched herself into the air and streaked across the sky.

Back inside the volcano, Bridgett and Gus were saying their goodbyes to Kenneth and Ero. As Osric walked through the entrance, Pebble ran up to him and Osric picked him up.

"I's is gonna miss you's bunches, but I's gets to see unicorns!"

"I will miss you too, Pebble, but we will see each other soon. Will you take care of Bridgett for me?"

"Yeppers! You's got's more colors now! Wanna play's I's see's somethin' you's don't?"

Gus distractedly started to correct his son, "Pebble, you must not use your gift to look at someone without..." He turned and looked over at Osric. "More?"

"Are you really going to start with the inspection thing again, Gus?" Osric asked, setting Pebble down gently.

"You better believe it, boy. Now sit down and look happy for a change!" Osric knew that he would not be able to deter Gus from inspecting him, so he sat down in a chair, arms crossed, and waited for Gus to tell him what he had seen.

Gus activated his gift and gazed at Osric from head to toe. Centered in Osric's breast was a bright red sphere that he recognized. "You picked up the dwarf's gift. Elemental Fire, by my reckoning." Pale-blue waves ran down his arms as well, in a hypnotizing motion he found all too familiar. "And somewhere along the way you acquired another Elemental gift: Water!" One more gift caught his eye, and again he found himself staring at something he did not recognize. Pastel yellow orbs hovered throughout his body, joined by long, transparent strands. "You have another gift I have never witnessed, boy." Gus shook his head in amazement.

Osric stood and looked down at Gus. "I am just as confused as you are by what is happening to me. I imagine this new gift is what allows me to be invisible, but I don't know how I acquired it. I don't know how I have any of them, but we don't have time to figure it out right now. Find out what you can from the unicorns, and I will return to Stanton and learn what I may. Contact me tomorrow." Osric walked over to Bridgett and took her hand, bringing it to his lips. "Be careful. I intend to see you again." He turned and walked away from her, unable to say more without emotion betraying him.

Gus watched him go, and Bridgett lifted him to her shoulder for the journey. As she picked Pebble up, Gus spoke in her ear, "The debate is over. He obviously has the wand from the prophecy. I just wish I understood why I can't see it."

Bridgett gently kissed his cheek, and spoke softly, envisioning her home, "Eo ire itum."

THE AUTHORS

Jack D. Albrecht Jr. resides in Colorado. He is a devoted father and a Pharmacy Technician. His new found passion for writing consumes most of his time, but once in a while he can still be found under the hood of a car or cooking fantastic meals for his family and friends.

Jack has been an avid reader for most of his life, with Sci-Fi and fantasy being his favorite genres. Osric's Wand: The Wand-Maker's Debate is his first novel, co-authored by Ashley Delay.

Ashley Delay resides in northern Colorado.

She is a single mother, full time student, and owner/operator of three businesses. Osric's Wand: The Wand-Maker's Debate is her first published novel, co-authored by Jack D. Albrecht Jr.

www.osricswand.net

www.facebook.com/pages/Osrics-Wand-The-Wand-Makers-Debate/201464756575335

On Twitter @jackdalbrechtjr

Made in the USA
San Bernardino, CA
06 April 2016